MAIN MENU

Director's Note 7

Part 1: The Prize of the Poor 9

Part 2: Nutting Up 59

Part 3: Desconocido Estrafalario .119

Part 4: Flipping the Script 177

Bonus Features 233

Photo still, courtesy Last Burn Films © 2006

 RESTRICTED

R UNDER 17 REQUIRES ACCOMPANYING
PARENT OR ADULT GUARDIAN

This film has been rated R for adult situations,
raunchy humor, gratuitous nudity, unpatriotic
music, violence, drug references, deviant sex
acts, and grotesquely offensive language.

Also by John Edward Lawson

Collections
Discouraging at Best
Pocket Full of Loose Razorblades

Poetry
The Troublesome Amputee
The Plague Factory
The Horrible
The Scars are Complimentary

As Editor
The Wicked Will Laugh
Tempting Disaster
Sick: An Anthology of Illness
Of Flesh and Hunger: Tales of the Ultimate Taboo

LAST BURN IN HELL

John Edward
LAWSON

RAW DOG
SCREAMING
PRESS

In memory of my father.

This book would not be possible without the efforts of Jennifer C. Barnes and Dave Lipscomb. I must also thank the following people for their support of my efforts: Mom, the Barnes family, Peggy, Abel, Mike, polycarp, Hal, satan165, Perry, Dustin, Vincent, and Brian.

Last Burn in Hell: Director's Cut Copyright © 2006
by John Edward Lawson

Published by Raw Dog Screaming Press
Hyattsville, MD

First paperback edition

Cover design: Jennifer Barnes
Interior images: riot image "Going Down" by Dave Lipscomb; all other images by M. Garrow Bourke or stock photos
Book design: M. Garrow Bourke

Printed in the United States of America

ISBN: 1-933293-25-X (hardcover)
ISBN: 1-933293-26-8 (paperback)

Library of Congress Control Number: 2005902655

www.rawdogscreaming.com

DIRECTOR'S NOTE

S O I WAS SITTING at a table in the local Todo Bell. There was a guy in a suit and sunglasses sitting nearby, reading a novel called *The Book That Birthed Itself*. It was really short, maybe 40 pages long. I went and acted like I was throwing something away just so I could read over his shoulder.

The story featured some interesting characters and scenarios, but when it got to the end I was all like, "Man, what's wrong with these clowns—you can't end it on that note! What about X, Y, and Z?!"

But I didn't say this. The man, he turned around and bared his teeth, probably because I'd been standing there for thirty minutes. He was creepy and stinky so I returned to my seat.

Sitting there in a cold sweat, my food long removed by some "worker," I contemplated what course of action to take. Grabbing a menu and a pen I scribbled my thoughts on how to improve the book. I suggested changing the title to *The Last Burn in Hell*, or maybe just *Last Burn in Hell*. I also pleaded with the reader to drop the suit and get some hygiene. Then I folded the note/menu into a paper airplane, threw it, and quite accidentally stabbed him in the eye—perhaps it was a bad idea to affix a shiv to the plane.

During the commotion I was able to sweep in and take his book. Surprisingly, nobody stopped me on the way out. The prison's food court wasn't high security, but you couldn't easily blow up the spot either. Instead of crashing the execution like I usually would I went home, got to work. That was in March of 2001. I kept tinkering with the words for four years and now here we are.

Thus, the half-baked product has finally become a hot potato. I hope you find the meditations on conformity, outrage, and self-determination within to be tastier than some Todo Bell carryout. To accompany the meal, might I suggest either Mad Dog '05—its piquant bouquet is delightful—or a can of kerosene.

—John Edward Lawson, Landover Hills, 3/16/05

THAT WAS, OF COURSE, the book's introduction. Now, a year and a half later, I'm proud to present the film version of my vision. There were some bumps in the road to production, but I'm more than pleased with the results. Since this is my first film I'd love any feedback, especially regarding the extra features. If you have any comments or complaints just send a message to john@johnlawson.org...thanks!

John Edward Lawson, Landover Hills, 11/30/06

PART ONE:

THE PRIZE OF THE POOR

"No one can see their reflection in running water. It is only in still water that we can see."
—*Taoist proverb*

"If you saw what the river carried, you would never drink the water."
—*Jamaican proverb*

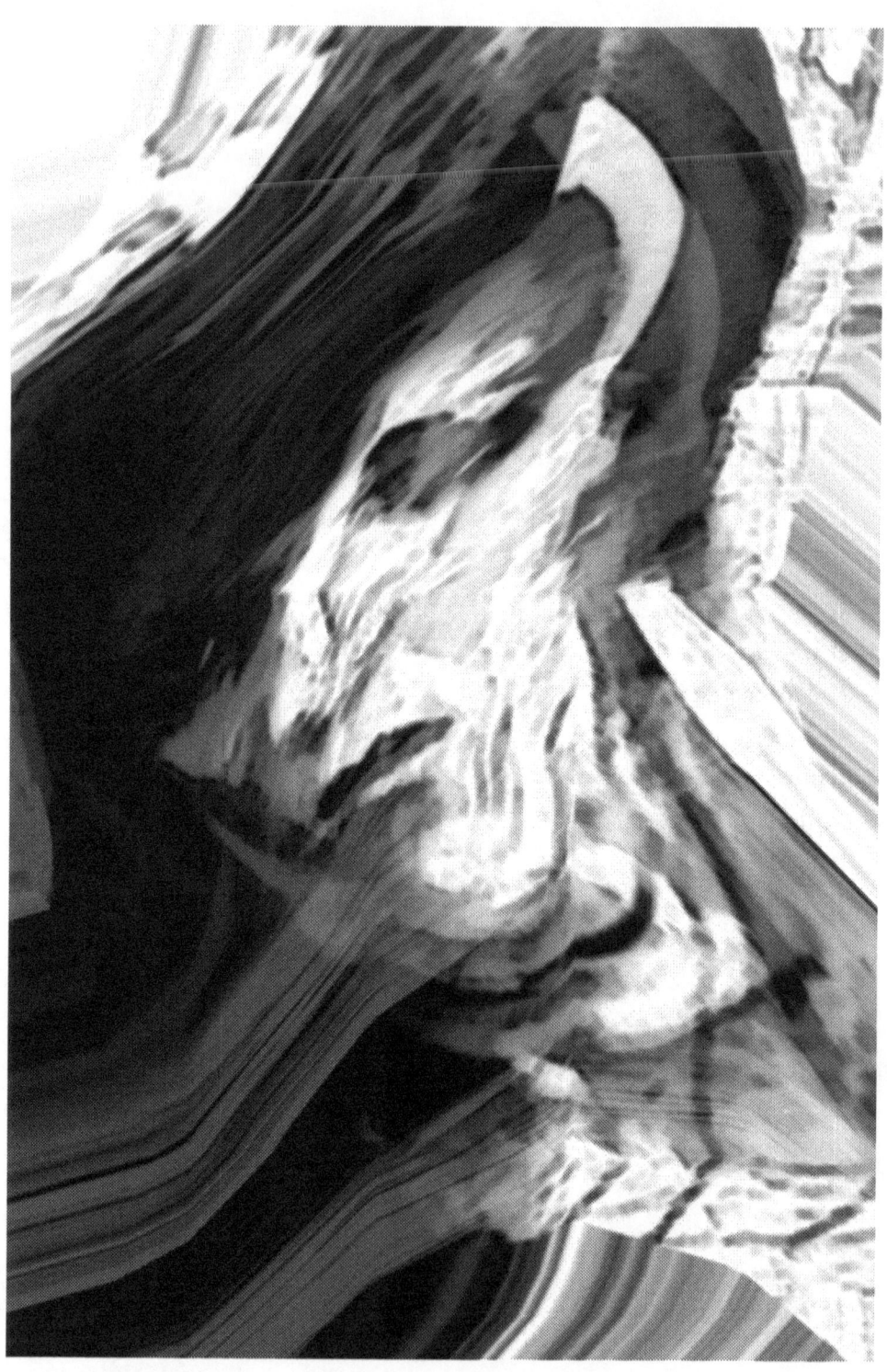

Promotional image, courtesy Last Burn Films © 2006

TRYING TO READ THE newspaper is like trying to get it up after imagining your parents making out. The headline that screams the loudest is *Vet Charged With Sexually Abusing Caged Animals*. The paper gets left behind on the dining room table. People like me, well, we already know more about that subject than we care to.

"Hey bro—you still there?" It's my brother, always bothering me with his whiney Sunday phone calls.

"Yes Shame. Still here."

"Damn man, can't you just call me Seamus? Like everyone else?"

"No."

"Well, thanks for thinking about it at least." He snorts. Then he adds, "So what're you up to today?"

"I'm waxing Ms. Clinton right now." And it would be a lot more enjoyable if he wasn't being so needy all in my ear.

"Mmm, Ms. Clinton, right. Tough old broad."

"Sure."

"She's what, pushing two hundred now, if I'm not mistaken."

"She's older than that, Shame." She is, and it shows. No matter how much waxing she gets it'll be the same story: elegant build, witness to decades of torture in some nutjob's dungeon, eventually recovered and put on display by authorities as evidence of progress. See folks? One less thing you have to worry about. One less torture happening in a world full of pain.

Shame snorts again. "Hey, that's between you and your Missus. Really, I figured you'd be doing, like, your ten-thousandth jumping jack of the day."

"There's no need to get sarcastic. It's in my contract. Got to work out, man."

When the buffing cloth strokes Ms. Clinton's dangerous parts you can almost hear the screams and wailing and sobbing. She's only getting a work over because she gives me a place to hide. There's a bogus telephone company repairman "repairing" the lines outside my apartment building. From this position the dude can be spied on by peeking over Clinton's left arm...whoa, was that a click in the phone line just now?

"Hey man, you just hear that?"

Shame snorts again. "Hear what?"

Oh well. No need to upset him by busting out with the 411. If it gets hectic he'll find out one way or the other. Or maybe he's already hip to it? Convenient that one of my brothers should just happen to call while a "repairman" is hacking into my line. The TV is on with the volume cranked up, just in case there are listening devices. A highlight of the Austin Ass-Rippers/Cleveland Clusterfuck game is running, sponsored by Todo Bell's new mild Green Card Chilli and Tortillera combo. The Todo Bell jingle plays briefly: "Get chipot-layed...tonight! Yeah!"

"There it is again. You heard that, right?"

"Dude man: you need to seriously take up medication or meditation." I inform my brother that where I work *meditation* means *solitary confinement*. "Okay, here we go with the prison slang again. You know what? Nobody cares about that, man. It's a language of anger and hostility and, shit, the language of death. I'm trying to talk to you about letting Buddha's calming power change your life."

"Not this Zen shizzo again. Buddha lived like what, five thousand years ago? What's he supposed to know about my life?"

"Didn't Buddha tell us that life is suffering?"

"Life is suffering? Life isn't a living thing, so how can it suffer?"

There's silence on the other end of the line, followed by what may

HERE'S TO YOU

MRS. CLINTON JESUS

LOVES YOU MORE

THAN YOU WILL

KNOW

Pillory

WO, WO, WO

Promotional image, courtesy Last Burn Films © 2006

13

or may not be another click. "Try to follow me here, Ken. For *living people* the *experience* of life itself is nothing but suffering."

My hand falls away from the wax container, my eyes drop from the window. "Shit man...that's some negative shit! How's that supposed to make anyone relax? Anyway, everybody knows life is about happiness!"

"Oh yeah?" he scoffs, hitting me with the day's forth patented Shame Snort. "Yeah! It is too!"

"Well, why don't you ask your friend Pillory Clinton about it and get back to me." Smug bastard.

Okay, so she's a pillory. What can I say, I'm an antiques collector. Since when is that a crime? "You know what? Now that you mention it, I think I *will* work out. It's *my* form of meditation. So..." No witty tell-off lines come to mind and it boils down to, "Put that in your pipe and smoke it!" The last thing I hear before hanging up is him laughing. That, and what sounds suspiciously like a suspicious sound.

Maybe I shouldn't have hung up; it's not like the phone rings every day. Then again, things are that way on purpose. Don't get too close, don't let anybody know what I do. As for exercize, going to my favorite place—the pool—really isn't an option. The staff has started making fun of me for spending more time in the water than on the land. "Living proof of de-evolution," they tell me.

What else is there to do, anyway? Zone out in front of the television, watch the Washington White Devils beat up on some other franchise, maybe let the thirty minutes of commercials per hour soak in. Sure. That's what I used to do anyway, before Leena. When we first met I was what she called "a five-corned square," so she set to hipping me up. Still, vegging to sit-coms and infomercials has its appeal because, let's face it, it's not like I'm going to have a real social life any time soon. A lot of people lose interest when you give them your job description, especially if you've got a job like mine. That's just it though: nobody else has a job like mine.

In my contract it says that I'm not allowed to masturbate. That's a *Code 21* in the penal system—the Powers That Be don't want inmates masturbating either. They for sure don't want an employee like me curbing his sexual appetite, since the ability to perform is my only worth in this world. How do they know if a person played hangman with the chicken? They have their methods. Code 21 is also known by the prison population as *killing*; masturbation is one of the few ways to kill time behind bars. You're not *beating off* thinking about your high school sweetheart, you're *killing* her, the same as *shooting* another inmate is *having sex with them*.

Everything is just words. If you call somebody something differ-ent, does it actually *make* them different? Is the way that you think of them different? Or are you just paying lip service, trying and failing to trick yourself, keeping up a lie just for the sake of living a lie despite the fact that everybody else also knows it's a lie. Well, maybe nobody knows. Maybe nobody cares enough to notice.

Lately the dictionary has been my book of choice, but the words don't seem to stick, like undercooked spaghetti thrown at a wall. Maybe it's because Leena is too much of a distraction. All paths flow back to her: we've got a "date" in just a couple hours and she still won't be impressed by my vocabulary. For just once in my life I'd like to have my mind noticed, to let it step into the spotlight—but it seems like you have to do something with your mind first. All this thinking is giving me a headache. Looks like some stretches are in order if I want to relax for our get-together.

Newscasters inform us that S.I.S.T.E.R. is on the attack again. This time they've burned down the home of a right-wing Supreme Court judge. There's probably not a need to listen to how insane the world is—I'll bet now that Shame isn't on the line the interest level has dropped. Sure enough, a peek around Pillory Clinton confirms the bogus phone dude is gone, so it's safe to lower the noise level.

Cute name, right? Pillory's a young gal, for her kind anyway. Only a couple centuries old. Pretty busted up though. I mean, what do you want after so many years of service? Not that she's been used lately. The hole for the prisoner's head is a bit decayed, and the wood is marred on both sides of the hole from where they nailed people's ears down. But the hand restraints are still in decent shape. Hawthorne said in *The Scarlet Letter* that there's "no outrage more flagrant than to forbid the culprit to hide his face for shame." In *Hymn to the Pillory* De Foe said, "Tell us, great engine, how to understand/or reconcile the justice of this land." Makes me feel kind of smart knowing all that, but the quotes came from Leena. She's always lurking in my thoughts, isn't she? In my dreams she's here, locked in this pillory.

The device itself is the main feature of my dining room, against the center of the wall, with small shelves on either side. One of the main features, anyway. The other is the dining room table itself: a long, flat item with ankle and wrist restraints at the ends, better known as *the rack*. This one doesn't have a name yet, but maybe soon. Hey, a guy's got to have hobbies, right?

Or a job. Usually they don't call me in on jobs, though, and that's something to be thankful for.

Sometimes I almost feel good about myself.

"Yo, we in da studio o' death, coolin' mental style an' gettin' buck wild...yeah, fool...rugged and stylish *por vida!*"

Here we are at Death Row Studios, some dude calling himself "satan" at the mixing board. This band is Taliban, Satan's brainchild. For us guards it's a break from the norm since projects here usually have names more like Everlasting Gospel or Super Trinity or Big G and the Bloody Nail. For the population of our all-female prison, well, their opinion doesn't count much anyway.

"Almost rioting, here," Rolli informs me. "Mofos poppin' off junk like this, makes the women flipping their shit. Oh yeah, baby."

I nod. "Of course the general population is going to get bent out of shape finding out the Taliban is in their back yard. Then again, what rap group isn't controversial these days? Got to admit, though, it's toe-tapping stuff."

He shrugs. "Oh yeah, baby."

Carleetha steps back from her mic and they rewind things. An overgrown homey calling himself Sodamn Insein is prepping in the corner, doing push-ups and jumping jacks and slapping himself. The sweat pouring out of his skin is either because of a cocaine jag or the fact that he insists on wearing his plaid jacket and bandana in here. Another one is decked out in Daytona Date Raper gear, with the words SCORE LIKE A DATE RAPER across his chest. How much longer is this going to take?

Hanging out with the guards, waiting for my appointed time, it can be a pain. Most of them are useless, some are okay; pretty much all of them want to knock my eye out with a baton. That's okay, their intolerance is understandable. As far as the rest of my brother peacekeepers are concerned I'm lower than a gigolo, a whore on retainer for the most despicable caste of criminals. Generally we bide our time standing in silence, eyeing each other for the first sign of trouble. They're worried I'll offer them my services or something, and that makes them want to open up a can of bodily harm all over my gigolo ass. Well, let's see them try it. On the other hand a lot of this stale time is spent with guys like Rolli. He's the one on duty here tonight so he invited me to bide my time with him.

Rolli is a middle-aged Sicilian guy, I think, or maybe he's from St.

Petersburg. Let's see...Rolli is about forty-five with folds of fat hanging off his body, and aside from being blue collar all the way he does his worst to be hip.

"Normally inmates would be running the equipment instead of this bugged-out white dude," I tell Rolli. "For the time being our women are just window dressing on this production. Fluff. Actually, around here *fluff* is *lipstick lesbian*—got to keep things straight or risk dissing somebody." Rolli nods, appreciating the explanations. I start to say something else, but Sodamn is ready to go. Drums and synths and sampled horns start to pound. The message:

Got wankstas exposed like Paris Hilton, serving bitch slaps by the muthafuckin' billions, call me Papa Insein cause you's All My Children, and As The World Turns ya get fuckin' burned, 'cause our mob rolls like Sopranos, so let go, you suckas can only flow...like a period, my skills are myriad, maddening, ill for your health like fattening, for the slaughter, bitch, and I'll take your muthafuckin' daughter, bitch, I already bought her, switch, I'm a hip hop marauder, rich, makin' suckas disappear like my name's Harry Potter, only it ain't magic—it's tragic when shit gets hairy and you're buried, in potter's field dead with your dick in the dirt, wearin' a damn skirt, tore your ass open with the Kobe Bryant hurt, 'cause I bust it out like underage cherry, got other MCs committin' hari-kari, look around and it's god damn scary, how many halfway muthafuckas I gotta bury, afraid to take the plunge, they just get the plunger, but son if shit floats you still goin' under

Rolli leans in and whispers in my ear, "What this means: harry-Carrie? Like unshaven woman?"

"Yo!" Satan barks. His eyes are like embers in a funeral pyre. "Shut it or get shut down, you fat bitch!"

Rolli starts to say something but I hold him back. This sound engineer may be trouble but he's got the state's seal of approval. Anybody spending thousands of dollars to rent a studio created as part of the inmate's vocational skills program, they bear the mark Do Not Fuck With Us. As for the vocational skills of the offenders, well, those can wait a month or two while this record gets made.

From the background one of the inmates adds, "Word, straight up representin' da X3 clica, an' if you's a fuckin' weezo we gonna split yo muddafuggin' wig!"

A member of the executive committee orders the recording to stop. There's a murmur among the other execs. "Does *weezo* imply something negative about cigarettes?" he wants to know. "As in one who smokes too much and is short of breath? If so, our sister company, Smoke Me Fags, will *not* be pleased." While the objecting exec mops his pink scalp I explain that weezo means *informant*.

The head lady seems satisfied with my translation and nods to the other five women and two men, all in power suits. "Keep the tapes rolling," the head honcho says. "We've got a deadline."

The verdict: it's okay to endorse shooting people in the head for disclosing crimes, so long as you're not badmouthing companies that spread lung cancer.

Rolli gives me a look. While this beats regular duty, it's boring as hell to sit through fifty takes of the vocals with a committee rewriting every line. Sodamn clears his throat and is ready to deliver the chorus:

Turnin' 8-Mile into 8-Mile Island
Blowin' shit up wit mad freestylin'
It's da Taliban—we don't give a damn
Bombin' muthafuckas from here to Afghanistan

One of the men gushes, "Ooh, this is gonna piss *so* many people off. We'll have race riots *and* political riots in every city we tour!"

"And just think," another adds. "Recording in an actual prison is going to make it all so authentic, all just that much more controversial."

One of the women, the least enthusiastic, chimes in with, "Instant gold. Or platinum. Or whatever. Problem is, how do you top masquerading as our nation's war enemies, screaming the most degrading slurs possible?" The execs look at each other. She adds, "Plus, where do you go artistically if you're a gimmick? We'll go gold on the first day of sales, sure, but it will just be a cage made with golden bars." The others, they stare like funeral attendees who are only there because they married into the family. "You know, a cage of golden bars? It's a common phrase."

The chief writes out a check and hands it to this upstart. "Ten million for your severance package," she says. "You're no longer needed, starting immediately."

Recording continues, and as the fired exec passes us we listen to her landing a job with another label via cell phone. We give each other "the look" yet again. Wonder if she'll keep all this under her hat, or tell the new label about a great idea like signing Osama Bin Laden to front some death metal band. Thinking about her keeping her mouth shut reminds me of something I'd rather not bring up to Rolli. The other day I had an anonymous note waiting in my locker. It read: *Leaks can spill both ways.* I'm not sure who left it but I've got a good idea. If they think stuff like that can shake me then they just don't know how many threats I've gotten in my life.

Meanwhile, one of the prison's money makers keeps on shaking:

We'll drive up Eminem's Hershey highway, y'all take it up the ass like a five cent lay, fuckin' America the beautiful with amber waves of pain, rammin' straight through like a fuckin' Soul Train, from coast to coast we're leavin' shit stains, step to Taliban your ass is profaned, fuck with Islam you catch two in da brain, leavin' wankstas burnin' like the world...trade...center—we'll forcefully enter, your hood and your ho and blow up your fuckin' show, shut the shit down, drag your ass to Mecca and sell you by the pound, turnin' hip-hop hatery into white slavery, and right now I'm startin' with your fuckin' family, there ain't no escapin' see, 'cause I'm Sodamn Insein and I don't just hate you, I'll fuck your shit up like Saddam's rape room, represent Islam, I'll take your sister and mom, add 'em to my harem and straight up fuckin' TEAR 'EM

While everybody takes five to plan the radio edit—*as if*—Rolli and I step into the studio lobby to keep an eye on the inmates. Carleetha grunts at us and we nod in return. Meanwhile Sodamn pulls out rolling paper, eyes us, then stuffs it back in his pocket. We hang in the corner, keeping our conversation to ourselves.

"Guess it," Rolli says. What an annoying turn of words, but it won't help to tell him. Two years ago his brother overdosed and he's still a little touchy about things. "Guess it my crewby. Tell ya what. USA, 1977, the laws G, this what I'm talkin', in the one nine double-seven dig it—prison sentence is fifteen years longer for smuggle of coffee than for smuggle of marijuana. Oh yeah, baby! Making sense?"

"Rolli...who taught you English?"

"Making sense?"

"Yes, Rolli, think about it. They use coffee to mask drugs from police dogs. On top of that, the penalties for smuggling something corporations profit from are going to be much more stiff because they have more influence over the government than some pot farmers out in the middle of Bumfuck, Ohio."

It wouldn't be too far off to guess the inmates have been teaching Rolli to talk like this. Can't blame them for wanting to make a joke out of the guards. Thankfully, the signal arrives—we are ready to proceed. Rolli has to watch over the recording sessions solo from here on out.

Leena's voice sounds like it's being strained through a little kid's megaphone, or that's how it comes across on this line. "Still giving that Olympic pool a workout, huh?"

"Yeah." It's surprising that even after all this time she keeps up with the compliments. Avoiding her smile I ask the receiver, "Listen, what was that book you were reading? You know, last time I was...over at your place?"

Her blue jean eyes examine those hard, short nails of hers. "Why do you want to know?"

"Well, was it any good?" Her laugh is as infuriating as it is heart-warming. "Come on. I'm serious. I want to read it."

"The only way you're going to find out is by coming to 'my place' and seeing for yourself."

"God, I hope not." Then, "You still have it?"

"So hopeful, huh? You'd trade my life for a book? You're one sick man."

"No, that's not what I meant—"

"Like you would even crack the pages." She laughs again, play-fully, and the short black locks of her hair call out to my hands, pleading for a caress. "If you keep acting this goofy I might actually start missing you."

"I think about you too." That yellowing bruise around her neck, the size and shape of an improvised noose. That's probably not some-thing we'll talk about any time soon. "So, nice weather today huh?"

We share a laugh before nervous silence seeps in, threatening to thwart another conversation.

"I heard you got another job. Good for you."

"Uh, I hope you don't take offense or anything...you know, like that. Offense I mean."

"No, no, the more the merrier I say. What the heck, you only live once right?"

"Leena, it's not like I'm some swinging dude or something, I'm just...I don't know, you know? Just doing my job. You know that."

She chuckles. "Can't you tell when a body's teasing you?"

"No, not usually."

"Listen, don't worry about it. She's a decent enough person."

It's good to hear her being so upbeat for once. "Cool, that's cool."

"Time's up," a voice says on the other side of the glass. Some new guard—or *new boot*, if you're up on the prison lingo—a woman, steps forward. Leena hesitates, says her goodbyes, then puts the phone back in its cradle. In her standard issue white jumpsuit my lady sits intently watching me, memorizing me, her domineering jaw set like that of a dog guarding its bone. Eventually this new boot grabs her by the shoulder and attempts to yank her to her feet. Leena rips her arm away and the two women stare each other down briefly, mad-dogging it with nobody to witness except me. For a second it seems like hoe check time, and sure Leena could take a new prisoner to the square and see what they're made of, but no way in hell can she go around doing that with the guards.

"Hey," I say loudly. "You know who I am? What's your name?"

The new boot backs off but her attitude has plain irked my nerves. Her last name's Kirk-something...shoot, she turned before I could read it. "I'm coming back there."

Leena motions to me to stop, that it's okay, but it sure doesn't feel okay. They shuffle away, a bright white suit towering over a dark blue one, one wearing shackles and one carrying an extra set—just in case. They're both shapely enough, in their own ways, but really that's not what makes my eyes linger.

Leena steps through the door without looking back, followed by the guard. This new woman pauses to turn and size me up with glowering intensity. Who knows what she's thinking exactly—whatever it is, it doesn't seem pleasant. Maybe I'm the one that's going to get taken to the square?

Chauntelle is superheated, almost uncomfortably warm against my arm, my ribs, my hip and thigh. Laying here like this, looking up at the ceiling of this conjugal cell—or this *canton* as most prisoners here call them—it's not too hard to imagine what restless nights in prison are like. Wondering if they remember you out there in the world, hoping those people in the other cells don't remember that remark you made the other day, hoping that the governor remembers you're one of his citizens. Hey, I have to remind myself, this cell is a step up for a lot of the women; they're used to spending time in meditation or in suicide watch cantons, or at the very least they grew up in the projects. Even though it's still public housing you don't hear insects crawling around in the darkness of this room, in this bed, and there's no mice scampering across your chest waking you at three in the morning. The women tell me about these things when we're alone.

My mind is starting to wander. To most of the African American women here I'm just an MO: muthafuckin' ofay. Chauntelle hasn't spouted any of that yet.

In an hour or two the sun is going to creep up over our world and put an end to all of this. It occurs to me that Chauntelle's lower lip is beginning to tremble—it's best not to look. This is always the end-sign leading to the final revelation. On the up-side these women get more than just physical comfort or release from my service. This thought is the most rewarding; that there can be spiritual and emotional benefit for the inmates makes every second worthwhile.

"I...I..." Her rough voice quavers, incapable of continuing.

"Chauntelle, listen. It's okay. Just take your time and tell me whatever you want. Whenever you're ready. Okay? Really." I tilt her head toward me so that she can look into my eyes. "I'm here for you." That's when she breaks down, blubbering self-hating syllables and regret and, well, snot. Tissues are kept on hand for times like this, and after restraining Chauntelle's wrists to keep her from clawing at her face I hand her a couple. These are the cheap kind and when she blows her nose she punches a hole in the flimsy tissue. "Sorry about that."

"S'okay, s'okay," she says to herself more than me. "Ken..." Chauntelle's voice cracks and she sobs before continuing. "I did it. I, uh, you know, I really did...it."

It's made clear from the get-go my name is Kenrick, and they can call me Ken or Rick, just not Kenrick. Not sure what she's referring to by "it" I stay quiet for the moment and stroke the cornrows of her hair.

"Rajhid, he was only three...wh-when I killed 'im. I threw 'im down the steps, down the steps in the 'partments, one floor and then I did the 'nother floor and the 'nother floor but he must'a been had his neck broke on just the first one. I don't..." Her voice trails off as her pupils seem to focus on something looming over us in the darkness. "Don't know why I gone done that." She faces away from me, ashamed or something. The heaving of her breasts as she hyperventilates is a little unnerving. "Ain't never told no one that. Not the laws, or the PD, or the sistas, or no one. Just you, white boy."

"It's okay. I'm not judging you." My hands massage her arm, her shoulder, and she rolls away from me. Not for me to stop, just to talk to the wall. This is the most physically intimate we've gotten the whole time. Up until now it's just been the occasional comment in the darkness, and laying here naked side-by-side, but not in an awkward way. She's just been enjoying the time at her own pace, savoring her last moments. "Chauntelle—"

"Why come you don't call me 'baby?' Ain't I your baby now?"

"Yeah, I guess so. Whatever you want baby. You like that?" My fingertips are gently dragged along her skin, from her neck to the small of her back.

She grunts in the affirmative. "His brains, they come out on the last fall. It come out all over th' floor. It was metal steps up in there, where we lived. And I just stood there, like I's simple, just lookin'.'"

"That's all behind you now." To say that it's over would be in bad taste, considering tomorrow's scheduled event. "It happened. Just don't let it keep happening in your heart, you've gotta let it go. You know?" As my lips brush her neck a shudder runs through her.

After a long while she breaks the silence. "All this time...if just one'a these head-shrinkers would'a said that to me!"

"It's okay baby."

"Whycome you don't shove me outta this here bed?! You ain't even mad!"

"I told you, I'm not here to be judging you. I just want you to take care of yourself."

"Don't you think it's all late for that and whatnot?" Despite her confrontational talk she seems to be calming down a bit. Suddenly she flips back over, facing me with wild eyes and rough, rushed hands. "Do me," she commands. I'm not sure if she wants me to execute her or give her lust, but I'll opt for that second one.

Every once in a while it feels like TV cameras are on me, the star of my own little show. One set is filled with torture instruments out of a dungeon, and the other is a dungeon. Which one is home and which is my job? When in doubt, look to the supporting cast. I nod to Cialis, better known as C.C., while she pushes buttons and pulls levers.

"What up, Mack Jackoff."

"Wonder what the consumers would think if they knew such a sweet girl was making their bread." She sneers and shoos me away, already starting to fall behind on the packaging. "Oh yeah, and try not to steal any of the product today."

She punches my upper arm. "I done stole *you*, son, how 'bout that?" *Stole* is *to have struck a blow*—not an all-out fight, in the traditional "fisticuffs" sense. Not abducted, not hijacked, not taken against my will, although maybe my standing with the sentry has got "stoled." His scowl is obvious even from here. Then again, Ritchie is always looking for a reason to scowl at me. He's already warned me once about "fraternizing"—what he probably thinks is this gigolo is trying to score more "business." It only takes a minute before I'm out of the bread packing station, some of the inmates hooting and whistling—everybody seems to know about my "secret" job.

One of them calls out, "I gots ta thank yo pops fo' givin' ya that ass, son."

Maybe my double lives aren't so separate anymore—the inmates aren't as dumb as most of my coworkers want to believe. Sometimes I almost slip up and call them the "mates" instead of the "inmates," but luckily that little problem has been kept in check. In reality, "female offenders" is the correct term.

Out of the seventy thousand women in the United States prison system less than one percent are death row occupants. Point-zero-seven percent. Of course, my home state is the leader of the pack with nearly a third of that doomed .07 percent locked behind its penal walls. What the general population doesn't realize is what life is like behind those walls, especially in maximum lockdown. It's like landing yourself on some space colony. Huge, fortress-like installations are so out, and pod design is so in. Circular units that allow 180 degree visibility for the officers, with inmates in the smallest possible clusters. Instead of long hallways everything is compartmentalized into tiny security zones: automated security for every room, every quadrant, and on and on. Motion detectors and vibration detectors have replaced humans on the ground. Gone are the barbaric days of having to see walls and barbed-wire fences surrounding our facilities; exterior upgrades include a continuous field of laser-activated claymore mines. All rooms and walkways are fitted with cameras, except for the cells, where cameras are replaced by "sniffers"—hormone detectors used to gauge when inmates become dangerously depressed or angry. Of course, sniffers don't work on the true sociopaths who kill or maim on a whim, but that's another story.

As for employees, most of the staff has been replaced over the last twenty years by drone carts and other robots. Why risk using people to do the scrub jobs in our prisons? The guards overseeing a pod, they're not armed with guns these days. Instead you get man-down triggers that alert the security matrix of trouble. Personnel are then dispatched to the pod, or in the case of a general riot the computer may choose to pump out nerve gas. Me, I never made it that far as a new boot. Of all the stupid jobs in my life Jack Mack patrol was my lamest, and it's the one that's most hated by the prisoners. They thought I was a G.I.—*gang investigator*—and called "Auguas!" to alert others I was coming.

Jack Mack is canned mackerel felons get from the commissary. A lot of times the cans are used for bartering, but mostly they can be put in socks and swung around as weapons. Since it's all canned the sniffers can't pick up on it. When inmates realize you're Jack Mackin' it, not G-eyeing them up, then they really hate your guts. That's because *Jackers*, as they refer to us, ransack what little belongings they have, half the time walking away with money, narcotics, or pictures of their relatives. If you're in the white state-issue jumpsuits nothing goes your way, or as they say around here: white ain't right.

"Hey. Hey Brimley!" Someone's coming up from behind. Fast.

It's Ritchie again, leaving his station in the bread packing area just for the chance to give me a piece of his mind. We get into it for the umpteenth time: the whole exporting of slave labor never sat well with me. Isn't that one of our main problems with China, that they sell goods their prisoners are forced to make? On the West Coast they export prison-made shirts, because our laws only say you can't sell the product in the USA. Down here in the South it isn't shirts, it's *white bread*, AKA *bolillos*. The Hispanic chicks, in their white state-issue jumpsuits, they call me and the other white officers bolillos too. But Ritchie, you could just call him a fuckin' asshole. And I do.

That's when he grabs me, and that's when I shove him, and that's when his fist slams into me, and that's when the inmates start jumping up and down cheering us on like it was the Birmingham Black Bastards versus the Washington White Devils in the playoffs. It would make their day to see us off each other, but a slew of other guards rush in and separate us. As much spy tech as we've got up in here it's a wonder we didn't get slammed soon as we raised our voices up a notch. You've been *slammed* when a guard *harshly takes you to the ground and restrains you.*

It's no surprise when the others slam me but let Ritchie split my wig. That extra quick little punch is gonna cost somebody, just wait and see. Punks. While they're busy getting the population settled down Ritchie leans in and whispers, "I got a long memory, boy."

"And a big fuckin' mouth!"

The fists come out to play again.

Can't even remember why I signed up with the correctional system in the first place. Up north, where I'm from, the weather wasn't nearly so hot and even now, a few years later, it still leaves me drained most of the time. So why stay here? For a new boot the pay was just so-so, and quitting to find a more pleasant line of work was my next step. That is, before an unusual sort of counselor job opened up. The rumors about an upcoming position were passed on by Fred in the cafeteria and Cindy the train driver—the *train* is the bus that drives prisoners from county jail to prison. Neither of them took it very seriously; after all how could such a wild rumor be true? Just to be on the safe side I lodged an official complaint about the matter.

"Kenrick Brimley. You ain't a relation of that actor, I don't suppose?"

"Um...pardon me?" I found myself standing alone in front of the warden, J. Marlan Dempsey, for the first time in my seven months of employment.

"That fella, Brimley, eats the oatmeals."

"Sanders said you wanted to speak to me about something. Sir?"

"True enough," he said, and tapped the ash from his cigar. "I'll cut to the chase with you. There will be, effective May 17, a new position available in our facility, one that is filled by appointment only—"

"So it's true then? It's true."

"Let me finish," Warden Dempsey said. He smoothed over the bristles of his mustache before continuing. "You are not in trouble here son. In fact, your decision to go against the grain and file that complaint caught the eye of certain individuals—who will remain unnamed—and, to be quite blunt is it, or is it not, true that you were once employed as..." He paused, checking his notes. "...as a male stripper?"

"Ye-e-e-eah, you could, potentially speaking, say I maintained an echelon of adult professionality—"

"What are you trying to say, boy?" He peered at me through the cigar smoke. "Yes or no is all I need to hear."

Looking at the floor, the walls, examining my uniform, none of that made it any easier to admit. "Yes."

"Right. So what this situation calls for is a stud with morals, if you will. Son, I appoint you as the first—"

"Wait! Whoa. What?"

Despite my initial reluctance things proceeded smoothly from there on out. The entire process was kept hush-hush because of tensions in the population of offenders, the population of correctional employees, and the outside population in general. The state board went into long debates about the details of my job description, and especially the fine print of my contract. During the debates I contemplated my sins while my lawyer handled all the legal jargon. It took a lot to convince myself it was the right thing to do: better me than one of the low-lives, better somebody who disagreed and could maybe change the system from the inside.

The right-wingers tried to slip it in the contract that "the candidate" would have to get a vasectomy in order to be eligible for work. My lawyer protested this as being highly inhumane. The argument the right-wingers gave was what if I impregnated one of the women? The next day she would be executed with an unborn child in her and that was completely immoral from their standpoint. It was during this stage of the negotiations that I flipped my lid. After kicking me out, the proceedings continued. My lawyer reasoned that to force a vasectomy on his client would be tantamount to killing thousands, millions of human lives—my sperm. He then quoted that part of the Bible about spilling your seed and the right-wingers gave in. It was all a total load, but this is the world we live in, right? Kill the mother, but not the fertilized egg.

"We aren't the first to hatch this scheme," Warden Dempsey informed me. "Historically speaking the practice originated with the French, or so the tale goes, and has been carried out by other nations too. We're just keeping with the traditions that make the system work."

On the evening before execution an inmate is given the privilege of one final sexual encounter. In the case of male inmates the prison will import a woman or a man, depending on the preference of those about to die. The problem here in female lockdown arose from our death row population being serviced by the guards, an obvious conflict of interest/abuse of power, at the least. With elections coming up, and possibly facing news leaks, the government caved to the complaints and modified the game, setting up an "independent contractor" on a leash. In the end, it was human rights activists that put me in this position.

Chauntelle's grave is unmarked, like so many of the others, just a little lump of a stone with a number carved into it. There aren't any flowers here. Heck, most of the graves could use some sprucing up or something. Like always, I'm the only living member of the party. Like always there's some remorse, some anger, and also some relief that I eased the suffering—if only a little. Chauntelle's was another case where I was the only witness. Imagine having to die alone, not even your friends and family coming to see you in your final week on Earth. In the end Chauntelle was able to look into my eyes as she drifted away from this world, her final thoughts locked away in a vault of flesh...and my thoughts, well, like always they were conflicted. These people committed murders, after all.

"Figured I'd find you here. Just you, me, and the groundskeepers hang in this neck o'the woods." He's standing here, casual as ever, like he hasn't killed anybody. Most people, when they take one life after another, you call them a serial killer. When the government gives them money to do it they're an executioner. This one, Bart, he's about ten years older than me and likes to pretend he's Southern.

"Oh, hey. Checking to make sure you didn't goof up?"

He's in his typical gray suit and wire-frame glasses. Is he trying to look like an undertaker or does it just come naturally? "Aw, come now Rick. Don't be sore with me. We both get paid to do our jobs, whether anybody else likes it or not."

Why bother getting into it with him? We're both here to relax—or at least that's why I'm here. He's pretty mellow too, taking his happy time finishing off sweet tea from that stupid mason jar he always carries around. So we talk a while. He's eating another one of those damn sandwiches. Ugh, it makes me sick just looking at it. Peanut butter and marshmallow creme, of all things.

"Fluffernutter," he tells me. "Elvis loved the things."

"Maybe, dude, but they're downright dirty."

He raises an eyebrow. "Dirty?"

"Filthy. Disgusting." He laughs. "Bart, you're living proof that it takes a cast-iron stomach to be an executioner."

We have a good laugh, then he changes the subject to the Internet, about wireless technology and all the information rocketing through the air. "No need for physical connectivity to anything else these days."

"And how would you know?"

"Been doing plenty of investing in that kinda thing. You'd be amazed."

"Sorry dude, I don't give a flip about the Internet."

"What? You don't mean that!"

"Why sit in front of a computer when I could be working out?" For whatever reason this cracks him up and his mood improves. "Say, check it out. Taliban's still here."

"Yesiree. They've pretty much taken up residence, as I understand things." A jeep follows the driveway, music blasting. Insein is hanging out the window thrashing his arms gangster-style in time with the beat. Inmates close to the windows hoot and holler. "Sons of bitches."

With that he excuses himself and runs off to do whatever it is executioners do. Bartholomew, the middle-aged and not-so-crazy dispenser of lethal injections. We get along okay, but once I asked him if he would consider taking a different job if it came up. "Why should I?" he replied. "I'm happy where I am."

Well, that set up a little barrier between us, but overall he's about the closest to understanding me. That is, aside from Leena. Everyone else that understood has been killed by the people who put food on my plate. These women took something from society; or as the prisoners say, they *hawged* it. In return society hawged their lives. Far as my own life is concerned, death hawgs it all. In the distance you can make out the buzz of chatter out on the yard, the revving of engines as trucks shuttle guards and inmates back and forth to their jobs. What about my job? What is my role, really? Isn't my job done once these women are in the ground?

I place a modest bunch of flowers on Chauntelle's grave, then sit in the afternoon sunlight reading poetry aloud, Lorca, for the rest of the afternoon.

I'm in Leena's arms again. She was my first job—it seems like a life-time ago now—but a last minute stay of execution changed things. Of course, the system's "independent contractor" had already been "put to work" by that point.

"Thanks for bringing the candy bars. You're getting to know my tastes too well, Kenrick. It's almost scary."

"Ken," I groan, "Or Rick. Is it too hard?"

"Let me check," she says deviously, sweeping me up in her arms and searching between my legs.

"Stop it you idiot! You're going to drop me!" We're laughing, and if she dropped me it wouldn't be the first time. I'm six-foot-two, she's six even, but we're both the same weight and it's all muscle.

"I'll break the little man to pieces," she snarls, tossing me up lightly and catching me again. The first time we were together she insisted on bench-pressing me.

Back on my feet I kiss Leena, then ask, "Are you ready?"

"Not yet. Not yet Kenny." She sighs. "I want to savor this. That's my problem, right? I want to live life, my way. That's what got me put in this place to begin with."

I settle onto the as-yet-unused bed. "What do you mean?"

"'The flame that burns brightest burns the fastest.' You ever hear that?"

"No," I admit. The second time they were going to overdose Leena we spent the night together, with her quoting philosophers between sex acts.

"In twenty-four hours I am going to be a corpse. Cold, not breath-ing. Dead. They...they're going to do it this time. Three strikes, I'm out. I wanted to let you know that I, I mean..." She doesn't usually get all emotional, but things are different tonight.

"Leena, honey, you don't have to say anything." I lay bare looking up at her, also naked, in the dim light provided by the room's single bulb.

"Did you just call me 'honey?'" She laughs and situates herself next to me. "Do you realize something?"

"No, I don't think so."

"Well, that's because I wasn't finished yet, silly. What I was *going* to say is that it's been over two years. This is the longest steady relationship that I've ever had. Too bad it has to e—"

My fingers move to her lips. "We still have tonight."

On lap seventeen Leena's coarse laugh creeps into my thoughts, the exaggerated cursive of her love notes blurs my vision. This pool is indoors, heated, and normally it's a soothing place to be. My heart feels funny and my stomach sours, because they did it again. It's doubtful the powers that be realize just how much torment it causes to keep jerking Leena around.

Still, my heart is flooded with relief. Lap nineteen comes around and I contemplate our "existentialist" conversations, her instructions for things she wanted done after she departed the world, her breath hot on my skin. During these last couple of years...whoa, it's going to be three years pretty soon! During these years there haven't been any other women I've even talked to, outside of work that is, only the inmates. Never really seemed like there was a void in my life but it feels like Leena has filled some part of me, and it's kind of exciting, kind of dark, and it's clear she's taking up too much of my brain power because I've lost track of the laps.

Due to a clerical error the execution had to be halted. Exactly what that error was has remained a mystery, but apparently somewhere down the chain of command someone made a boo-boo with the paper work. Our next "appointment" is scheduled for roughly three weeks from now.

But more importantly, how can a guy concentrate on good stroke mechanics like sculling technique, hand position, and angle of entry when there's a gaggle of people spying on him 24/7? Those hipster chicks on the other side of the pool, they're so totally out of place here. They're not even getting in the water! How much more obvious could they be?

It makes sense. The new wave of threats left at home include a whole bunch of feminist propaganda. Could they have found out about me somehow, maybe hacked the prison's computer system? And what about that stuff Bart said—information traveling through the air. Everything's wireless now, so there's any number of ways they could get the info. If you adjust your TV or radio reception just so, can you pick up computer files rocketing to Tokyo? Five to one odds it's that S.I.S.T.E.R. group.

Back in the changing area somebody has busted my locker open and taken all my stuff. When I get to the apartment in my cold, wet swim trunks and robe—which cost so much you have to wonder if the pool staff doesn't steal your stuff just to scam you—the door isn't locked. Soon as I step inside there's the sound of a window being thrown open. Running back to the bedroom doesn't help. Whoever it was has already jumped and run.

Okay, it's happening again. That means it's time for me to take the offensive.

Bully Boy Barnes Settles With Accuser
By Jim Bean, AP Writer

HOUSTON - With a terse written statement and an even more terse court filing, the sexual assault case against Bully Boy Barnes that gripped the United States abruptly ended in an agreement ensuring the basketball star never stands trial for what allegedly happened in a motel parking lot two years ago.

Few experts believed in the civil lawsuit, in civil liberties, or even in civility. "This kind of thing will never be heard by a jury, nor should it," stated prominent law analyst Ricky Mardnt. He added that Barnes and his accuser, a 19-year-old woman who is convinced he raped her, should shut up once and for all instead of revealing intimate details to the court.

The case elevated the public profiles of both Barnes, 27, arguably basketball's most brilliant player, and the accuser, a high school dropout who once auditioned for "Are You Hot?" and was subjected to wild Internet speculation.

Although the terms were not released, law experts assure us the agreement spells out financial penalties, and possible sexual penalties, for revealing details.

A two-syllable statement faxed to AP by Bully Boy's attorneys said only "Fuck off," forcing media outlets and experts to fill in the blanks.

"The attorney's party is a birthday suit affair," another statement said. The one-sentence filing for dismissal stipulated the case can't be refiled, and was filed in Houston federal court.

The Los Angeles Layers' spokeswoman said Barnes has declined comment on his name change, music career, or the settlement. Barnes scored 66 points Wednesday night against Boston's Booty Bandits, but the Bandits still pounded the Layers 194-171.

Barnes, married father of seven, apologized for his "rampant ho-pumping and the consequences of getting caught," but insisted all sex was at least semi-consensual.

Texas law impedes plaintiffs in civil cases from winning more than $3,000,000. The accuser's attorneys have said the amount was too low for compensating the woman, or for their time and effort.

Marketers estimate Barnes gained $12 million to $18 million in endorsement contracts after being arrested. He has appeared in Fly Right commercials since the allegations first surfaced, and Todo Bell renewed their deal with him.

"The defense team for the criminal case made sure the victim got reamed by papers loaded with rumors and innuendo regarding her sexual history," said Marndt. In the end experts are left wondering why she bothered.

AP Writers Tanith Lemler, Sandra Tsui and Eric Hadner contributed to this article.

People tell me that I'm too sentimental, a softy or something, and it might be true. Just so happens that there's a journal in my living room filled with mementos: letters from the weeks leading up to the event; maybe a lock of hair they gave me for posterity. I used to be worried that "posterity" was some religious thing, or maybe a hard task like something to do with their families—no way do I want to get involved with their families—but it turns out that posterity is good and necessary. We need to remember the past, and to occasionally look up words in the dictionary.

Hope, Anita, Althea, Lavonda, Malloree, Whitney, Blossom, Gizelle, Daphne, Treshana, Claudia, Chauntelle. Bubble gum wrappers, panties, hair, notes on napkins, scrunchies, lipstick, letters in marker or pencil, the shiv Claudia tried to use on me, a curious envelope that is marked "dont open til u dy" (and I haven't...uh, opened it, that is), a cassette single of "our song" (some obscure seventies song that Anita really liked), a nude instant photo that Blossom forced me to take of her on the threat of "doin' somethin' insane-like" if I didn't comply. There's so much in here. And throughout it all, time and again, weaves the name Leena, with her army of forget-me-nots like a network of roots threatening to crack a foundation. That's what weeping willows do, or so my brother tells me in his whiney Sunday afternoon phone calls. Like this one.

"Don't you think you're overreacting about things? It's not like you haven't overreacted before."

"Can't let 'em jug me like this, bro. You know how it is. They don't back off until you split their wig once or twice."

"Uh, 'jug?'"

While I explain that *jug* means *to harass with the intention of inciting violence*, there's another clickety-click on the line. Bastards! "Shame, you get any visits from the phone company lately?"

"Ken—"

"Or little bro. You heard from him recently?"

He sighs. "Remember what Mom always said about living by the river? It always looks the same but it's completely different water." I remind him that our mother said a whole lot of stuff, none of which was worth remembering. "But still," he insists. "Those times are gone. The freaks aren't out there after us anymore. Nobody even remembers, except you. Stop holding onto it."

"Maybe it looks the same because it *is* the same."

Speaking of looking the same, my apartment still looks the way I left it. Stopping in like this to make it look lived in is a hassle, but what can you do.

"Look, let's not get into the family again. All right? You and I never can talk about things nicely. It always turns into...this."

"Whatever. Listen, tell me about the whole wireless thing. You work with computers, so give me the goods."

While Shame ticks off a list of tech details nobody could really use I start to wonder about my antiques. What if somebody gets in here and messes them up while I'm hiding out? The upkeep alone costs a small fortune: maintaining not only the devices, but all their pedigree papers—court documents, historical references to the various trials and punishments with dates and names, even old judges' journals. Just look at them all, collecting dust while I'm playing hide-and-seek with maniacs. Nobody's even talked to them today. Some people talk to their plants, I talk to my antiques. And do tormented spirits still huddle around the pieces, do they pay attention to the current world? If so I better spice up the conversation next time around.

"Yo! Kenrick. You even listening?"

"Sure."

"Then what did I just say?"

"Shame, don't start playing Mom's stupid mind games."

"Oh Christ, here we go again..."

Take the iron maiden for instance. When you want some quiet time you can step inside for a bit—of course, the door has to stay propped open enough to keep you from becoming a pin cushion. When I'm in there, are spirits peeking in on me, squeezing into my ears to hear my thoughts?

"...all three of us went through the same crap, but you're the one with a martyr complex. Just get over yourself, man..."

Most of my babies were designed for public ridicule because it used to be that your public standing was all you had. Words were the most feared thing in the world. They may not break your bones like sticks and stones, but they made you dead in everybody else's eyes.

"Okay, you wanna hear about the Internet? Here's something you can relate to: all the 'models' on those amateur porn sites, they're all the same people. Put a wig on them, give them contact lenses, cover their tattoos, change the name next to their pics. Different porn, same model. Or maybe it really isn't the same bunch of people over and over again in some nudie conspiracy. Maybe, just maybe, they are all different and I'm trying to hold onto something that isn't there."

"Subtle, Shame, subtle."

"*Seamus.* Is it so freakin' hard?"

The phone line goes dead. I hang up and slip out the back window, just like those perps did the other day.

Sometimes, when I'm chilling in the iron maiden, I wonder what it must be like for all those demons in Hell, torturing folks. Sometimes I wonder if I'm not already there.

Miles make champions. That's right up there at the top of every page in my notebook. Well, swim log. We'll call it a swim log, but it spends most of its time being my private journal. Your swim coaches make you keep detailed records, like *100m x8, 12 second rest intervals, -3 sec.* and so forth, with commentary. It's supposed to track your progress, but really they want to snoop. The easiest way to tell if your athletes are getting burned out is to monitor their swim logs for signs. Signs like muscle/joint related complaints, decreasing body weight, any mention of intestinal upset, etc.

Technically, it's not *burnout*—that's passé. No, it's really *maladaption*. The theory is that physical and psychological stresses combine to weaken the physiological processes. ACTH production goes haywire and starts interfering with your other hormones, especially within the cortical region of your adrenal glands. You hit your adaptation wall. So, there's a limited amount of adaptation energy, and beyond that there's just maladaption. On an even more technical level they call it GAS—General Adaptation Syndrome.

Me and the others? We just wanted to swim.

Miles make champions, miles and miles, then you slam into the wall and derail. But miles of the same car behind you, that makes for being followed. I accelerate. They change lanes, maneuver around the car separating us. It would have to happen when I'm on the way to my dealer. Well, maybe the trip can be salvaged; I've still got some moves left from my days on the run. The question is: who wants to chase me down this time? The safe money is on the lesbians.

I've been receiving a new wave of threats lately. The first was a photo of a bleached blonde woman with a buzz-cut and stern-looking glasses. She was staring angrily into the camera with her top hanging open and her skirt bunched up to reveal a lack of hair. At the time I figured it was some pissed off law student who got my address by mistake. A week later the second one came in, some kind of nude neo-hippy with paint on her face violently strumming an acoustic guitar. Maybe it could be a coincidence, I told myself. Then came the third, some businesswoman in her late forties wearing only the top of her suit. She was pointing to a financial chart that was all in the red.

My car veers to the left, my pursuer follows suit. They're driving one of those fucked up Vanagons from back in the...what, 1970's? Has to be on the antique list, or, well, not my antique list anyway.

They get close, too close, dodging other motorists left and right. Feels like I'm back in my old racing days, each competitor barreling down their own lane. These curves prove too dangerous, forcing a deceleration, and they pull up alongside me. Up front are two women—a bleached-blonde and a black/pink combo—both naked. The blonde, a metal stud accentuates her pouty lower lip and her barcode tattoo is menacing for some reason. The black/pink, her tattoos aren't nearly as

Photo still, courtesy Last Burn Films © 2006

disturbing as the strips of metal implanted in her arms—the surrounding scar tissue makes me swerve all over the road. In the back there's an Oriental woman, maybe Japanese, also nude. Her long hair flows freely, but she's got chains wrapped around her arms. She shakes them at me, her angry eyes unblinking, and I lose control.

My car skids off the shoulder, fishtails on about fifty yards of grass, comes to a halt against some thorny bushes. I'm back on the road heading in the other direction before they can turn around.

"The *branks* were known also as the 'scold's helm' and the 'dame's bridle.' As you can see it is made of iron and incredibly heavy. This is a replica, so the cage is actually large enough to fit over the head of modern man. Not that it would ever come to that!" The broker, thin as a twig and about as charismatic, pauses to chuckle. "You'll note the spiked bit of iron that juts in from the mouth plate. This fits into the mouth and causes excruciating pain to the tongue any time the wearer attempts to speak. As you can guess, our forefathers really did think women were better seen than heard."

I nod, pretend this is as interesting as usual. But something's missing. Is it that the job is getting to be a little too important? Aren't things on the outside as good, if not better, than the hours spent locked up with all those women? It's hard work, an all-nighter by nature most times. We're talking in the neighborhood of six, seven orgasms. Sometimes more, sometimes less. And the women? They usually double that.

My modus operandi is that I'll start with a general body massage, beginning at the hands and feet, working slowly toward center. Not only does this work the blood toward the erogenous zones, heightening sensitivity in those areas, but it builds the trust that we both need to have a successful night. Then they receive the Yoni massage moves—something that, in most cases, is totally new to these women.

Yoni is "sacred space" in some language called Sanskrit. One day I'll have to visit Sanskritistan—is that what it's called? Anyway, those Sanskritinese don't dis their women by using crude terms like *cunt* or *twat*, instead using the term Yoni, and Yoni massage isn't some goal-oriented event, unlike what stressed-out Westerners go for. More often than not the night eventually heads toward MO—major orgasms, or at least moderate orgasms—but that's all much later. If an orgasm happens here it happens, but really you're just trying to create an experience of ultimate pleasure and arousal. In fact some sex therapists use it to assist in breaking through sexual fears and all. Sometimes the experience is so intense the women flip their shit, but that isn't the norm. That's a different MO: *malfunctioning orgasm.*

Of course, every once in a while the inmate will go all loopy on me without even getting to the Yoni stuff, having been the subject of all sorts of abuse once too often. Or maybe they didn't give her the proper dosage of meds that day to save money since she'd be gone soon anyway. There's even been times when some of the guards fill a lady's head with all these stories about the horrible things I do to the women, but really that's only happened once and I managed to calm the woman down after a bit—Daphne was her name. Never did find out which idiot set that one up but he'll get paid back some day.

Don't get emotionally attached is always a good mantra to have. *Don't get all numb and crass either.* Another important thing is to respect even the strangest requests of the inmates, because really everybody has something they've never done that—no matter how off it seems—is important to them. Smuggling in the cookie-dough ice cream might've been the most difficult. Unfortunately I'm not the be-all, end-all; I can't fly people to the Great Wall for one last scenic view before oblivion. I do what I can though.

My antiques broker is still rambling. "These implements come from China, circa 1950. They were used most frequently during the so-called 'struggle sessions' in which suspected enemies of the Communist Party were publicly forced to renounce their crimes. The workmanship is crude but you'll be hard pressed—so to speak—to find another set in such pristine condition."

Normally visits to the broker calm the nerves, distract me from all the job-related stuff boiling in my head. Instead everything reminds me of the women. "How about these? What are they, branding irons?"

"No, that one was heated and put through the tongues of Quakers found distributing their 'heathen writings' in Massachusetts. The R-brand next to it, though, was used to brand the shoulders of Quakers. It stood for 'heretic.'"

"Aren't Quakers harmless? All they do is ride around in buggies and eat oatmeal."

"That's beyond my area of expertise. Obviously, these items haven't fared very well and are being offered at a reduced price. Now, over here, we have..."

Question: do the ghosts of the tortured hang around, sort of stuck to the instruments of torture, or do they get shuffled off to Purgatory or Hell or whatever? And if spirits get stuck on these things, then what about the women I work with?

The broker tenses up. "I'm sorry sir, but viewing is by appointment only."

Who? I turn only to find Ritchie partially concealed by a ducking stool. His face is a mask. "That one," I say. "Tell me about that one."

We move in on the ducking stool and our unwelcome guest. "Seventeenth century, England, crafted by William Holmes Ellsworth. Used in—" He pauses to retrieve a photocopy. "Seventy-three punishments in Essex."

"Punishments in sex?" Ritchie asks.

The broker looks up, glares. "Sir, if you don't respect our posted hours I'll be forced to call the authorities."

Ritchie ignores him, taking in our surroundings. "You sick bastard, I shoulda known."

"Should've known what?"

"That a sick fuck like you would collect torture gear!"

"This is an antiques and collectables clearing house!" the broker shouts. We ignore him.

"Is this the kinda kinky shit ya get up to with the gals?"

"Aren't there still some empty tree limbs? I thought you'd be out prowling for Black folks."

Ritchie cracks his knuckles. "Keep on jokin', man-ho. Keep on jokin' and see what happens." He stalks out, nearly busting the glass door.

The fragile little broker looks to me nervously. "You know what," I tell him, "I'll just take the branks and brands today."

Top US Singles:

1. Baby I Want You To Be The Glove (Wrapped Around My Throbbin' Love)

   B-3, *Invasion Of Da Poo-Poo Snatchas*

2. Bust-in Loose

   The Notorious T.I.T., *Liberating The Rack*

3. It's Da Taliban

   The Taliban, *It's Da Taliban*

4. Beat the Rendezvous

   The Tomatoes, *It's The Night*

5. BRIMSTONE HEAVEN

   Hellmonger, *Fuck the World*

6. BRA BUSTER

   The Notorious T.I.T., *Weapons of Mass Distraction*

7. WOMEN OF THE NIGHT

   Down for da Count featuring Dre-Coola and DJ Renfield, *Goth Milk*

8. UP YOURS

   The Hating Forkful, *What's Your Price Tonight?*

9. BUNK BUSTER

   Moby with Korn featuring Jennifer Love Hewitt, *Peace vs. Resistance*

10. BEAT YOUR FEET ON MY SHOULDERS

   The Tomatoes, *It's The Night*

Top Import Single:

CHAMELEON

Nikki, *Chameleon*

"What is it this time?" These days Warden Dempsey doesn't bother to look up when I enter. He would rather not be reminded of my role in the penal system. We haven't talked in months—okay, we don't talk, we argue, so we stay clear of each other. After a while you decide not to bite the hand that feeds you, especially if it's a masturbating hand.

"You heard about the fight between me and Ritchie?"

"Sure." He keeps stuffing his pipe, looking over papers.

"I want to lodge a complaint. He's been way out of line lately. Always harassing me every time I turn around."

"And?"

"And for starters he's been following me all over the place!"

"Feeling a bit paranoid again, are we?" When one of the anonymous notes left in my locker gets thrown onto his desk he takes his time reading it. "'A gigolo in the ground is worth two in the bushes.' Didn't Jefferson say that?"

"Look, if you don't start taking this seriously I'll have to deal with it myself. Sir."

He sneers. "Ain't you supposed to be a lover, not a fighter?"

Maybe it's time to blackmail him. "You know, last time we talked you said there would be visible changes in three months' time. I've got a little news: it's six months later. Know what the only changes have been?"

Dempsey signs a document, then grunts. "Please. Do enlighten me."

"When they cut education programs to the death row inmates you said they would still have books. Now all hardcover books are banned—"

"They can't keep weapons in their cells—"

"I think we know why *law books* aren't allowed in the cells. Oh, did I say that? I just meant 'books.' And Varney, I warned you about him before, he's started strip-searching the women again."

"For the love of God, who do you work for boy? You know that's perfectly within the bounds of the mandates set forth by—"

"Why is it we're the only industrialized nation where prison workers of the opposite sex can conduct a stri—"

"Is there anything else? I'm rather busy here." At least he's looking at me now.

"Yeah, there's plenty." Having said that I turn my back on him and exit his stuffy office.

The television is running in this pod. I'm looking for Leena, but maybe they've got her doing work, or she's set off in meditation. On the screen a talk show is playing out. Looks like one of the people on stage has a turntable set up.

The host crosses his legs, glances at his notes. "My first question regards the recombinant DNA of hip-hop. Given its divergent roots what could one say is hip-hop's proper lineage; what cultural movements and musicians are its ancestors, its inheritors? Does it belong solely to the DJs and MCs who went to the creative laboratory to create it? Or—as it employs guerilla tactics—is it truly the music of the people?"

The DJ smiles. "Excellent question. I've been traveling the country proselytizing about this very subject for some time now, and—"

"Gawd damn bama-ass *faggots!*" Somebody switches channels.

Rolli says, "Oh yeah, baby. The women, they are pissed."

On the next station is another talk show, a host and some sort of brainy expert.

"...examining the state of lookism in the 21st-century," The brainy lady says, "we can see that 'face' is indeed a four-letter word."

"Bama-ass ho!" one of the women calls, and again the channel is changed, this time to a police show.

If Leena were here she'd go into her regular spiel: the crime shows have two murders per episode, sometimes more, making for at least one-hundred-four murders per year in their city...however, murder rates have dropped so low that there's more murder on prime time than in real time. She'd rail against fake crimes generating real fear generating certificates that say corporations have real money, because there's more wealth on paper than there is in the real world.

"Hey man, you seen Leena?"

"Lawyer," Rolli says.

"Right." One of the women, in the corner, she's watching me a little too closely. Like she knows me. She trying to jug me too? And what's up with that bandana on her head? "Yo, what's her story?" I ask.

"Oh yeah, baby!" Rolli's eyes grope every inch of her.

"Knock it off. I mean what's her problem."

"She's upset about her sister. I'm knowing how this feels—my brother, he left me all alone in the cold world this is being."

Sister? Oh shit. Now I remember where I've seen those bandanas before. Without another word I slip away. Time to check into my hidey-hole.

Okay, so why don't you start by telling us who you are.

Maddox Blayde Kadeen, age 69, CEO of Facility Management.

Maddox Blayde...? That's a hell of a name.

Sure, sure. Go on in the sandbox if'n ya want, but I won't be joinin' ya.

Still though—

Named after grandparents on both sides.

Ah. And you're a chief executive officer?

A wisenheimer, huh? Ya know damn well I's a janitor.

Some might even call you a maintenance man.

I call myself the last human person workin' up in this bitch.

Pardon?

Not if you live here, not too likely.

[pause]

So how about the non-human entities here?

Look, I's an old fart, see? Can remember before all the animated bool-shiet. This here man is the last member of the non-security personnel. Everything else is machines, or they get the women to do it they own damn selves.

You harbor resentment toward the automated help because you have to repair them.

Hell naw! That's all contracted out to pals of the governor.

What is it you do then, exactly?

Install shit.

You don't say. And this post-organic matter is deposited where?

Huh? I's talkin'—

Surveillance devices and the like.

Sometimes, sure. After the contractors do the installment, if something needs replaced I's the man.

Let's say a person were to slip you an extra bit of cash on the side. Would you be willing to install extra security cameras on the "down low," as they say?

[pause]

That's what I thought. Now we're getting somewhere.

S.I.S.T.E.R.: Sapphic Interventionists Standing Together as Empowered Radicals. They're freaking out in my living room, throwing back beers and setting their bottles on the rack, on the pillory, I mean damn: don't these crack heads know condensation leaves those fucked up rings?!

One, two, and breathe...

Okay, so it is them after all. At least it's not New Age freaks and weirdoes. Just need to keep sitting pretty over here across the street. When you know somebody's about to make a move on you the easy way to trap them is setting up shop nearby, somewhere you can keep an eye on things. Just like old times. Mom would be proud. Only, it's not exactly like the old days—these chicks blow up porn publishers and filmmakers, burn down right-wing political organizations. Doesn't take too much to figure out they're not here to congratulate me for being paid to have sex with female prisoners. Probably they think I'm one of these male pigs who abuses his power like, well, too many people in the judicial system.

Watching them long enough might give me an idea who slipped them the goods about me. When they leave they'll be easy enough to follow. Who knows when that's gonna happen, though. It's already been twelve hours. Wait—what's that? One of them is making the rest go hide. Shit, the lights just went out! Lucky for me spy cams are cheap. Let's see what those puppies are picking up.

```
                                    FADE IN


INT. BRIMLEY APARTMENT - NIGHT

The front door is opening. Somebody slips in. At
first it is only distinguishable as a man. He takes
a few cautious steps forward and we can make out
the features of RITCHIE.

Ritchie checks his weapon; it is still tucked into
a pocket.

A dark form rises from behind the furniture and uses
a stun gun on him. As Ritchie cries out several oth-
ers lunge at him with stun guns.

The shades are drawn by other shadowy forms, and in
the resulting darkness there is much activity. When
the lights are turned on eight WOMEN are kicking
and stomping Ritchie.

                    SISTER #1
          Over there, just like we planned.

The women stop kicking him, and with the help of
SEVERAL OTHERS they drag him to the pillory.
```

Holy shit! Will you look at that. His own gun is being shoved in his face, smacked upside his head, crammed in his ear. They even pull down his pants and shove it where the sun don't shine—like anybody really wanted to see that. He's still not telling them what they want to hear though. All kinds of beans get spilled, the little weezo, such as he's just a prison guard, the one that turned S.I.S.T.E.R. on to me.

The women look at each other.

> SISTER #2
> Like we're gonna believe that, you
> misogynist bastard!

> RITCHIE
> Please! You've gotta—

> THE WOMEN
> (chanting)
> His name is Kenrick Brimley...his name
> is Kenrick Brimley...his name is Ken-
> rick Brimley...

They circle him, overpowering his pleas with their
chant. Two of them bring forward the branks.

Sorry Ritchie, old buddy, but you got yourself into this jam, not me. There's nothing I can do when they stuff the branks over his head, when they hook him up to the rack. No, I *could* call the police, but then what? Would it go against my confidentiality agreement? Would it lead to a more thorough background check digging up all sorts of other stuff from my past? Can't have that. A man is stretched out on my dining room table screaming for mercy. With every yell the branks scrapes his tongue bloody and the women, they laugh it up. Can't shake the feeling this is some kind of Internet snuff film. It's creepy and makes me feel ten shades of dirty. And maybe if you put a wig on him, gave him some contact lenses, cover up his tattoos, maybe he would look something like me then.

Those little voyeur cams keep pumping out the images. Women in hemp jackets and earth-tone colors twist the crank, popping Ritchie's joints one by one.

Oh yeah, baby.

Promotional image, courtesy Last Burn Films © 2006

PART TWO:

NUTTING UP

"The underlying attraction of the movement of water and sand is biological. If we look more deeply we can see it as the basis of an abstract idea linking ourselves with the limitless mechanics of the universe."
—Sir Geoffrey Jellicoe

"It is a fascinating and provocative thought that a body of water deserves to be considered an organism in its own right."
—Lyall Watson, *Supernature*

Photo still, courtesy Last Burn Films © 2006

NE OF THE FIRST things you learn in swimming is the law of action/reaction. Kick one way, you move in the other direction. Natural laws make sense: belly flop and it's going to hurt. Things would be a lot different if we used natural law to decide who went to prison. In fact, I might be on the other side of the cell doors given the stuff going down lately. Then again, I haven't acted yet, so maybe I'm not guilty of anything.

"What's the difference between search and seizure and medical seizure?" Rolli asks.

There's nothing like prison humor to pass time. "Okay, I can tell this one's going to be good."

We stand for a while before he finally says, "No, I'm asking."

This is what I get for tutoring Rolli in English. Like I'm any great master of the language, or like I have time to worry about pronouncing things when there's all these rumors about a coworker named Ritchie failing to show up. People are griping that we're already understaffed. And Rolli, what does he want to know? Only the important stuff.

"Jigger means this is a good dancing person, no? Or is man who sells sex?"

"No Rolli. *Jigger* is prison talk for a person who acts as a lookout while somebody else does something illegal. A *gigolo* is a male prostitute."

While explaining *X3* has nothing to do with porn but everything to do with California's Hispanic gangs, it's hard not to think about cleaning up all the fast food containers, the bottles and wrappers. While explaining *hyna* has nothing to do with hyenas but everything to do with Hispanic prison lesbians, the look on Ritchie's face doesn't play over and over in my mind. While explaining other slang, I don't think about all the blood or the stains it might leave. While explaining *bull* has nothing to do with the animal and everything to do with masculine lesbians, I really don't think about the bits of skin stuck in the iron maiden. While explaining *bull dagging* is lesbian sex, I don't wonder what happened to the body, no way.

"*Sister* isn't a relation, it's a weaker inmate you force to have sex with you." Here I am at work, nothing out of the ordinary here, folks. "*Clica* isn't people making sounds, it's the group you travel in." My bags aren't packed, no, not at all. That would look suspicious if anybody happened to find out. "No, your *carnal* isn't like carnal knowledge, it's your Hispanic homeboy."

Rolli finishes off a cookie. "Homeboy? So, if you're my carnal, you're a shut-in?"

No, I'm for sure not thinking about the screams. Uh-uh. And still Rolli keeps on with the questions.

"*Laws* also means a police officer, like a pig is a cop."

"What about male pig?"

"That's a *hog*, not to be confused with *hawging somebody's property*."

"No, I mean like I'm saying 'Oh yeah, baby!' and a woman is saying back at me, 'You male pig!'"

"That one you'll learn on your own. Just keep dating. Now, why don't you tell me something I don't know."

Turns out he's a fountain of information. Over in Eastern Europe they have ways of passing the time we don't have here in our prisons, according to him anyway. One thing they do is chain two prisoners together at the neck and force them to run in opposite directions. Another is called *tails*, where you make them walk around naked with your truncheon stuck up their backside. A third thing, and the most original, is called *scales*. That's where you line the inmates up naked. One lays down and another prisoner is forced to lift him by his cock and balls. He grimaces, "No can do with female type of prisoner, but you feel me."

Two guards pop around the corner. "Okay, she's ready." Time to get to work.

This is Juanita: five-feet-two-inches in height, midnight black hair tied back painfully tight, green eyes, the bottom of her left earlobe missing from the time somebody bit it off, beige skin and darker lips, a jagged scar across her throat from a rival gang member's knife, armed robbery with seventeen homicides under her belt, and she'll be twenty-one next month.

This coming birthday means death, probably on the day itself, and the state is nearly salivating over her. Juanita's case caused a big stir in the media four years back when she and her girlfriend took out a bank on their own. Two sixteen-year-old locas make good. From what I can tell Juanita was just along for the ride. Her girl Yvonne was the one who decided to firebomb the place with everyone still tied up inside. But since Juanita wouldn't roll over on her main squeeze the DA decided to set an example. That, and they were pissed at not being able to catch Yvonne or recover the money. So here we are.

"Awright esé. Let's talk terms." Juanita is sitting across from me with the air of a thug, posturing like some kind of godfather...it's always like this. For once in their lives these ladies have the final say, full mastery over what will happen.

"Terms? Okay. Let's talk."

"Right on."

We sit for a second, thinking or something. The pen and notebook are at the ready, and so are my standard issue mace, restraints, and revolver. This is the only time we are allowed to be alone prior to the act; these "strategy encounters" are where we introduce ourselves and work out any requests. A guard will check in every five minutes to ensure that we aren't jumping the gun, or to make sure I'm safe, or maybe just to try and overhear the juicy stuff.

It's hard for me to concentrate on the business at hand instead of getting worked up about the state's newest decision to postpone Leena's execution. They're waiting until it can be televised, which by the time the bill passes would be, oh, next month. I clear my throat. "Look. I'm aware of your, uh, sexual orientation—"

"Aww, come on now, don't be sayin' that! Do it up right or don't do it at all. Go on ahead and say it."

You learn not to bring up sexual terminology directly with the inmates. "Yeah, right, well, this is all, you know, this whole thing...I'm optional. It's an option? You don't have to be doing this. I mean, being a lesbian and all."

"I ain't even told you what all I got in mind yet." She stews for a bit, arms crossed, not looking at me. "So what's up with you? One of them fashion-boys?"

Flattered I say, "No, no, just an employee of the penal system. You know. A workaday guy." She's eying me skeptically so I add, "Well, it's not your regular job, but I guess somebody has to do it?" Pause. "You want to know more." She nods so we go into a detailed history, family and all, even though it's strongly advised against. So far none of the women has had the time or clout to use this kind of info against me. But this is all boring stuff—nobody cares about families and jobs and whatnot. "Okay, let's get more personal." I reveal my abdomen. "Lady by the name of Brandi. She was sitting right where you are now, she got me with a nail burned into the top of a cigarette lighter. The Ford said she almost put a hole in my kidney." Behind bars, a *Ford* is a shitty prison doctor, or prison doctor who conspires against inmates.

The scar isn't exactly what she's looking at. "So you two ever hook up?"

"Let's just say the kidney stab is a deal-breaker."

"Yo, check it." Juanita places both feet on the table and works to uncover her calves. Horribly thick burn scars circle the area above her ankles, with tattoos spreading out from them. "Papa Number Four, wasted and bored off his ass. Woman he was with, who didn't know about Numero Quatro Mama, got tired of his shock treatment lovin'. So he gets me—"

"How old were you at the time?" I'm writing furiously.

"Twelve. Right, so's I'm all tied up on the floor with these metal shizznits all around here, on my legs right? Old man jacks up the juice and passes out. Leaves me fryin' all night."

"That's...um...freaking sick. I'm so sorry."

"Wha's up young? Show me the next one!"

"Okay," I say, still too disturbed. Even while I lower my pants, the interrogation continues. "So, you were in the foster care system?"

"Yo!" she exclaims, looking at the faded scars on the rear of my left thigh. "What in—what is that?"

"Sand shark, Nag's Head, North Carolina—"

"Yo! You got bit up by a muthajackin' *shark?!*"

"No lie. Juanita, um, I don't know how to say this..." My pants get pulled up just before Rolli opens the door. "Hey Rolli. It's all good in the hood." For some reason he gives me the "power to the people" fist before leaving. Juanita and I have a good laugh at his expense. "Like I was saying, did your foster father, if it was a foster thing, did he do, ah, other things to you?" This is territory I hate going into.

Juanita snorts. "Ain't none of 'em had time for that. 'Sides, it's more fun to just watch a girl bleed, seems like. If ya all pressed, then yeah, I'm a—I uh, ain't never, ya know...done..." She's too embarrassed to finish. Instead, she makes the crude hand gesture that universally translates into *sex*.

"So you were in the foster system. And the juvenile correctional system."

"I lived in foster. Yeah, and the juvie, sure. So what?"

"So...the government, if you follow me, they trained you to do all the stuff you did. I mean it's like you were raised by the state right?"

She just looks at me.

"So it's the *system* that needs to get whacked right? Not you. That's the point I'm trying to make, that's the argument I'm taking to the warden, to the governor—"

"Shit. Ya one of them 'save-the-whale' sissies? Step off with that yah-yah."

"Listen...I'm trying to help you, to help all of you, I'm not in it for myself."

"Ya know what the word is. If it ain't fixed ya can't break it." Her logic is eerie. "Yeah see, that's how it is. If it wasn't me it'd be somethin' or someone, somewhere. Ya's all the same. If I don't get strangulated or capped in the head or some shizznit ya got nothin' goin' on. Get yaself a life."

"So we're going steady, huh?" I'm taking my time getting undressed; Leena and me, as a couple, are past the insane passion stage.

She leans back in her chair, smiling as a cigarette burns away between her fingers. That smirk of hers says she knows something I don't. Again.

66

"What?"

She takes a drag off the cig. "You have a problem with relationships."

"Oh yeah? And what's that?"

"All your girlfriends are dead."

I carefully fold my pants. You learn to wear virtually no buttons or even zippers. In this line of work the layer of fabric separating you from sex-crazed clients has to be easy to remove or it ends up destroyed. Really, it's not too cool trying to walk out to your car the next morning with shredded clothes hanging off your limbs.

"You're crazy," is the only response I can think of.

"That's exactly right. I'm crazy. The doctors say so, but I just consider myself liberated."

"You know, I was just reading that insanity isn't, like, some sort of freedom."

"Oh? You were reading?"

"Well don't be surprised and all. I mean, I do read when I have the time."

"When you have the time!" She's laughing pretty hard at this.

"Yeah, well, like I was saying, it's supposed to be this ridiculous theory and all. Some kind of—surrealist?—writer deposited this theory in a movie—"

"*Posited*," she says in a scolding way, for some reason, then stops to let me continue.

"Okay, so the guy posited this theory about a bunch of people, right, nose-pickers I think he said, they would go out to this thing, it didn't really have a name or anything but it was weird, a really weird circus-like atmosphere, like a bad Fellini movie he said—"

"Listen. This is going nowhere. Fast. Give me your cock."

Every once in a while I think that maybe romance isn't so romantic after all.

The system's gears shifted after a witness stepped forward, causing Leena's case to draw media attention, and the government was forced to scrutinize her appeals for the umpteenth time. The same witness recants, the media makes sure a sympathetic public becomes a jilted public, and the death machine gets rolling again. Which puts me back in with my girlfriend, and has the workers here laughing behind my back.

We're both spent now, with not much left in the way of time. Leena looks at me. "How was it?"

"That's usually my line."

"But, still, how was it?"

I pause, and maybe the lack of words that follows is awkward for me alone. "Like, a revelation that God is in your lover's face. Sort of."

"So where did you read that?" Leena asks, looking at the ceiling instead of me.

"What do you mean? Read it where? I didn't read that."

"You just made it up, just now."

A little puzzled I say, "Right."

"Right."

Nearing the five-minute mark we race to throw our clothes back on. Our planning sessions are involving less and less planning every time, but maybe we actually do have something important to discuss today. After the guard checks on us, that is. What I want to tell her is I've gotten phone calls every day this week. What I want to tell her is my Hillary got used against her will the other night by some nuts out to do in Kenrick Brimley. What I want to tell her could get us both killed.

"Ricky?"

"You never called me that before..."

"Okay, *Kenny* then."

"Yeah?"

"I've got a recipe. I want you to take it home and try it."

"Um, okay. What is it?"

"Something hot..."

"Mack Jackoff. What, you here to steal my raisin jack?"

"Hell no! I wouldn't drink that stuff if my life depended on it." *Raisin jack* is homemade liquor the inmates brew under their beds. Another thing confiscated regularly on Jack Mack patrol.

C.C. grins while she works. The bread loaves are already bagged by this point, in red, white, and blue packaging with a satisfied cartoon mother watching her smiling cartoon kids eat smiling cartoon bread. Would those kids still be smiling if they saw where the bread was made?

"Hey, I was wondering where the flour storage is—got a second to show me around?"

C.C. checks left and right. With Ritchie still AWOL she can afford to take five and give me the lay of the land. For a few cans of food, that is. We walk past cartons filled with bagged bread. Even the boxes have cartoon kids all over them. Is this supposed to be some kind of added punishment? Eight out of ten women here are mothers and haven't seen their own children in forever—about four hundred of those kids are born here in the facility every year. From what I hear at least half of the inmates took the fall for their man. You'd think these dudes could at least remember to visit the women inside. Instead all they see are guys like me and Rolli and the warden, and instead of their children they get these smiling cartoons that are shipped off to consumers God-knows-where.

"This is it. You need a key to get inside. Whycome you wanna know 'bout flour?"

"No reason."

On the way back we bump into Warden Dempsey and that new boot Kirkmoor, who still looks like she wants to slam me. "Brimley! What in tarnation you think you're doing here. And you! Why aren't you at your station?"

"Just trying to take a shortcut and got turned around," I lie. "She's setting me straight is all."

Kirkmoor sneers. "That all you two were getting up to back there?"

Dempsey displays the selective deafness that made him boss of this place. He tells me it's my day off and warns me not to buck the system. "Thought you would've learned your lesson after that row with Ritchie. Be thankful he isn't here, and skeedadle. You too, little miss."

C.C. and I share a look. "Yessir." When we get back to her station I offer extra jack mack.

"It's all good. You keep it esé." This is the first time she hasn't called me that other annoying name. Her glance says that she knows I'm up to something, and that makes us cool.

On the way to the parking lot Bart crosses my path again. "Hey man. What's up?"

He grins, sloshes tea around in that mason jar of his. "God's hooks." Then, "Oh, don't give me that queer look. I ever tell you 'bout God's hooks?"

"No."

"Come with me then." He explains himself while we walk, heading over to the medical pod. His job gives him clearance for the morgue, so he takes me along for the ride.

"All right, you know how when the inmates want to send messages to each other, all locked up in their cells, they go fishing? They make a little rope out of some torn linen, tie one end to a note, and fling it through the tiny crack under their door. Way I understand it, it takes a lot of practice to get it under another door, much less the right door. Then, the person in the other cell can attach a reply to your linen, and the two of you go back and forth as need be."

"So far, you're not covering any new ground."

He sloshes the tea around in his mason jar, smiling. "Then there's religion. When you don't have any hope—like being stuck in the back-woods of some third world country, or in a hardcore prison for instance—hope becomes a big commodity. You seen how the chaplain snatches up the minds of these women on his mission for Jesus Christ. The Fishermen of Men, as the chaplain calls Him. Well, I hon-estly can't help thinking, when they find the women dangling from linen wrapped around their necks, that the Lord delivered a message. Or, they're being used as lures to snare the rest of us." Seeing that I don't get it, he adds, "You know, God's hooks. That's how He goes fishing, if you will."

We stand in the chilly morgue just kind of looking at each other. "Are you high, man?"

"God's hooks? The nails of the cross."

"That's some kind of freakin' stretch, if you don't mind my saying so."

He laughs and pulls the sheet back from the suicide's face. "Check it out, they just found her hanging in her cell. Guess that makes her God's hooker." I don't laugh, not that he notices. "Peaceful, huh?"

I recognize her—different porn, same faces. Pretty much looks White but had a Hispanic name. What is it again? It's tough holding onto it if it's not in my scrapbook. Need their pedigree papers to keep them straight.

"Young meat. Wanna take a gander?" Bart playfully pulls the sheet down further.

Promotional image, courtesy Last Burn Films © 2006

"What the fuck, man?"

"Hey, easy now. No need to grab me like that, Ken, I'm just dickin' around a little. Listen bud, while we're alone down here, there's a bigger fish I wanted to fry. You heard about the new Gov's first move?"

I haven't, and it's the worst kind of news he could lay on me. Why the hell haven't I heard about this yet? The Governor died of a pulmonary something last week and has been replaced by Holstead, a guy who's pretty much frothing at the mouth. His first act has been to modify the existing laws regarding our death penalty. Hey, why should that be a bummer? We're actually doing something that's a first: reverting from lethal injection back to the firing squad. On top of that it has become known within "the biz" that he will not tolerate any of this pardoning foolishness.

Bart watches my reaction. "Bet you'd like to kill his sorry old ass, wouldn't you? Given the whole situation with your lady friend."

What's that supposed to mean? "No. No I wouldn't."

"Oh come on. An eye for an eye and all that. It's the Christian thing to do."

"Huh? No, it's the opposite of Christian!"

"Kenny boy, we could stand around arguing semantics forever. Now, you criticize me for doing my job, but at least I have the guts to take harmful people out of society. It's not so easy to kill somebody, is it—not even to just say you'd do it. How about this. You ever had a pet that you put down? To put it out of its own misery, if you will."

"Nope. Can't say I have."

"Waddaya mean? Don't you have pets?"

"I...collect antiques."

"Okay. Tell you what, bud. Responsibility for the death of a pet is quite something. Imagine how the vets feel, performing the task." He digs one of the lethal syringes out of his briefcase.

"What's that?"

"Freedom in a bottle my friend. Magic like a genie."

"I mean what are you doing with it?"

"Me? Shucks, I ain't doin' a *damn* thing with it." He forces it into my grip. "You're the one gonna snuff a stray dog or cat tonight."

"I'm a-*what?*"

"You heard right. Then you'll sleep on it and tell me how you feel about the killin' of things next time we're rapping." He studies me a second, then adds, "Hey man, count yourself lucky. You don't wanna know what I charge most folks for that stuff."

Does he know about my double life, my triple life, the life sentence I'd get for Ritchie? No, when I dig around it seems like he's not playing games—he honestly thinks killing some animal will help me out. I press him about the fact that he sells these things, but his lips are sealed. Probably he's just flapping his gums.

The door swings open and Kirkmoor checks things out. The needle gets crammed down into my bag, but her attention is on the naked suicide, not us. "I don't know, Brimley. The rest of us have to go to the firing range to keep in practice for our jobs. But the things you do to keep in shape for yours..." She shakes her head and turns to leave.

A comeback is at my lips but Bart grabs my shoulder. "Pick your battles, friend, pick your battles. One thing I've learned is the guards need their corpse-fucking humor. There's ways to get 'em back, though."

"Oh yeah?"

"Oh yeah, baby."

What is your position in the penitentiary?

Doctor. General practitioner administering care to a population of

7,590 inmates. Medication, emergency care, case/time of death, the whole enchilada with extra chipotle.

A Ford, in the terms of the inmates.

Mm-hmm.

Why do they call you that?

Story goes that a few decades back there was this really messed up prison doctor by the name of Ford. Kinda stuck.

But they don't refer to the prison gynecologists or psychologists as Fords.

The gynocologist is always a she, and they call her the Hootchie Mama. The psychologist, they call him...it's kinda weird. Had this political prisoner a few years back, a highly-educated fucker who called the psycho a Maori, and that stuck.

Maori?

As in the tribe of headhunters/head shrinkers in the South Pacific.

Right.

They're the ones with the ritualistic cannibalism that had to be stopped because they started coming down with the human equivalent of Mad Cow.

Human Cow Disease?

From generations of people eating each others brains. You see—

We're getting off topic here. How about the most common cause of death in prison?

That would be...prison.

Favorite type of death?

Heart attack, or any other death that involves little to no exterior traces.

Oh? And why is that?

Uh...no reason.

Kenrick Brimley, you two hang out?

[pause]

Uh, I'm not sure I know who you mean. Is he the janitor? Always got a bad feeling from his type and kept my distance. He's the janitor, I'm pretty sure.

No. No he isn't. The executioner, Bart Judson, you ever spend much time with him?

No. No, we don't even know each other.

A little quick on the draw with that denial, good doctor.

Look, I said I don't know him.

Are you sure about that?

Quite.

Because work records indicate that you and he do a lot of overtime after the executions.

That's only natural. The state wants everything to be as in-depth as possible. Very thorough. Every T crossed, every I dotted. Sometimes families try to sue if there are any irregularities. Executions, they can be a very sensitive thing.

The darkness that falls brings with it an unfortunately busy night. This is my first "double-header" so to speak. Tomorrow they aim to execute two convicts in one day, and that means I have to work for my money. Might be difficult with this burn on my ribs, but what do you want for nothing. First up on the agenda is Juanita.

Of course, the main thing is to actually get inside the facility. There's like hundreds of protesters/partiers this time, maybe over a thousand strong. They're huddled around in cliques and subgroups, each band of demonstrators with their own colors, their own signs and slogans, their own chants. Some wear face paint, some are going buck naked, some grill steak while others are grilling veggies. If you didn't know any better you'd say this is all G.I.-approved gang activity, disgruntled clicas that won't bump it on down because they intend

to handle up on their business. The road into prison is the line separating them all, loaded with guards. Each side has an obvious tank
boss shouting orders to their people through megaphones.

After parking I'm stopped by a news crew who is talking with
Warden Dempsey, getting ready for some last minute PR interview type
deal. From out of nowhere a nut job in a beaded robe jumps out, yells
"Somebody better call my mama!" and whacks me in the face with an
omelet. A freakin' omelet! The place goes crazy, and in the chaos my
case full of goodies nearly gets lost. When the show settles down it
becomes obvious some of my coworkers have slammed the dude; he's
face-down on the pavement right outside the main entrance, sobbing
about his executed mother. Dempsey is sweating bullets, insisting nothing like this has ever happened before. The reporters are furiously taking
notes about the "alleged omelet" that is being collected by officials. They
don't bother to ask if the "alleged victim" is okay, they just collect the
globs from my clothes and hair like my body is some kind of crime scene.

If that fool can act up in here, even with all the extra security, then
who knows? Might just set the tone for the evening. Didn't see any of
those freaks in the crowd but it feels like *they're* here, somewhere,
watching. Following. Waiting for me to slip up. No need to look over
my shoulder—*they* won't get the satisfaction of being acknowledged.
Different porn, same faces—and those faces might get a black eye if
they're not careful.

After signing in and briefly shooting the breeze with the guys it's
off to the locker room to get ready, and then make the last minute
preparations Leena asked for. Luckily the omlette-tosser caused
such a stir everyone else has been called down to manage the crowd.
After this it's off to Pod 9. Leena told me that's an appropriate name
because nine is supposed to be the number of finality, whatever
that's about. All that matters is it's where we "do the deed."

Just outside the pod is the last security checkpoint, and look who's manning it. Kirkmoor would be on duty tonight, of all nights. She eyes me suspiciously, then looks at my case. Nobody else is around. "Tools of the trade, eh?" she asks, gesturing to the case.

"How badly do you want to find out?"

She doesn't appreciate the suggestion. "Right. I'm going to have to conduct an inspection, given the circumstances tonight. You read the pa—well, you probably watch TV. You know how tight security has to be."

"I *read the papers*, sure, and nobody told me that about a search or anything. When I have time." Then, "About the papers I mean."

"Save it. Put the briefcase on the table Mr. Brimley—"

"Oh, it's 'mister' now, is it?"

"Just put the briefcase on the table and this will all be over sooner."

"Fine with me," I say, placing the case on a little black table to the left. "You do realize that I'm, like, an employee here? A privileged employee?"

No response. Instead, she takes me to an examination room. Normally they rely on the robots and scanners to figure things out, but they keep private rooms like this handy because there's still no substitute for human intuition. That's what the warden tells us, anyway.

This is my first time getting a really good look at Kirkmoor. She's got pupils the color of dead wood. That, and she's older than the average rookie. With a buzz cut. And, a smirk. "Geez, what's that on your face?"

My fingers probe around until they snag some egg by my ear. "Oh, uh, just some omelet." She doesn't need to know the details.

"Sloppy eater?"

A Shame snort slips out. "Wouldn't you like to know."

"Okay, that's it." Her hand is on her billy club all of a sudden.

"Look, *why* do you wanna jug me like this?"

"What'd you say about my jugs?!" She's got me pinned against the wall, her left forearm against my throat.

Wow, she really is new here. An explanation might do the trick, but instead my eyes go to her chest. "Don't flatter yourself, honey."

With her free hand she pats me down, then forces me to face the wall. What's next? Are my clothes going to be piled in the corner while she plays amateur proctologist? No, wait. What's that sound? Some kind of contraption she wants to use. It doesn't matter what it is—stun gun, vibrator, or some other unidentified object—this dude ain't going out like that. The spin-and-shove move that was supposed to catch her off guard turns into a block; my forearm collides with her wrist. The syringe she intended to stick me with clatters on the floor—the needle is busted and some funky-ass florescent goop seeps out.

We give it a moment of silence, then she says, "On to Plan B."

Despite a good attempt to dodge, her finger-jabs strike my belly and throat. Even with the excruciating pain I know I'm lucky to have been in motion, otherwise these kung fu moves of hers would've probably killed me.

"Listen, tell S.I.S.T.E.R. they're safe! I'm not a weezo!"

"You have a sister, huh? That's good to know. I'll make sure she joins you in hell!"

Her hands and feet are everywhere, slamming into my arms and legs so hard that pain rockets through my limbs, shoots through my body. Fuck it, I charge forward and at this close range she can't fully toss me to the side. The two of us plow right through the cinderblocks. What the fuck? Oh, right—there was a stink about walls crumbling on account of all the water leaks. They must've put off repairs, like usual.

We land in a storage room, with her on top thankfully, because she catches most of the cinderblock fragments with her back. Instead of taking her out of the game, though, it revs her up. All of her hate goes into one killing blow, but my head slips out of the way at the last second. When Kirkmoor pulls her fist back up it's shaped like a partially deflated basketball. That's what she gets for punching concrete. Instead of screaming or passing out she just turns really, really scary-looking.

Getting to my feet I offer, "Hey look, I'm sorry I busted that needle back there. Why don't we just call it even, huh?"

Her backhand makes the world flicker, almost go out. Her boots play my ribs like piano keys, turn my head into a soccer ball, use my shins for target practice.

That's it. My fist slams into her jaw, connects again, then a third time. She grabs my wrist and flips me. What the hell!

It shouldn't have come to this but I've got a syringe of my own, compliments of Dr. Bart. Problem is the damn thing's in my bag! Dashing for the hole in the wall seems like a good idea but then my feet are gone. Just fucking gone. Face first on the floor. The world flickers again, maybe gets turned off for a second or two. My legs kick out trying to hit anything at all. Don't hit her, but do knock over a stack of crates. They crash down on her, giving me a chance. The world spins, a wall slams into my shoulder. Where the hell am I going?

All of a sudden Bart's present is in my hands and my bag is spilled open at my feet. Arms wrap around my chest from behind, like bent iron bars. Finding a vein isn't the problem, staying conscious is. Using me as a shield she runs through another wall filled with mildew like some kind of cancerous Twinkie—somebody has to hear that, or the shouts and curses and howls. At least my hand shielded the needle from the wall. Come on, how do you get the cap off this fuckin' thing?!

The fact that she just sank her teeth into my shoulder isn't a surprise but the pain sure as hell is. Note to self: if you plan to throw down with a freakbaby keep this needle real close next time. Oh thank

81

God, watching it sink into her arm is the most beautiful thing I've ever fuckin' seen. But wait. What's taking so long? Was he just yanking my chain, or could she be immune or...

No, her grip's loosening up. My feet are square with the floor again. When you see a freak-ass enemy struggling to stay erect do you run for it or try to finish them off? Don't want to start running, not yet. Her glazed eyes don't even flinch when my fist connects with her nose. Blood sprays everywhere. This wigs me out and the next ten or fifteen punches are wild, bouncing off her ribs and shoulders and belly. They take her down, anyway, or maybe it was the delayed effect of the drugs. A couple good kicks later and she isn't moving.

Minutes go by, according to the clock on the wall, and my only thought since killing her is: *the first execution didn't get televised after all. Governor's sure gonna be pissed.*

A laugh creeps out, and because my mouth doesn't know what else to do it just goes with the flow.

Juanita is chilling, leaning back against the wall and smoking like she's got no worries in the world. She doesn't seem miffed about the marks on my skin, the state of my clothes, the fact that I'm already sweating. It's fine if she never asks about it, because frankly I'm not interested in ever thinking about, well, what just happened. It's enough simply keeping up conversation.

"So was there ever any skeezas ya turned down? Ya dawg?"

"No, no. I mean, there's been some rocky moments, and uh, really there was only one woman I was philosophically opposed to being with, but I swallowed it."

"Oh," she laughs, "You swallowed it. So it was all like that."

"Huh?" What's that supposed to mean? "Back to the topic, she was this freaked out neo-Nazi, shaved head and the whole nine yards, named Malloree. That was all...messed up."

"So's there any hoochies what turned ya down, shark-boy?"

"One time, right, this chick, she canceled the whole deal because I eat pork."

"You eat pork?"

"Yeah. I do. Is that a problem?"

"Dunno. Have to think on that one..."

What is all of this? Everything that just happened, and she's worried about pork. Not like I told her about any of it, but still. Meanwhile the scorched area on my ribs is bothering me again. "All right then, if that's it, the station is set and everything. Just turn it on and adjust the volume thingy on top, next to the headphone plug."

"Awright." She greedily takes the portable radio, dying to hear the final game of the World Cup. "Thanks Sharky," she says, giving me a pound, and it's time to leave her be.

Instead of enjoying our "date" Leena is nervously staring at the small view of the world allowed by this cramped cell window.

Her days as an incendiary specialist have paid off. Only now she has to torch things vicariously through me—her words, not mine—although it gets the same end result. To boost her military knowledge I bring to the table stuff they don't want you to know about this facility. That includes being able to pinpoint the three weak spots on the grounds. Not like I'm a mastermind or anything, no, it's just that these are the places we used to sweat about when going over riot scenarios.

Outside, one large group is chanting for death, while another cheers life on. Their cumulative din is enough to mask the polystyrene and gasoline combo, your basic napalm, as it undermines the cellar below the kitchen. But the plume of flames on the other side of the grounds, rising fifty-some feet into the dark sky? It's more than enough to catch people's attention, and even though a sparkler-bomb is harmless the place goes haywire.

"All right, let's get a move on."

The change of clothes from my bag looks almost ridiculous, but the wig is convincing. "Don't look at me like that," Leena says. "Just tell me we'll make it out all right."

"We already have."

On that note we skip out of the conjugal cell, and it feels very strange to be walking around with Leena unsupervised, unshackled. Finally the fire alarms in the cafeteria kick in, perfect timing really, because by now most of the night staff have either gone to the armory, or the alley behind the incinerator to find two-hundred-fifty sparklers stacked up, sparking like all get-out. The timer, the thermite, it all worked like she said it would. On top of that, the disabled alarms in the empty kitchen let the fire get out of hand. Now it's crucial for all available hands to get down there and keep any potential fires from reaching the highly volatile stores of flour. Luckily the designers had the foresight not to use natural gas lines inside areas that prisoners can access, because the place would undoubtedly blow sky high.

We pass by a familiar door, the auxiliary conjugal room, and I can't help stopping. It only takes a second to unlock the door.

"What are you doing?!"

A peek inside reveals Juanita aggravated to no end by the sirens disturbing her soccer enjoyment. Even so, she notices me, and once she sees Leena in civilian clothes she puts two and two together, realizing that the time for fleet-footedness has arrived.

Photot still, courtesy Last Burn Films © 2006

"You can't be serious," Leena says once the three of us get moving down the hall.

"Hey, you know the deal. They're set to punch her ticket tomorrow too." Here we go...weak spot number three. The area behind the back-up generator in Building Services is dangerously hard to view via security cameras. Just outside of Building Services is the water management building, which leads nowhere but down. If a person can get into there and access the little-used service duct number three it's possible to enter the underground river system the prison relies on.

"Check it," Juanita whispers. "Door's unlocked."

Before I can stop them the women push through to the open air beyond. Rolli is standing in the damp night air, alone, twirling his baton around like he's trying to impress a date. He's facing away from us, looking out over the wilderness. Leena freezes up; Juanita walks into her and almost utters a complaint, but hushes herself on seeing the cause. I slide past the two motioning for them to keep cool. Leena produces a revolver from under her top—who knows where the hell that came from.

"Hey Rolli," I say, frantically waving my hands in a cease-fire motion to Leena. "Looking for something? Or did you just get lost again maybe."

"Thinking I heard a sound."

"Oh? What kind of sound?"

"Like it could be, I don't know slim, love birds flapping away in the night..."

I step out further, motioning to the women to do likewise. "Bats Rolli, bats. Didn't you hear about that? We've got an infestation of them."

He turns ever so slightly away, keeping pace with the sound of our footsteps, so that we stay just out of his vision. "Flying rodentia! How terrifying. Ought to be gone inside then. It can be scary out here in the night, Rick."

86

"That's what they say. You take care man."

Rolli strolls back inside not once looking our way, much to the shock of my companions. As the door locks behind us there's no need to stop and explain, in fact it's all I can do to try and catch up to the women. They discover that the door to the water management building is locked, but soon enough I have the code punched in and we make our way down to the river as fast as possible.

Below the building at the edge of the water, the roar of machinery around us, darkness waits to swallow us up. "All right," I say. "One quick swim to freedom."

"I can't wait," Leena says and wades into the waters, giddy.

Juanita grabs my arm, a strange look on her face. "I can't swim, Sharky."

"What?" That's not in the plan.

"Tough luck, sister," Leena calls out, waist-deep at the very edge of the light.

"Hey, Leena, wait up. I have an idea." I grip Juanita's reluctant hands and, turning, wrap her arms around my waist. "Whatever happens you don't let go. Got it?"

"Gonna carry me all the way?"

"Well, just don't let go. Once I get going I don't stop." Having said that we rush on into the freezing water and her small frame jumps, arms and legs clinging, and she climbs higher, rubbing my burn raw. "Careful! Careful now."

"What?"

To Leena I say, "My ribs, I wasn't going to mention it, but I had a bit of an accident testing out your napalm recipe today. I'm charred."

"You're who?" Juanita asks.

"I said I got burned. Never mind. You hear that Leena? I was testing out your..." For the first time it hits me she's gotten so far ahead that you can't even hear her swimming anymore. "Don't worry, I can get us through here. It'll only take about five minutes or so, got it?"

In up to the armpits we go and soon enough all those long hours of aquatic workouts get put to use. Blueprints replay in my head while my ears stay trained on the sound of the water's flow, wary of ramming into the stone walls or, even worse, somehow getting turned around in here. Images creep in: a life with Leena on the outside, no bars, no panels of inch-thick glass, nobody to observe us or decide when we live or die.

"Yo!" my passenger barks in my ear. "Keep it—" she only stops to spit out a mouthful of water, "—can ya keep it up above the fishes? Huh?"

"Aye aye captain," I mutter.

"I'm just sayin' is all. I'm just sayin'." After that she keeps from shouting, even though she's still shivering against me.

Sliding through the darkness again without any distractions it's hard not to think about the barracks that burned to the ground, the ammo dump that lit up the sky, the brig that roasted with some of the people still trapped inside. The news footage was shocking, and nobody could forget the twisted wreckage that used to be a row of Humvees. They never pinned any of that on Leena, instead settling for the twenty counts of murder for the preschool that burned down nearby. Maybe they just didn't have enough evidence to convict her for the military arsons? Not that it'll come up while we're swimming, but maybe sometime...

Soon enough we're out under the open sky again, away from the chaos back at the prison, and Leena's nowhere to be found. Taking the first chance she gets Juanita leaps from me, splashing in the water and then righting herself to walk up the muddy embankment.

Panting, I drag myself up onto the muck next to her. There's no sign of Leena anywhere, not even footprints, and it occurs to me that she might not have made it after all. But really that's just crazy talk. Right?

Juanita hawks up a lugie. "Never thought I had rabbit in me." In prison a rabbit is an escapee.

"You're a regular Bugs Bunny," I joke, not sure how funny it is.

Her eyes linger on me, and any traces of contempt are gone. This look is familar—oncoming confession in three, two, one: "I wasn't even there when mi hermana and Yvonne gone and done that bank."

"Who's Herman?"

She's just shaking her head. "My sister, it's Español. Spanish? She looks enough like me for uppity bolillos to convict my ass. But I ain't no rat, no way."

"But—you didn't do it?"

"What I'm s'posed to do? Throw my sister in jail and watch my mama's heart break? Nuh-uh. They grabbed one of us, but it's all good, we'll be familia again now." She pauses, then asks, "What about you and...?"

"I'm not worried about it. We had a plan. Getting separated just means that we meet up again at a place we decided on, down south."

"'Down south?' Where down south?"

Kenrick the dummy almost blurts it out. "Well, really, I'm not supposed to tell anybody..."

She nods to herself. "Ya ain't no rat neither."

Sitting here, dripping in the moonlight, it's tempting not to wonder if the car is still waiting on the other side of the hill. Either way we made it out of the fire, and even if it means finding yourself in the frying pan...where is this thought going?

Juanita stirs and forces herself to rise. "That moon is always lookin' down on me, white as The Man, all the way up there like that, ya know? Moon! Kiss my *Latina ass!*" She's only been out from behind the bars a few minutes and already she's nutting up.

The sound of alarms going off barely makes its way to us out here.

Soon enough helicopters and all-terrain vehicles will be swarming the immediate area, and there's going to be trouble if we're still lounging around shouting at the sky.

"You coming, or what?"

Juanita inhales deep, checking things out. "I ain't no leg rider. Ain't no thang. Good lookin' out for the fence parole, my man...I won't forget." That said, she takes off into the underbrush on her own.

The scenery speeds by, a reminder of the fix I'm in. Everything is moving way too fast. The world out there looks to be parched, and it isn't getting better.

"Ever been to the desert, boy?" one of them asks.

Kenrick the dummy killed a woman and helped two dangerous convicts escape from prison last night...and now he's supposed to have time for small talk? "No."

They rattle on about anything and everything, this pack of hobos. What a bunch of experts. Like they wrote a book about it or something? My head nods, my throat grunts, all just to be polite. This rickety old hulk we're in has been in motion for hours and hours. Must be near the border by now. There doesn't seem to be a leader here, but there's for sure one or two that dominate the conversation. A couple others get their comments in when they can, and the other two keep busy sucking on their gums and cheap wine.

"C'mon, boy! We'll show ya a bit'a dat thar Spanish. Uh-huh. Ya be speakin' some right Spic talk when we get done wid ya. Uh-huh."

What was I supposed to do anyway—not just sit back and let them execute my girlfriend, that's for sure. Sometimes you just have to say fuck the system. Sure, but what happens after that? You fuck the system and slip out in the middle of the night, but when the system wakes up and finds you're gone you've got hell to pay. Nobody likes that one night stand feeling.

"Jus you r'peat after us. Lissen 'n learn ya somethin'." They said this train was going to Mexico, but it could be going anywhere. Who knows what these dirty bastards might tell you. I'm supposed to listen to them now when it comes to learning another language? "Matter uh fact, gimme dat paper Leroy. Gonna write dis all down fer da lad. Uh-huh. Can ya read it?"

"Mu...mucos...mucosidad." They nod and giggle. "What's it mean?"

"Means 'good eats.' Here, pass it back an' we's gonna write ya up ever'thin' ya need ta know." The others are all quick to agree. They sure are having fun helping me out. Better leave them to it then, it'll keep them off my back a while. Right now the train is rocking back and forth, back and forth, and I'm too warm and comfortable to move...

Ungh...

What the—I'm waking up with feet kicking me, a lot of feet, no. Wait. They're fighting. Dumb-ass drunks are stepping all over me! Scrambling to my feet I yell at them to watch out, try and grab my stuff, but only end up getting my hand on one bag before one of them gets punched and falls into me and—

FUCK!

Can't believe I'm not dead. Crazy bastards wanted to leave the side panel hanging open to ventilate the car. No problem with me, those old geezers were pretty ripe. But nobody said you could fall off a moving train that way! Ah hell, is my shoulder broken? No. No, it's all good, sore but good. The train? By the time I scramble up the sandy embankment the thing's gone daddy gone. As for my stuff, it takes a while to collect everything that fell out of my bag. At least those notes the hobos gave me are still here. Might come in handy if this is Mexico. There's nothing left to do now but follow the tracks.

Seems like an hour or two go by but it's hard to tell with the sun beating down like this. Remember: miles make champions. Maybe even another hour or two go by before it's clear a person might need to find some shade and rest when marching through the desert. Every step sucks the fluids from my body. Never imagined anything could be this hot.

There's what looks like a stand of trees off to the right, so that's where I go. Or try to. Takes forever to reach it. Actually, it's a bunch of rocks with spiny shrubs growing on it. Whatever. There's enough shade around back for me to lay low. Never heard of a third degree sunburn before, but hey, anything's possible.

At first it's exciting when the sun goes down. No more hellish burning. Seems like as good a time as any to get moving again. After a while my smile fades. Which direction are the tracks in again? And nobody ever warned me that it gets cold in the desert. At night. Cold as a bastard! No sun, no heat, no life. "How come nobody warned me?!" My yell echoes around in the empty landscape. That gets me listening to something other than my heavy breathing and clumsy feet. After a minute I finally have to stop and let my eyes follow my ears.

Is that Kirkmoor out there in there darkness, dragging her busted self along just as slowly as me? Maybe it's her ghost. Yes, that's it. She wants to torment me. Or, maybe she's like those spirits that cling to the torture devices. No, that's something made up in my head. Plus, she'd be haunting that needle, not me. Right? Shut up and keep moving, man! You're gonna die out here in the dust under a black sky. All the nighttime critters are gonna tear me apart if I fall now. Have to keep moving.

Shit, no—that was for sure a sound just now. The mirage of Kirkmoor seems a hell of a lot closer now. Just to be on the safe side a faster pace might be good. Anyway, the faster I move the faster I get somewhere, right? That's right. Conserve strength? Hah! Nobody needs that crappola. No sir. Not out here in the desert, on the run, freezing my ass off with the ghost of some freakbaby after me.

That shuffling sound, it's for real. These old ears aren't making that stuff up. And it's getting closer. Way too close. When I look back over my shoulder something whacks me and knocks me on my ass, oh God, but I ain't going down with no fight, no way, I took her outta the game before and I can do it again and—oh. It was a wall. I walked into a wall out here in the dark, in the night, and it would be funny except that damned shuffling sound is getting closer. The adobe wall isn't too high for me to climb over, but damn if they didn't stick a bunch of broken glass up on top! Agh, shit! Hopefully nobody heard me scream going over. Actually I hope they did. They can come and deal with Kirkmoor. Me? I'm just going to lay here and close my eyes for a while...

Things to Be Scared of in the Desert

1. The smell of hobos.
2. Rattlesnakes.
3. Insects.
4. The smell of your own skin cooking.
5. Weird lights in the night sky/hallucinations.
6. Getting hungry when you smell your skin cooking.
7. Gila monsters.
8. Cleaning sand out of your shoes again.
9. Being stomped to death by stampeding jackrabbits, ala *Night of the Lepus*.
10. Sticking your hand down a hole.

When I wake up there's a dark-skinned angel looming over me. It takes a few seconds to realize this is somebody else's bed, somebody else's house. Her house? One can hope. She makes exotic X-*hot*-ic. Her words are in Spanish so there can't really be a conversation, but neither of us is complaining, at least it doesn't seem like it. Those phrases the hobos taught me would get put to use except they're folded up in my pants, and my pants are...somewhere else. Someone else's clothes are on me, and I feel like a different person.

"What happened to my clothes?"

She smiles warmly but says nothing. That white dress of hers is almost blinding in this sunlight. Sitting on the edge of the bed, she runs a damp cloth over my forehead. Inventory time: there are bandages on my hands, arms, knees, feet. Other than that everything's where it should be. While she keeps patting me down with the damp cloth the rest of it comes into focus. There's a clock running on military time, so who knows *when* it is. Flowers, really nice wood furniture, a bear skin carpet. Okay.

"Rosario," she says, pointing to herself.

"Rosario. Pleasure to meet you. I'm Ken." I scribble my name on the pad that's on the night stand.

"Cain," she says. It takes a couple tries before she gets it straight.

We spend some time saying things that the other doesn't understand, but why not—it's fun. After a while a woman comes to the door and Rosario shifts gears. Judging from how they talk to each other this must be her mother. Pretty young to be the mother of somebody who's got to be in high school or college, or whatever kind of school they have in Mexico.

Burnout, or maladaption, is defined as depleted your reservoirs of adaptation energy. Your body fails to keep up with the evolving situations your experiences produce. Your joints creak and ache, your back stiffens, your lymph nodes swell, your nose starts to run, you experience every kind of intestinal upset. I've got a belly full of General Adaptation Syndrome. The only known cure for burnout is rest, so I allow myself to sleep.

The next few days float by like this—sometimes awake, sometimes unconscious, with Rosario always hanging around. Talking, bringing me food and water, her mother stopping by occassionally, and it seems a little boy has been spying on me too. It takes this whole time to realize I'm on edge not because there could be cops busting in the door any second, but because these women are so close with no bars, no restraints, no guards. Is this what normal male/female relations are like? Here I have no belongings, no privacy, depend on them for daily rations of food and water. Here, I'm the one living on borrowed time.

Still too weak to leave bed I crawl over to the other side of the mattress and peek out the window. There's a little path under the window sill, and a wall blocking the outside world. Somebody was cool enough to plant some flowers in front of it. Still, can't help but think it's a bit too much like a prison here.

Later, when I get the tour of the house, it becomes clear we're on a pretty huge property. These people must be filthy rich. Introductions are made: Rosario, her father Juan Eduardo, mother Maria, sister Jordana, brother Felipe—they're the Diaz family. We stand and watch some Latino cowpoke taming a horse. Okay, so this is a ranch. The several nameless men stone cold lurking in the background don't get introduced. One of them has a tattoo of a fist clutching a lightning bolt; it's the same image in a lot of sculptures and paintings around here.

One room seems like a study or library type of deal, another is locked, a third has leather seats and a huge television with surround sound speakers. One room is full of nothing but gear for the Daytona basketball team. No wonder that logo was familiar. It's all over the jerseys, the sweatshirts, the shorts and jogging suits and shoes and head-bands and pricey boxer shorts. That's weird. Aren't Mexicans into soc-cer? Maybe the Date Rapers have a crossover franchise down here.

The more strength returns, the more time is spent wandering around. Seems like they don't want me going outside, and that's cool with me. My skin's had enough of the Mexican sun for a while. Sometimes I let Felipe stalk me with his toy gun, other times I jump out and surprise him. One time I did that he was with his dad. Señor Diaz just sort of looked stern and went on his way. He doesn't come around much—he must be busy running the ranch from what I gather. Any time I spend with Rosario or her mother or sister, those tattooed dudes lurk around in the background keeping an eye on things.

It crosses my mind that these people saved a stranger from the desert without so much as a a question. Well, the stranger climbed over their wall. And, if they were trying to ask any questions it's not like I can understand them. Not that wandering the desert and crashing somebody's house was part of the plan. If the car had just been waiting for me after the prison break...well.

One night I almost walk in on some kind of religious gig. Instead of interrupting them I listen in from around the corner. Who knows what they're saying—the last week of banter with Rosario hasn't rubbed off. On the other hand, she's a quick study. My Ingles words are coming to her more and more naturally. Her voice is in there, chanting along with the others. There's somebody called a despojo, like a priest or something. After the dude starts sacrificing animals the bed seems like a better place to be, so I beat it.

The next day there's a second woman hanging around. She's older, sure, but easily five or ten years the junior of the parents. At least, I *thought* they were Rosario's parents? In Mexico they don't get down like folks in Utah, do they? No, no, I never heard about polygamy south of the border. Rosario's older sister? No, no...physically impossible, unless you believe those tabloid articles about five-year-olds being parents. Family friend or some other kind of relative, must be. She's the only one here with green eyes—those eyes pierce me as I try to drink my sangria. The family introduces her as Lupe.

Lupe has a friend with her—he comes off as the strong silent type. Long black hair, black snakeskin cowboy boots, black jeans and a black button-down shirt. Very suspicious. He doesn't stop to talk with anybody. Instead, a couple of the ranch hands lead him to a room in the back of the house. For some reason Felipe gets excited and drags me back there with him. The room has crazy aquariums set up all around, filled with...huh? There's sand, rocks, branches, and tarantulas. Oh, and scorpions too.

Señor Diaz sees us in the doorway and says something harsh to Felipe, who scampers off. One of the ranch hands makes a move toward me but Señor Diaz looks me up and down, then gives a dismissive wave of his hand. They go on about their business, leaving me to wander from tank to tank looking at the critters. Hard to tell if they're alive or dead. Guess one pet is as good as another. Did Bart go around snuffing stray dogs and cats, or was that some jive? And did he ever try his hand at putting down something like these scorpions? As for my pets, it's a safe bet they're starting to get dusty back at home. This new guy, this friend of Lupe—maybe it's just me, but he's staring. What, he got a beef or something? It sounded like somebody just called him Enrique, but it's hard to keep up with the conversation.

A new box full of scorpions gets opened and I jump back. Diaz's men laugh.

"Whoa, you collect these around the property or something?"

The scorpion dude surprises me by answering the question. "Actually, I bring the scorpions in for Señor Diaz. Hey, you'd be surprised how well smuggling arachnids from country to country pays the bills."

"You speak pretty good English for a bug smuggler."

"Heh. I was schooled up norté, know what I mean."

"Uh-huh."

"Now check it out. These here are Bark Scorpions, the only deadly ones found in North America..."

It's easy enough to nod like this is all impressive information. There's a scorpion resting on his palm that he points to like a biology teacher. "Why do you keep calling it a 'he?'"

"You can spot the males because they're smaller, less bulky..."

And this is what I get for asking questions. He goes on to mention how 90% of scorpion stings occur on hands, how the pincers are called pedipalps, on and on it goes. Señor Diaz gets tired of the lecture and has a servant take me to the kitchen for a snack.

Now that everything has healed it's time to show some appreciation to the Diaz family. We're all gathering out here in the courtyard relaxing, having some drinks. Can't think of a better time to deliver the words I've been practicing. Getting everyone's attention I clear my throat and begin. Gesturing to myself, I say, "La ingle. Si?" Gesturing to their home I add, "Que preciosa colonia de denudistas!" Hopefully that statement shows them even us English speakers have some culture and manners.

Must still be dehydrated or something, because there's this really weird vibe all of a sudden.

Stepping up to little brother Felipe I say, "Usted muy mal educado."

To little sister Jordana, "Conozco a la deshonora y...embarazada."

To mother Maria, "Usted mi madre de alquiler...um...gracias por la llamada obscena."

To father Juan Eduardo, "Usted un certo ateo."

Standing in front of Rosario, I say, "Yo...ah...quiero violacion ocurrida durante una cita con un conocido a Rosario este despatarrado."

They all look at each other, then at me.

Juan Eduardo mutters, "Me lleva la chingada," then motions for me to stay where I am. Is he going to grab some kind of gift or something? It's not clear what the customs are here. Jordana looks a mite anxious. Maybe he's going to get something for her instead, like a...what're those little flower arrangements that a girl wears to fancy occasions...cummerbund? Corset?

Nope, it's not make believe. There's for sure a weird vibe coming off everyone now. Maybe it was an insult to speak Spanish to them, with my sloppy uneducated pronunciation and all. Yup, that's it. Great. Now I've gone and insulted them in their own home. Worse still, Juan Eduardo is some kind of big wig in these parts—insulting a prominent man in front of his family has to be a major offense out in the sticks like this! Hell, I wish I would've practiced more before opening my big mouth. What kind of way is this to repay them for saving my life?

Lupe looks to Maria, who in turn leads her children inside. Rosario looks back over her shoulder at me, the look on her face one of...what? Some kind of sadness or hurt. I look to Lupe and might as well be staring at a lump of granite. What about this Enrique guy, the one that's been glaring at me the whole time? His expression has not only softened, but is a mix of what looks like suppressed laughter and maybe surprise.

"Uh, what gives? Is my Spanish that bad?"

He walks up to me, leans in close so Lupe can't hear. "Listen man, you need to get out of here. Now."

So that's his game. He considers himself Rosario's "betrothed" or some such, the original man on the scene, and this here bolillo is busting in on his game. Petty jealousy never ranked high with me, and I tell him as much.

He looks back to the house; a man is shouting inside. Seems like a couple of the henchmen are moving around in there too. Rosario's suitor puts his hand on my shoulder. "I'm not sticking around to see this. My car's the red convertible out front. It'll be running, but once the guns start blasting I'm outta here. Peace." That said, he walks off at a brisk pace.

Guns blasting? The guy must be pretty desperate if he's going to resort to threatening my life. Splitting his wig is what most people would do, but watching him go I only spit out some phlegm. Good riddance.

Behind me, from the doorway, there's the roar of "*Me lleva la chingada!*" followed by the roar of a shotgun. The statue next to me loses its head. A second later Juan Eduardo is reloading. His men are hanging back, preparing guns as well.

Damn!

The red convertible is still out front, engine revving. I jump in like my last name is Duke. "Come on!" I shout. "Let's get the hell outta here!"

The smuggler looks over at me and smiles, then snatches up a scorpion by the tail. "Keep him safe," he says, dropping the thing in my lap. It's not clear if he catches my girlie gasp—seems like he's too busy squealing the tires. Some of the gunshots hit a little too close to the car for comfort, but the driver knows his way around a steering wheel. When we're in the clear he reclaims his pet and puts it in a box behind my seat. Five minutes go by in silence. It takes that long just for my heart to slow down after all that craziness. The smuggler—Enrique?—finally speaks up. "From here on out you're *un Suicidio*."

"Uh...what did you just call me?"

"Suicide. That's what it is, walking into a place like that and talking so much shit."

"What's that supposed to mean? Bunch of people turn homicidal and it's my fault all of a sudden. Maybe you should pull over and let me out."

"Tell me one thing: where'd you learn your conversational Español?" After explaining the situation he asks to see my cheat sheet. He glances at it while driving. "Okay. See this here? Next to 'I want to take you out for dinner?'"

"Yeah."

"This doesn't mean taking someone out for dinner; it means date rape."

"What?!"

"Uh-huh, and that's not all. You're better off not knowing some of the shit you said back there. I mean damn, you told Señora Diaz she was your surrogate mother and then you thanked her for the obscene phone call."

"Bullshit!"

He laughs. "Think what you want, man."

"I will."

"So tell me why the mood changed and people started grabbing guns. Hmm?" Well, maybe he's got a point there. "Okay, Suicide. Where we heading? You got people around here?"

"Who knows where we even are?" He fills me in. Quick geography lesson: the Sonoran desert is in northwestern Mexico, the state of

Sonora is next to the state of Chihuahua, the compound we escaped from belongs to the biggest crime lord in the north, and I'm in trouble with a capital FUCKED.

Mexico has its pros and cons, but one thing for sure is the weather up north was way more humane. How can people live down here? Enrique was quick to notice my sorry state of affairs and offered to buy me some drinks on the way to Mexico City. Never asked him why he saved my ass, and it doesn't much matter. People with his background and connections don't go to the cops.

So here we sit, enjoying air conditioning for the first time since leaving the Diaz ranch. If the thugs or the lesbians or the laws don't get me, this heat sure will. We passed by a roadside stand on the way into town. It was loaded up with chocolate skulls, little paper skeleton puppets playing little paper guitars. Kids were hopping up and down, impatient for their souvenirs of death. Enrique told me it was something called la feria del alfeñique. All kinds of facts and figures followed, making it clear we weren't on the run but on a field trip. What I want to know is how the heck they keep those chocolate skulls from melting?

He laughs again about the whole translation problem earlier. "Probably nobody's ever fucked with him like that. He's not gonna let it go, you can bet on it. Guess you didn't hear about the mass grave that was just uncovered. It was full of Diaz's enemies." He laughs harder. "So what's your next move? Cry in your beer?"

"Heh. Life's too short for that."

"There's a saying in Español. Life is short but wide, my friend. Short but wide."

"Wide? I used to do salt water races. Try swimming in the ocean. Then you'll know what wide is all about!"

"I'll drink to that, Suicide." He raises his glass and we toast something important, but it's not clear what exactly it is. "So you're a swimmer, huh? Maybe you'd be interested in this. A friend was just telling me about these huge, shallow pools down here in Mexico. They're manmade but you can only tell that they're related to each other from the air. They represent the solar system, spaced exactly to scale over a span of three miles."

"Wow. Who was cool enough to do that?"

"It's pre-European."

"I didn't know the natives were into swimming."

"No, not swimming pools. These can be used as a seismic monitor. The slightest movement in the crust disturbs the water."

"Whacky stuff, man." We sit here drinking in silence for a bit, and I feel something brewing in my gut. What the hell, this guy saved my life, and I need to get some stuff off my chest. Three, two, one, and the details of my job spill out. Everything: the politics, the personalities of the women, the whole weird situation with Leena.

"Damn," he says, nodding. "Impressive."

Still, things can only go so far—there's plenty of dangerous subject matter there, like Ritchie and the lesbians, Kirkmoor, the breakout. So we move on to safer topics, such as deadly bugs. We talk about how scorpions mate, how your view gets distorted when you look down through water, the swim competitions I used to do, that kind of stuff. Eventually it all ends up leading back to our near-miss with the drug lord who has northern Mexico in his grasp. How do you make good with somebody who has everything at their fingertips?

"That's what the problem is," Enrique tells me. "Carpe Diem isn't enough for Diaz; he doesn't want to just seize the day, he wants to snatch all power and keep the people in a strangle hold forever."

"Um...carp? He wants to catch fish?"

He laughs. "That guy catches plenty of 'fish' on the side his wife don't know about, I can tell you that much."

I laugh along, like I know what he's talking about. "The people won't always put up with him. Nobody can keep on power-grabbing forever."

"Hell no. You and me are men, we're born with power. I don't care who it is, if they wanna reach for this they're in for some hurt."

"Born powerful? I don't get it."

He grabs his crotch. "This is our power, bro, right here. We didn't have this we'd have nothing."

"Hell then, back when I was working that prison job I must've been the most powerful dude in the state."

He chuckles. "Then maybe Diaz met his match this time."

"Hey, teach me some real Spanish so we don't have any repeats of today. Like how do you say man or male in Spanish...malo or something, right?"

"No, no. That means 'bad.'"

"Bad?"

"Yeah, like her." He points out a woman in a historical-looking mural on the wall.

"She the Mexican Mona Lisa or something?"

He smirks. "Malinche, that's her name."

My eyes close. I'm trying to visualize the Spanish to English dictionary out in the car. "Wait. wait, I got it: malignant. That's what it means, right?"

He keeps smirking, takes another drink. "Maligned might be more like it."

"All right, what's that supposed to mean."

Don't ask me how friendly drinks managed to turn into a history lesson. Actually, it's kind of interesting. Story is this Malinche character was a native slave girl Cortez used as a translator when he lead the

Spanish invasion centuries back. He called her his "tongue" and that makes sense, but it's creepy at the same time.

Three Coronas later and it's time to hit the road. Before getting in the car Enrique pulls out a little handheld black light and flashes it around the interior. He explains that in the "hyaline layer" of a scorpion's cuticle there's an unidentified chemical that makes them fluoresce under UV light. The hyaline layer is incredibly tough and is one of the only things left when they become fossils.

"What, you can make them glow in the dark with that thing?"

"Pretty much."

I laugh, but then he sweeps his arm exposing one on the passenger seat. "Uh-huh. Can't be too careful around the little buggers."

On the way into Mexico City we picked up some sunglasses and some stuff to put highlights in my hair. Hopefully it'll fool somebody—Enrique says it's how the stars are able to go out in public. With me, it's not a problem of signing too many autographs. It's the lingering look of every thug hanging out on every street corner.

The real sweating went down when we got caught up in the so-called virgin traffic.

"Hey, it's the straight stuff," Enrique insisted. "We're near the Basilica de Nuestra Senora de Guadeloupe." Then, "The Virgin of Guadeloupe."

"No joke?"

"It's no joke man. They get like thirteen million visitors a year."

"And they all crawl on their knees?" Up ahead the cross-street was filled with people crawling and praying, crying, nutting up, and I couldn't help thinking of doing the crawl stroke.

"It's a holy day so they're going all out. We're still a mile or two from the damn place."

Miles make champions. Those folks were trying out for the Heavenly All-Stars.

Enrique spent about half an hour explaining how this Virgin used to be the Aztec goddess Tonantzin—that, and cursing while he battled the other drivers. Day two of the field trip.

The story of Tonantzin didn't make sense though. "How can she be a mother goddess *and* a death goddess?"

"Yeah, well, it's all mixed up." He found a break in the traffic and charged ahead. "Come on, how about some ice cream? Soft serve."

"They even have that down here?"

"Sure. Just keep your eyes peeled."

That was two hours ago. Now we're at the base of some kind of monument, and still we don't have any ice cream. "So what is it?" I ask, unimpressed.

"El Monumento a la Madre, erected in commemoration of motherhood. Hey, it's a big whoop in these parts."

We're right smack in the middle of Mexico City, at the intersection of Paseo de la Reforma and Insurgentes, some militant-sounding roads if you ask me. Only, there's nothing militant about motherhood. There's a woman holding a baby, with a huge column behind her. Damn thing must be, like, fifty feet tall. On either side are kneeling men, just out of the mother's reach, one holding corn and the other holding a book.

Enrique says, "Check out the dudes with maize and learning. I figure that means agriculture/industry and learning/society are being held away from the woman who takes the path of motherhood. The inscription translates to: 'Because their motherhood was voluntary.'"

"Should I be taking notes? Is there going to be a quiz later?"

"I'm just saying is all."

I sigh. "Okay, so what does it all mean?"

"I don't know man. We shouldn't stay in one place too long."

"Hey, I'm not the one who brought it up."

"It could take a while—there's a lot of concepts put out there by the academics, in terms of Mexican psychological identity."

"Oh yeah?"

He fidgets a bit, looks around. The coast, it seems, is clear. "See, the way I understand the theories from my psych courses is—"

"Whoa! Sorry to interrupt dude, but when did you take psychology classes?"

He balks. "In college!"

"College?"

"I said I schooled up north, didn't I?"

"Well, you know, I just figured that was some bug-smuggling jive."

He laughs. "Right. Like I was saying, the idea is that Mexicans are peculiar about their cultural identity because of their isolation. They're cut off from any possible European roots by the fact that the Europeans came through and savaged their ancestors. At the same time, they've got European blood, making them impure—the monster's blood is in them, so they're cut off from their native heritage too. Mexicans consider themselves a bastard race."

Trying to come up with something thinky to interject, I spout, "It amounts to the solitary confinement of an entire nation. Ask anybody in the penal system and they'll tell you it's only a matter of time before somebody cracks up in solitary."

He sizes me up. "Quick study." Glancing back at the car he continues to elaborate. "It's like this: Malinche bore Cortez the first mixed child. She's the *chingada*, the 'fucked one,' and Mexicans are children of the chingada. Chingar, it's an incredibly negative concept, and I'm not sure there's really an equivalent en Ingles. The Virgin of

Guadeloupe though, the Mexican nation worships her almost on the level of Jesus himself. They're seeking asylum with the maternal embodiment of native purity. She's virginal mother, the one who sacrificed herself, kind of a counterbalance to Malinche. They're the two most famous Native Mexicans, but here's where you get to the difference between fame and notoriety since the whole Spanish invasion is Malinche's fault."

"Her fault? Dude. Aren't slave girls, like, rape victims? Aren't translators people that use words, and didn't you say something about Cortez having an army and the plague, not to mention a shitload of enemy tribes working for him? Plus the prophecy of the natives…didn't you say they let the Spaniards grab a lot outright just because of their own beliefs and predictions that Cortez took advantage of?"

"Look man, Kenrick, stop being logical about shit. I'm just telling you how these people are. All the blame is on Malinche. Sure, she underwent a transformation later…got baptized and became doña Marina, but that's not important. These people want their women to be pure mothers and nothing more, all right? They've got centuries of betrayal—or rape if you want—to make up for." He lights up a cigarillo.

"And what makes you so different? You're just sitting back spitting smack like it didn't make a bit of difference to you."

He laughs again. "It doesn't. My family's from Spain, by way of Argentina. Me, I was born in Wisconsin. I'm a fuckin' American, man! This shit doesn't mean shit to me."

Well, you really can't judge a book by its cover after all.

Just when I'm about to ask when we'll be stopping for food he speaks up. "Look, I'm gonna grab something outta the car. Be back in a minute."

While he goes off to do whatever, I take some time to check out the statue, and those guys holding commerce just out of the mother's reach. Not like she's really paying attention to them or anything. Speaking of paying attention, who's this dude looking at me? Shit, is it some kind of Fed or something? He's white as all hell, wearing a suit and tie and sunglasses in this fucked up heat. My God, I think I'm going to be sick.

Trying to look casual, trying not to let the nausea get to me, I glide away. There's a guide in my pocket that could tell me where to go, but it's best to ignore it. You're not supposed to look at maps in metropolitan areas because it makes you a tourist. I'm not on the run, I'm from here see? This is a harmless regular guy. Not a criminal, not at all.

"Excuse me," a starched voice croaks. A rigid, powdered white man in a suit and sunglasses stands before me. Several of these robotic wackos are milling around, zeroing in on me. "Excuse me, sir. A moment of your time." His mouth doesn't open nearly wide enough when he speaks, and his facial muscles don't move at all. How's that physically possible?

Nope, for sure these are not Feds. Their circle is closing in on me, and there aren't any witnesses around. Where did everybody go?!

"Sir, it is in your best interest if—"

Punching this creep's face lets me know that there's absolutely something wrong with him. Can't stop to think about how his face is like foam, not when I'm running for Enrique's car. Not when those six or seven suit-wearing fools are chasing me down like a pack of mad dogs.

And definitely not when I discover that Enrique's car is gone.

Yelling and shouting doesn't bring him back and there's no sign that anyone in the area gives a flying freak about what's happening. Sprinting down a major street in Mexico City, dodging people left and right, and there's an avalanche of white coming down on me.

"*Excuse! Me! Sir!*"

No time to figure out what this is about, can only focus on all the people and cars in the way. Over a sleeping hobo, bouncing off a trash can, down a side street, an alley, another alley—oh God, what's that stink?—out onto another side street. And still their freaky shouts are keeping pace just around the corner, but at least I've got them blinded, but for how long?! Wait, what's—

After catching a glimpse of what's on the other side of the wall I leap up on top, then over. It's all I can do not to cry out when the shards of glass embedded in the top of the wall dig into my hands, my legs, or make a sound when I hit the paved courtyard. With my mouth against the brick I have only two thoughts: don't let them hear my crash landing, and please don't let this give me a swollen lip.

Oh, and my third thought is: *Juanita, please don't make a freakin' sound!*

"Ya sure ya dint lead them laws up in here?" she calls out.

"I ain't no rat, remember? Said so yourself."

Juanita's at least keeping an even tone now. She was convinced my surprise appearance had ruined everything. She'd be deported and executed, her wealthy extended family who let her stay at this compound would get screwed by the Mexican authorities, her mother's heart would break, and her hermana too, and no matter what I said or how bad I felt it was the end of the world—plain and simple. Even an hour after those white-faced freaks ran by. It's pretty clear now they didn't realize where I went.

"Look," I told her. "You can't let your fears dictate things. You've got to take control."

"How I'm s'posed to do that, huh? 'Specially with you blowin' up the spot!"

"I'll help you." When she asked how, I told her that with my supervision she could overcome her fear of water. Then, when she revealed this crazy crib has a huge indoor pool there wasn't any choice in the matter—and now, after forty-five minutes of her excuses we're finally ready to go. If she'll ever come out of the changing area, that is.

More time passes. Who knows whose swim trunks these are, or if the guy's worn 'em yet. Could ruin the experience to think on it too long. "Hey, what's a...a...I guess you'd call it, like, a mansion, huh? What's a mansion doing in the middle of a Mexico City ghetto?"

Her cryptic reply is, "Best kept secret in town."

Water lapping at my sides, pasting my hair against my skull: I feel at home for the first time in forever. Okay, so maybe it was all just a scam to get into the pool. Being out of water too long can make a body edgy.

"Ready?" her voice calls out.

"Man, I was born ready. Waiting on you is all."

Juanita pokes her head around the corner from the changing area—it's still weird seeing her hair cut this short. Probably to keep from being recognized on the street. The green of her eyes is somehow accusatory. "Don't be makin' fun of me and shit like that. Makes me swoll."

"I never laughed at anybody learning how to swim."

She nervously steps out. "Ya so simple sometimes. I mean this swim suit getup. It's all..."

She found one that pretty much fits, but it's a nasty teal one-piece with leafy orange frill spiraling around it. Brings to mind grandmothers on acid and I fight back a smile, only halfway successful.

"Hey! I done tol' ya, I'm *firma* ese—just 'cause we on fence parole together don't mean shit if ya make me flip my shit!"

"Okay, okay! No need to take it to the square." I gesture for her to come to the edge of the pool. Maybe she's just sensitive because so many of her scars are visible this way. "Look, it just clashes with your tattoos is all. Personally, it doesn't matter what kind of suit you're wearing, you look fine." This seems to do the trick, and she takes a few timid steps toward the pool. "Let's stop procrastinating and get this show in the water. By the time we're done here, you'll be jumping and flipping all around like Shamu. If you're *really* good, you might even get some chopped fish."

The hardness leaves her features. "Ya so simple minded sometimes!" Once she's sitting at the edge I explain that your body naturally floats *in* water, but not *on* the water. Takes a while before she gets the difference. "So how long's that take to learn, this 'buoyancy' move?"

"No time. It's just how you're built—you don't have any choice but to float. Now here, get in with me, and stay facing the wall." I help her ease into the water, and she chides me not to try copping a feel. People get afraid and start mouthing off about any and every thing, especially when it comes to swimming instruction. "Okay, now keep two fingers from each hand on the wall, and lift your feet back, off the bottom. Then release the wall."

"Let go?"

"Don't worry, I'm here if anything goes wrong. It'll be fine, you're just going to drop a little bit in the water. This way we find out how much buoyancy you have. It's different for everybody."

"Yeah, well last time ya had my back ya was dunkin' me like bread in gravy."

She goes along with it and discovers that letting go isn't so bad. Putting yourself in nature's hands is certainly a lot less of a struggle than going against the flow. Pretty soon she's floating like a champ, ears submerged and grinning like a fool. Of course, she's got my hands lightly supporting her back, but we all need guarantees sometimes.

While learning to adjust the position of her arms and legs to achieve balance, she says, "This ain't half bad!" There are a couple rough spots when she begins to freak out and thrash a little, but that's only natural.

Overall she does pretty good for her first swimming lesson, and I tell her as much. Quick to dismiss her progress, she blurts, "Sure. Floating's a real big deal."

"Sure it is. All swimming *is* is floating, moving from one point to another while floating. Without it you'd lose control and drown. And if you're ever involved in some kind of disaster out on the water—"

"Dios mio, *please* don't say that, it's always been my..." She hesitates, then decides she can tell me. "Ever since I can remember, my worst nightmare always been being on a plane crashing in the ocean, or maybe a sinking ship or, well, one time it was my school and it was sinking. Guess that's stupid."

"You don't have to worry about that anymore. Any kind of emergency, you can float. Plus knowing how to do it right'll keep you from getting exhausted and drowning before help can find you."

"Dint think about it like that."

"This is what I really love, doing this. It's cool to think maybe I taught a person something that'll save their life."

She splashes me. "It's just an excuse for ya to get all close up on the girlies."

I teach her a little about breathing, and she uses it to help regulate her buoyancy. For the first time I've managed to forget the fact that I'm a fugitive from the law, that weirdoes and crooks are chasing me up and down and back again. At least she's managed to stop freaking out about those suits who ran by here. Soon as we have it, it's over. Juanita's climbing out and talking about dinner options.

"Is there a shower I can use?"

"Right back here," she says, heading into the changing area.

"What, like some kinda YMCA thing?"

"Somethin' like that."

Cripes, how rich are these people? Before I changed in the little guest room she set me up in. Actually, it wasn't so little. And neither is this shower area! It's the size of my bedroom back at home. Only thing is, it doesn't have individual stalls.

"Uh..."

"Yeah?" She looks over her shoulder while she slides out of her suit. "What, you need an invitation?"

"Just wondering if it's cool for me to shower now is all..." She laughs and gets on with it. Maybe that means this is how they do things down here, or maybe it's the same as two guys showering since she's a lesbian, or maybe she's just used to prison showers. Whatever. After all the long hours at the pool, showering off with the guys is the norm.

So, we make small talk about this and that, how it's my first time in the country, and she tells me about the stuff she's been up to since we left. After a while she turns and asks, "Ya know...was ya listenin' when I said it was my *sister* that done the bank job?"

"Uh, yeah."

"So, ya know, it was *her* girlfriend helpin' her and shit like that?"

"Um...uh-huh."

"So?" Our eyes lock, the answer rolling around close to the surface of my brain, but nowhere near close enough. "I'm not a lesbo!" She gives me a playful little shove and laughs.

All sorts of questions and exclamations come to my lips. The one that wins out is, "What the—?!" She laughs again and bumps me with her hip. Is she freakin' coming onto me now? "Then what the hell was all that grief you gave me about your sexual orientation way back at our, you know, 'meeting?'"

She laughs. "I just got's ta make a MO squirm around sometimes!" So now I'm a muthafuckin' ofay too? She knocks me with her hip again, then wiggles her fanny around going, "Nyah nyah! Nyah nyah!" with her tongue sticking out.

Even with everything else going on, this is a little mind-blowing. Isn't anybody really the way they seem on the surface? "Well, look...sorry about this whole shower thing, if it's improper and whatnot—"

"Nah. You get used to group showers inside—and sharks." A *shark* is a guard who makes a point of always observing inmates as they shower.

Our first meeting flashes across my mind, when she ogled my bite marks, and later when she called me Shark-boy. "Look, I'm not a guard—"

"Then what are ya, G-ride?"

"Huh?"

She laughs again, rinses her hair. "Tha's ya new street name, dig it? G-ride."

"Sure, I get it. Like those pimped-out cars you see driving around the 'hood or whatever."

"Naw, tha's a *gangster* ride. Ya's a *gigolo* ride. Naw mean?"

I kinda liked the name, before she said that.

The sound of water drumming against the tiles is awkward now, ever since her little revelation. Surrounded by these smooth white walls her bronze skin is a magnet—a magnet my eyes are trying to resist. What if Leena caught us together like this? And why does the word "caught" jump to mind, as if we're doing...well, *something*. I thought we were just, like, sharing a moment, a bonding moment. Like friends do. Buddies. We were buddies! But you don't take showers with female buddies, do you? I just didn't consider her a chick before. And what about Leena, anyway? Were we ever buddies, or did we just have a lot of sex? Jesus, now everything's screwed up.

"Yo G-ride." Those emerald eyes of hers feel more penetrating than ever before. "Anyone home?"

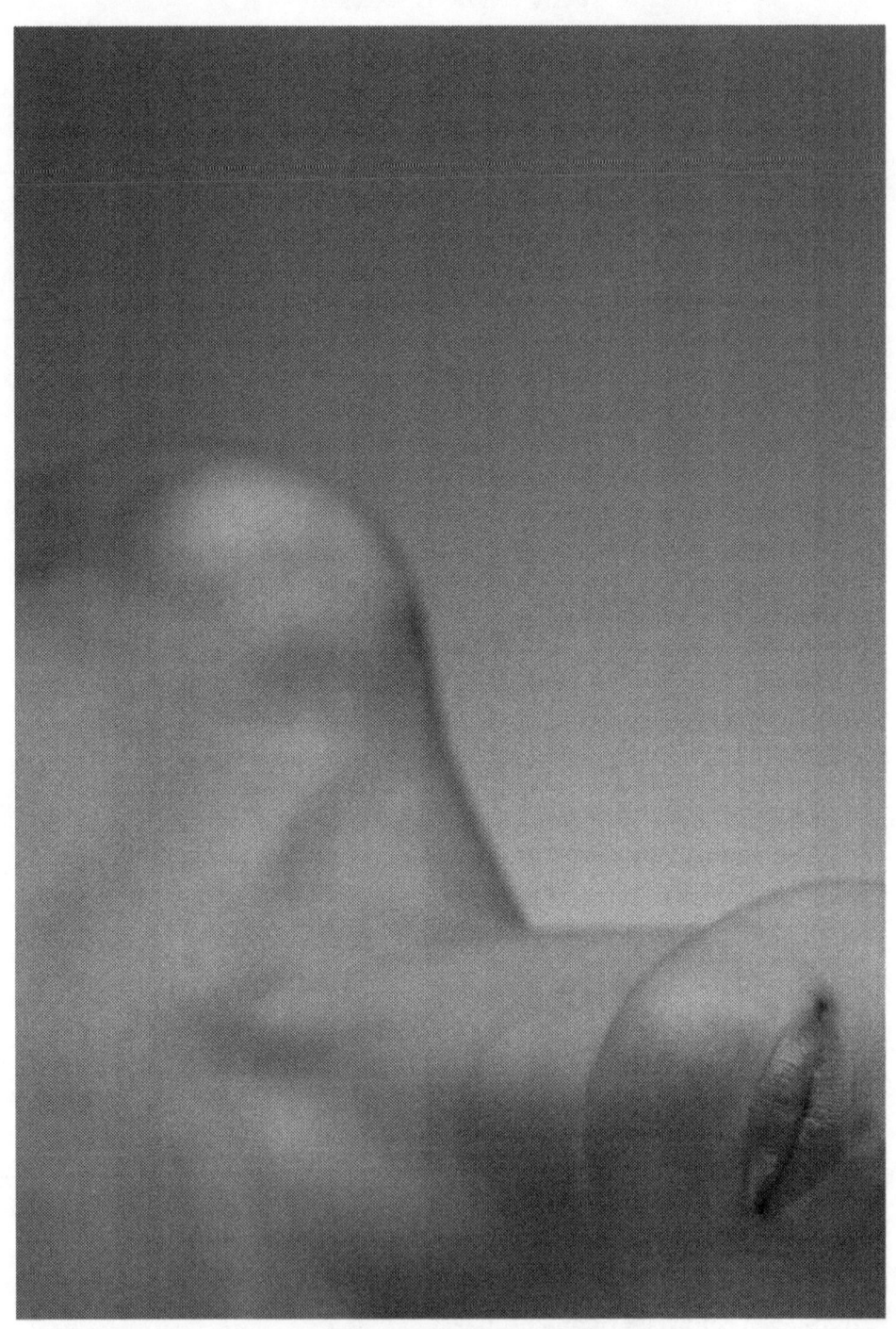

Photo still, courtesy Last Burn Films © 2006

"Sure, sure."

Snapping back to reality I realize she's fully facing me for the first time. What was that I was telling her about letting go and letting nature take its course? My eyes develop a mind of their own and I become one with the water that cascades over her hair, down her face and neck, stuttering at the scar slashing across her throat, guided to the center of her chest by her collarbones, gliding between her breasts and spreading over her clearly defined abs, only welling at her belly button momentarily before moving south to the darkness between her hips: her tattoo.

Holy shit! That tattoo!

"Fuck me..."

She takes this the wrong way and starts to fondle my chest, her stilted gestures indicating that she's not familiar with touching people this way. I jump back, slipping and almost cracking my head before catching myself on a soap dish. Suddenly I'm not so buoyed up.

"What?" she yells, hugging herself, looking all hurt or something.

The tattoo on her lower abdomen hypnotizes me. Just below her waistline is a left fist clenched around a jagged lightning bolt, its lower end descending down into the dark shroud of her pubic hair.

That means Diaz. That means maybe I'm not the only one leading a double life. Suddenly we're not floating on the surface any more.

The sound of the pool room door opening snaps me back to reality. A man calls out. That means trouble. With a capitol D.

One, two, and breathe...

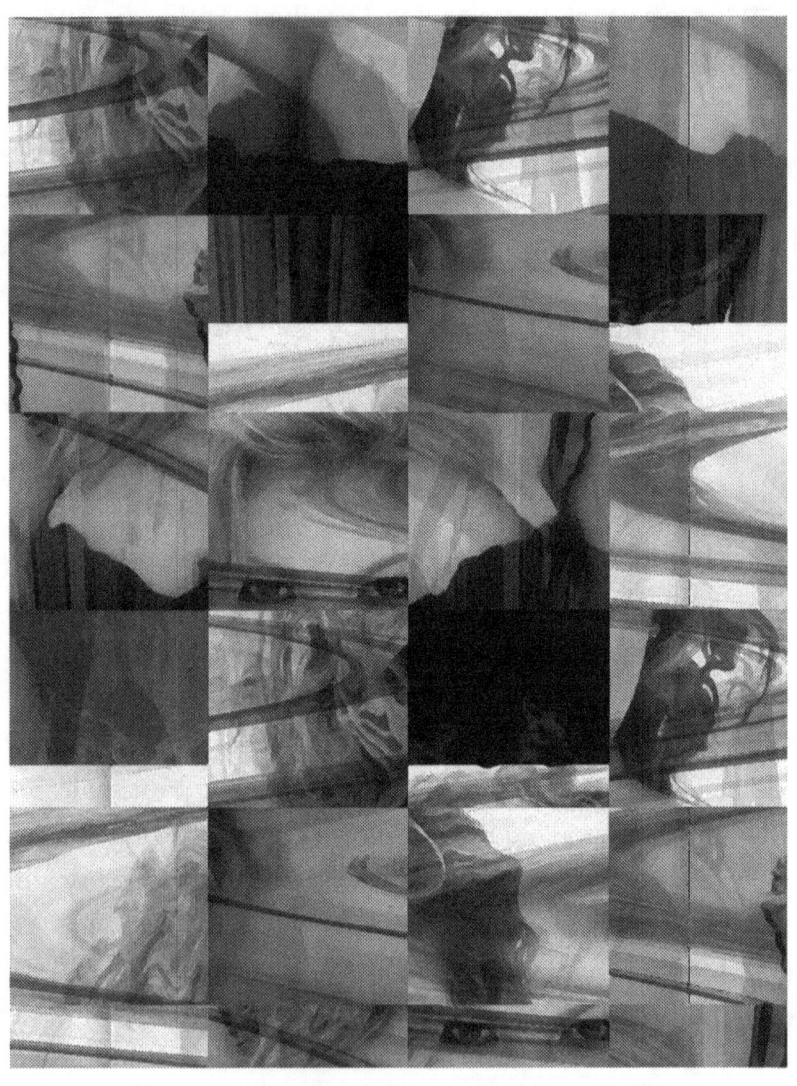

Promotional image, courtesy Last Burn Films © 2006

PART THREE:

DESCONOCIDO ESTRAFALARIO

"Parva saepe scintilla contempta magnum excitavit incendium." [A spark neglected has often raised a conflagration.]
—Quintus Curtius Rufus, *De Rebus Gestis Alexandri Magni*

"A little fire is quickly trodden out; Which, being suffer'd, rivers cannot quench."
—William Shakespeare, *King Henry the Sixth*

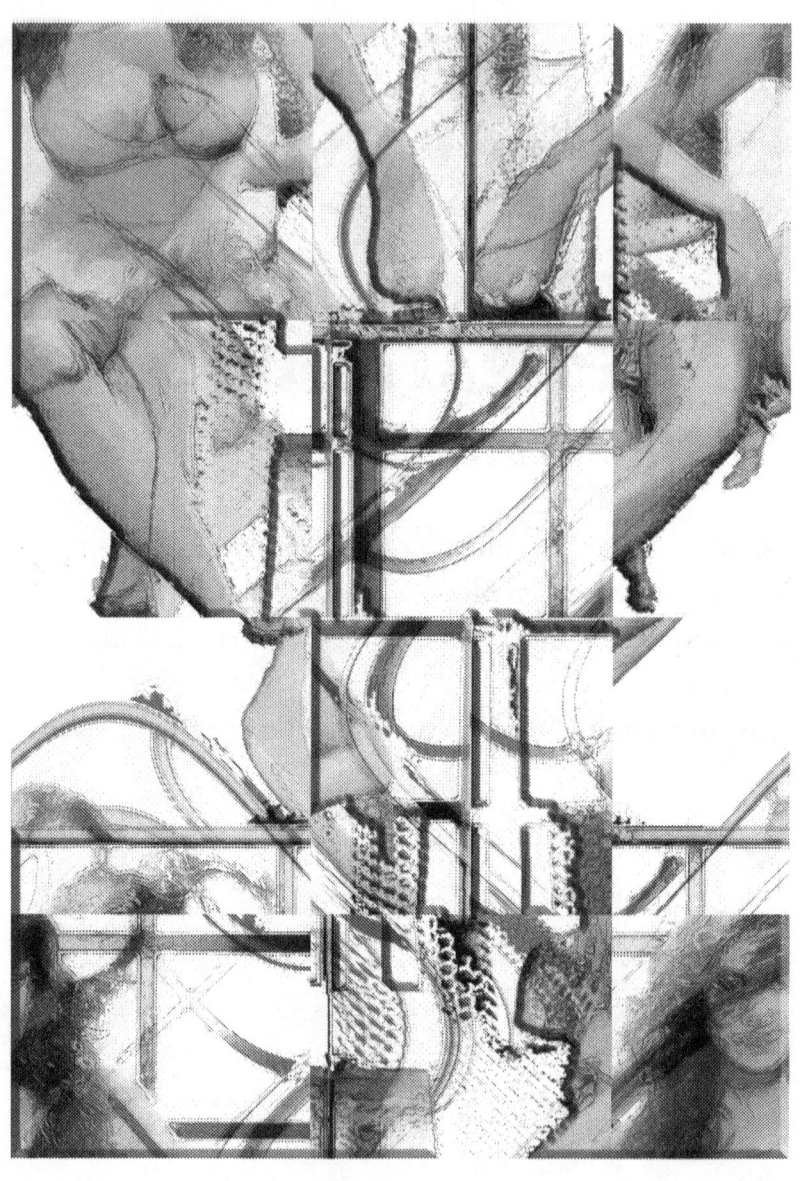

Promotional image, courtesy Last Burn Films © 2006

I T WAS EASY ENOUGH slipping out the window while Juanita distracted her uncle. How could Diaz be her uncle, of all people? It just doesn't make sense. My pal the bug smuggler tells me Diaz has his fingers in every type of crime imaginable. Guess it figures about Juanita's sister and the bank—it runs in the family. Maybe she was even doing the bank job for him, who knows?

Either way, using the car keys she gave me wasn't as easy as it was supposed to be. Finding the car wasn't any problem but, of course, Diaz wasn't alone. His guards were hanging outside and must've figured I was boosting their boss's property. Or maybe they recognized me. Either way they're still chasing me down at 140 KPH. Every now and then we have to slow for the crazy curves, the pedestrian traffic, a stray llama or two. When that happens they pull up close and let loose with their guns. Somehow, that manages to convince the pedestrians and llamas to hurry the hell up.

Was that a bullet that just whizzed by my window? Shit, it was another bullet!

They're getting closer. This keeps up and somebody's getting hurt, no doubt. I'm no kind of stunt driver and these other guys aren't either, so there's plenty of near-misses along the way. Do traffic cops exist in this stupid country? Whoa—what was that? Something's happened to the rear tires and the street's jumping around like crazy and fuck it, I'm heading right into this telephone pole ain't I?

Ohh. Ohh man, just take me back out to the desert again. Take me back to the prison and let the State do their worst. Let rabid lesbians put me on the rack, in the iron maiden. Ohh *hell* no. Must've broke every bone in my body. That's how it feels anyway. How bad is it? Well, this car isn't going anywhere any time soon. As for me, I might be able to walk away from this.

They screech to a stop down the street, then turn around and come back to finish the job. Where the hell is there to run?! Maybe that store over there...

Somebody steps out and fires a handgun. Two more shots and the car starts to swerve all over. Diaz's men lose control and plow through a row of wheelbarrows, then ram right into my car! Fuckin'-A, thanks to the damned good samaritans out there. My whole body just got bruised a second time. And Diaz's dudes? A wheelbarrow went through their windshield, 'nuff said.

For a second everything's quiet, then it's clear the good samaritan is getting closer. Shit, are they Mexican police? It's impossible to stay still and play dead with my heart beating out of control and my limbs shaking from all the adrenaline. Broken bits of plastic and metal are all around, but really it's not that bad. If I'd thought fast enough I'd have spread some blood around to make it convincing.

"Come on out Kenny. Who are you trying to kid, anyway? You don't even have any blood on your face." Holy—it can't be. Leena pries the door open, yanking me out onto my feet. "What, no hello?"

"Leena, babe, I don't know if I ought to suck on your tongue or rip it outta your mouth. I mean, damn girl."

"Gee, look who woke up on the wrong side of the car wreck."

Just when my legs get steady a tattooed gorilla jumps out of the other car and clobbers Leena a good one over the head. She does some kind of kung fu type kick, lightning fast, smashing his gut—too much like Kirkmoor for my tastes. Both of them fall back and I jump on him. We wrestle around, neither one of us getting the upper hand. Seems like there's blood everywhere, both of ours. And, blood from his buddy, not to mention brains and organs and oh God, my lunch is gonna spew. Sliding behind him my arm hooks his arm, my other arm wraps around his throat. His elbow is an explosion of pain in my side, twice, three times. With each swing of his arm you can hear his broken ribs grinding together.

He tries to kick Leena, but she blocks him with one hand and stabs with the other. Her knife slips up under his ribcage and straight into the heart, seems like, because he goes limp instantly. Just like that, as if she's done it a million times. The one or two people peeking out through the surrounding windows scatter when she turns to scan the area. She's pretty scary right now with the blood dripping from her hand and her forehead.

When I start to freak about her cut she informs me, "You can never bleed too hard." As tough as that may sound she doesn't look too good, but she shrugs away my concerns. "The water here, it's killing me," she says. "My stomach's giving me shit like you wouldn't believe."

Okay then, so I'm not the only one who's a fish out of water down here. Time for me to tear a scrap off one of these dude's shirts and press it to her wound. Once that's in check we get the hell out of Dodge. It just so happens that she has a room outside of town, in a place she affectionately calls a "shit hole." Once we're chilling in her crib it's easier to understand where she's coming from with that.

"Trick to keeping rats out? Chop one in half; stick the front end in one hole and cram the back half in another hole. Keep it up until all the holes are plugged with the corpses of their buddies. Usually scares 'em off. Rest of the time it turns 'em into cannibals, which I find somewhat amusing." Soon as she spouts this wisdom she has to spend half an hour on the john.

The next few days are spent caring for my woman. Sure, she left me high and dry, but she also saved my ass. Seems to me that should balance things out. Either way, we don't talk about the breakout. It would be kind of weird, and besides Leena's sick as a dog. The blankets soak up her fever sweat like a sponge. Between drying them and feeding her and trying to figure out what people around here are saying to me there's no time to worry about police and such, or how it is these people keep finding their way into my life.

Turns out my bedside manner involves more than orgasms. By the week's end Leena is getting back to her old self. She's back to being witty and sarcastic, instead of laying there all washed out. Pretty soon she wants more than just a massage or a hug. After the two of us spend a day in bed together she is pronounced officially recovered. And sure, maybe it helped that I walked the extra two miles every day for bottled water.

Later, I'm shaving and Leena is in a tub full of bubble bath, striking muscle poses while she grins at me over her shoulder, a smoldering cigar clamped between her lips. This is the most lively she's been since we hooked up again. Seems like just a few days can do miracles for a couple.

"Ricky baby, this calls for a celebration. Why don't you be a dear and fetch us some brewskis?"

"What calls for a celebration?"

"Oh, you'll see. It's a surprise."

Everything's a surprise lately, but if she's in a good mood it's better to flow with it. No, "brewskis" aren't on my to-drink list. All the same I find myself down at the local store buying some. Never mind the unnecessary public exposure, but what the hell—our pictures aren't posted behind the counter, aren't on the covers of the newspapers, so it would be too paranoid to stay holed up around the clock. Paranoia tends to be a side effect of being an international fugitive, or witnessing murders, or taking part in them. I pay the burnout behind the counter and get back to the hidey hacienda. It's goofy, but a little of that bounce is back in my step after working things out with Leena. Seeing her up ahead standing in the parking lot makes me feel a lot better about things. After all, she's my woman, I'm her man, and we've been through things that would wreck most people's minds, much less their relationships. And...

And who the hell is this chick? Some tall model-type is on the scene, getting a little too comfortable with my honey. Even though Leena towers at six feet this one is almost as tall, but the similarity ends there. She's got none of the muscles that make Leena so scary, and she has long blazing red hair, huge boobs, what looks to be professionally applied makeup. Damn, is she some kind of movie star, and holy hell—*did they just kiss?!*

I clear my throat as I draw near, and the redhead looks annoyed. She says something in Spanish and shoos me away.

"O*kay*. Good to meet you too. Uh, here's the stuff," I say, indicating the bag and looking to Leena for answers. There aren't any.

"What *stuff?*" the redhead asks.

Leena puts an arm around her waist, drawing her in. What the fuck, man! "It's okay baby," she coos, "He's cool."

"You know him?" Red looks like she smells something funky.

"Does she know *me?*"

Before I can finish, Leena takes the bag and claps me on the shoulder. "Kenrick, meet Nikki. Nikki, meet Kenrick."

"Ken. Or Rick."

Nikki the model chick has already gotten bored with me. "Whatever. Are we ready to go now or what?"

"Sure."

"Go where?" You step out for some beers and this is what happens. Is it any wonder I never drink?

Nikki laughs, like I said something funny. My first impression of her is a whole lot of posturing, a mannequin with revolving faces. We're moving to a blue convertible. Leena informs me what little supplies and clothes we have are already packed up and loaded in the trunk, so we're good to go.

"Go *where?*"

"In the car," she replies, her voice dripping with mock whininess. Again Nikki laughs. There's only a front seat in this sonofabitching thing, so it won't be pleasant, but they're not shaking me that easily.

"Not that I'm ungrateful for the ride or anything, but, uh, why are you here?"

"Oh come on, Kenny," Leena says. "Play nice with my main squeeze, or you'll find yourself hoofing it."

Nikki chimes in with, "Frankly, I'm not even sure why I'm letting him sit in my car."

All I can say is, "*Main squeeze?*"

"You know, my girlfriend?"

Okay, this is messed up. I'm on the run in a foreign country, sandwiched between my escaped convict girlfriend and my girlfriend's girlfriend. Leena's the bull, Nikki's the fluff...and I must be nuts, making this a bullshitting fluffernutter sandwich.

One, two, and breathe...

Leena sneers. "Aw, how cute. He's doing his special breathing exercises to stay calm."

"Oh? Some kind of swami come down from the hills to enlighten us with his meditative ways? How magnanimous," Nikki sniggers.

"Okay, look you two—"

Nikki cuts me off with, "No *you* look. I don't have an inkling as to what your hang-up is, and frankly I don't care. Leena and I were doing just fine before you crawled out of your hole, so why don't you scamper back to whatever kennel you escaped from?"

On the radio, a familiar voice is soulfully crooning, a soothing female voice. Still, the look I'm giving this Nikki lady could get me three consecutive life sentences, easy.

Leena's arm finds its way around my shoulders, a python's embrace. "Oh, come on you kids. If you can get along Daddy'll buy you ice cream."

Nikki chimes in with, "Oh really, Daddy? Wow! Are we there yet, are we there yet?"

While they have a good laugh, I weigh in with, "Oh look—it's the lesbian Abbott and Costello. The funniest women on the planet are right here in this car."

"Sorry hon," Nikki quips. "Your mother already took the title of funniest woman when she put out a joke like you." This earns her a stiff fist in the shoulder from Leena. The car swerves and we nearly collide with at least four other vehicles. "Ow! You *bee*-otch! That hurt like hell!" This earns Nikki a second punch. Only this time one of Leena's knuckles is sticking out, burrowing even deeper into the flesh. No doubt, Nikki's gonna feel that every time she moves her arm for a week, at least.

We ride the rest of the way in silence.

Instead of ice cream we end up wrestling with a waiter at some restaurant. It takes forever to order because this Nikki person can't bring herself to behave like a human being. One table doesn't have enough light, one's too drafty, one has people sitting near it. Then she has to find out how the meals are prepared, and changes all the ingredients around. Mainly, she can't find anything that's strictly vegetarian.

It figures she'd be a vegetarian. Before I can even comment on that she "enlightens" me: "The primary source of energy for our solar system is the sun, the emanations of which are harvested directly by plant life, making plants a cleaner source of energy. You wouldn't put used oil in your engine, would you? I *thought* not."

"I don't know about you, but my engine runs on gasoline, not oil." This earns me a swift kick under the table from Leena, who quickly changes the subject.

After a fairly brutal dinner Nikki and I find ourselves abandoned by Leena, who's gone off to meet up with a "contact." We're standing behind the restaurant by some thorny type of undergrowth, looking up at the stars. Everything is so much clearer here than back up north.

Nikki decides to break the silence. "So, don't you ever have anything interesting to say?"

It takes a second to come up with something conversational. "I like your hair."

"Shut up." She takes a sip of her drink, then looks me up and down. "So what are you, some kind of drug connection she met in the joint?"

I laugh. "Why would you even ask something that weird? That's just a weird idea."

"Look me right in the eye and tell me you didn't dope her up just now."

I step up, face to face with her. "I didn't dope her up a minute ago, a month ago, or a year ago. Who the hell are you, anyway?"

Suddenly my nuts are being crushed. "I'm the only person in the world that ever gave a damn about her is who I am, and you're some prison scum bag. Now *you* tell *me* why she's walking around like she's on sedatives!"

"For Christ's sake! I'm a prison guard!"

She lets go and the ground rushes to meet my elbows, my knees. "You're her inside connection?"

After panting for a bit, flooded with relief that my gonads weren't ripped off, it comes out. "I set up the devices, I had the security codes and schematics and all that. Okay?" A moment later, "What are you talking about, 'sedatives?'"

She doesn't answer. Instead she leaves me to clutch my groin in peace. Waiting all alone in my apartment are antique iron testes crushers from China. They're forged to look like a crude alligator, and they split down the middle with a hinge at the tail's end. The alligator's mouth is where the nut-mashing action takes place. If that weird contraption ever enters my life again I'll be sure to name it after a certain redhead.

By the time I get my groin under control my ears pick up noises out here. Weird animal noises. Hanging out back at the car is real appealing all of a sudden. Turning the corner the women come into view, both waiting in the parking lot. Leena's pacing back and forth, waving her hands around violently while she rants about something. Nikki sees me getting near and almost looks relieved.

"Uh, Leena?"

She turns. "Oh! Rick. Where've you been?" She's never been like this: eyes frantic, short of breath, veins wriggling under her skin like worms on fishing hooks. She insists her "meeting" went well, and that nothing's wrong. Even though it's uncomfortable being around her when she's this agitated it still feels good to see Nikki cowed.

When we're back on the road it becomes clear Nikki is splitting. Says she's got some talks to do or something. When I ask how we'll be getting to the next town they both give me an "oh brother" type look. Whatever. While they're busy talking my eyes stay on the night sky. This one star, it almost looks like it's following us. One of those tricks your mind plays on you, or maybe a shooting star. Nope, that's out of the question, because shooting stars move really fast. There's no point in bringing it up. They'll just make a slew of stupid UFO jokes.

We go to a swanky hotel and pull around back. This seems like as good a time as any for Nikki to lecture me about discretion. "You'll figure it out sooner or later anyway. I'm not just Nikki, I'm *Nikki*." There's a pause to allow that bombshell to sink in.

"You're...Nikki."

"Right."

"I don't get it."

This inspires another fit of drama from the redheaded queen of the spotlight. Using a string of ten dollar words she informs me that she's a pop star south of the border, bigger than Madonna. She has to leave because she's booked to speak at some schools on Mexico's west coast, and I'm not to think she's a stranger to educational institutions, because she graduated at the top of her class at Brandeis.

"Um...is Brandeis like a university or a college, because there's a difference, right?"

Nikki turns to Leena. "You deal with this monkey. Just make sure he doesn't screw things up."

"Yes *mother*." Leena says.

Nikki makes sure to embrace her, planting another huge freakin' kiss on her before leaving. She eyes me all the while over Leena's shoulder, trying to figure me out. She honestly doesn't know about me and Leena? Whatever. It's probably better to keep a big dork like her from getting any more ammunition than necessary. My God, what is she trying to do to Leena? Is she gonna pork her right here in the parking lot?

"See you in a few days. You know where." The diva marches off, and it dawns on me that we get to keep the car.

After she's out of sight I tell Leena, "You can't be serious."

She gives me this look, one I haven't seen before, and it doesn't seem like a good thing. Then something gives and she cracks up like mad.

"What? I'm just saying. Who does she think she is?"

Leena ruminates, "I ought to suggest she title her next album Does Not Play Well With Others. Look, forget about it. She's just not used to considering that maybe everything in creation doesn't revolve around her."

"High maintenance girlfriend?"

She makes a gun with her hand and fires at me. I hope that means, like, "right on target" or something. Either way she's way more relaxed now, the Leena I know and...love? Is that what we are, in love? Back on the road we decide to listen to the radio and that song is playing again.

"Man, this tune really drives me nuts. Who is that? She sounds so familiar, but with it not being in English and all, well, is this like some foreign version of a real song?"

Leena laughs, tickles me. "Of course it's a real song, you dummy! You're listening to it."

"You know what I mean. I just can't put a face to that voice."

"You just said goodbye to her, slick."

"Ahhhh, shit. Are you serious? This whole pop star thing is for real?"

"Tell you what, Ken. Why don't you call us when the mother ship lands."

Whatever that means.

How to Make a Bed of Nails

Nails, typically, are only harmful when driven into flesh by a hammer. This is a rare occurrence; one is much more likely to get hurt in the attempt to hammer a nail into wood. When examining the tip of a typical nail it becomes aparent they aren't so sharp after all. However, if placed under the weight of an entire body, this single nails could penetrate skin and muscle tissue.

A "bed of nails" is an althogether different proposition. The average person is 150 lbs, so distribution of said body weight over 600 nails reduces the burden to merely 0.25 lbs per nail. The skin is a resiliant organ, capable of bearing 8 times that force per nail before registering pain. If outer garments are added to the equation an even higher threshold of force may be achieved. Thus, physics demystifies the "bed of nails." *

To construct your "bed of nails" you will need 1,500 nails, 3" in length; 1"-thick plywood, 35" x 70". To ensure straight nails pre-drill each hole, creating 60 rows of 25 nails, spaced roughly 1" apart. (See Figure 6a)

The second phase of construction involves the arm rests necessary to lower oneself onto the "bed of nails." You will need 7/8"-thick plywood, 4' x 4", cut into 1' segments. Two lengths serve as the armrests proper, and two as braces. Arrange as per your body size, preferably after drilling the nail holes but before actually hammering in said nails. (See Figure 6b)

Please note: Participant should always have a cloth, pillow, or board placed under neck as a precaution, due to the number of critical blood vessels close to the surface in this region of the body.

For extra amusement, place a wooden block of at least 35 lbs (min. 20" x 12" x 4") over the chest/abdomen of the participant. An assistant then strikes the wooden block with a hammer of at least 3 lbs weight. The wooden block, while not heavy enough to signifigantly raise the per nail pressure, has enough mass to defray the hammer's impact in and of itself, leaving the participant without even slight discomfort. Audience members will be mortified, then amazed. **

If executed properly, the "bed of nails" can provide hours of enjoyment for you and your family. Impress friends and colleagues by demonstrating your ability to be a human pincushon! ***

It is not advised that you attempt this without the assistance of professional carpenters, physics professors, or sideshow performers. Not recommended for punishing children or pets. We are not liable for your actions.
*** This activity is strongly advised against. We are not liable for your actions.*
**** Be sure tetnus shots of all involved are current. If uncertain get a booster shot. We are not liable for your actions.*

Leena folds her arms across her chest. "Funny running into you here."

"Word. But maybe ya comin' after me, right? Keep them beans from spillin', or ya cut a deal wit da *laws*." Juanita folds her arms too, probably trying to press her muscles up so they might compare with Leena's.

Shit, the prison yard stare down again. Shouldn't we have left all that baggage behind? Worse, it's impossible to tell how many of these people are here with Juanita. Could be the whole crowd for all we know.

Stepping between them I say, "Nobody's following anyone, or making deals with cops, or whatever. We're in town waiting for our hookup to hit the scene. And you have relatives here, right? Didn't you say something like that?" Juanita's stare flickers my way long enough for her to agree. "It's just a weird, you know, coincidence is all. So everything's cool then, right?"

"Awright Sharky, I feel ya. But best we don't be seen all three of us, jus' standin' 'round like this."

Leena does a 360. All of a sudden she wants to hang out and see the nightlife together. Juanita gets all suspicious again, and guess who has to keep playing diplomat. Tonight it's easy enough, though, because everyone is happy and dancing, playing guitars, laughing about some unknown joke. Incense is burning everywhere we go, and Nikki's song is blaring from every damn radio. Don't these people have, like, anything else to listen to? Leena tells me the title means "Bizarre Stranger," as if anybody cares.

After a few drinks the two of them are getting on like sisters. It's not clear if that's a good thing or a bad thing. I mean, what about the stuff that went down between me and Juanita? It's getting more uncomfortable for me every second. Am I the only one thinking about the shower by Diaz's pool, what the hell would Leena do if she found out, and how do I even feel about her after the whole Nikki revelation? Shit, man. This has become a BLT&A sandwich.

Over drinks Leena shares a little something. "Nikki was the one driving the getaway car."

"Huh?"

"Think about it. With her behind the wheel it was no problem for us to get over the border; I wore bandages over my face, posing as a wealthy friend who got cosmetic surgery from a famous US surgeon. The customs agents didn't care; they were too busy getting Nikki's autograph to pay much attention to some mummy stretched out on the back seat."

Wait—is that who I think it is? Up ahead that looks like Enrique finishing off some roasted meat on a stick. He sees the three of us and moves in, beaming. "Hold on now my man, you got the juice. You got the juice!" He laughs and tosses his arms around me. "Kenrick, buddy, you got to hook me up."

I start to say something about him calling me that, then decide it's better to be polite. "Enrique, allow me to introduce some special people. This here's Leena."

"I'm his 'main squeeze,'" she jokes, vigorously shaking his hand.

"And this is Juanita."

He says something to her in Spanish. Whatever it is, it sounds graceful. Then he kisses her hand. Enrique, you old dog you!

It's strange, the four of us meeting up like this, but what the heck. Or, maybe if you save somebody their spirit is drawn to you. Kind of like that old Asian philosophy thing they're always talking about on TV shows, when somebody's life belongs to you after you save it. That would explain the women being drawn back to me. And, me to Enrique.

Enrique and Leena, they get along fine. Both of them like to talk brainy, and each of them has left me high and dry at one time or another. Their conversation about the subjugation of the female identity is kind of a snoozer. Me and Juanita, it's a little more complicated than either of us would like. After that whole shower incident we have to go through tons of small talk just to keep anything from getting too "real"—especially with Leena around.

Juanita nudges me. "Yo man, smoke on the horizon."

Enrique asks, "Something burning?"

"Maybe our asses if we stick around," Leena states, grinning at the thought.

What is it now? Diaz's thugs? Rabid lesbians? Robotic-sounding foam-faced freaks? New Age radicals bent on kidnapping me and my brothers?

Juanita nudges Enrique. "The laws, naw mean?"

He nods philosophically, and the four of us move away from the approaching police. It crosses my mind to ask if they refer to arrests as *getting stung* in his line of work. Right now, though, the only thing that stings is my ego. Everybody knows in prison there's no such thing as running away from a problem, and there's nothing but running in my future, seems like.

Back at the hotel we wait for what feels like forever. Nothing beats standing around in public to make you sweat when you're trying to keep a low profile. After awhile a massive tour bus with tinted windows pulls up, all sparkling silver with Nikki's face and her album cover painted on the side.

Enrique and Juanita look at each other. "Yo, what the hell?"

"Here's our ride," Leena says.

"Yeah man, she did that 'Bizarre Stranger' song." They look at me like I just graduated from the third grade.

The bus door opens and a familiar redhead sticks her head out. "Anybody call for a taxi?"

A tip from the hip: Kenrick Brimley is a *himbo*. That means *male bimbo* in pop star talk. From the sound of it every diva keeps at least one himbo in her entourage so she'll always have somebody to put down. Lucky me.

"Come on, baby," Leena says when everybody's distracted by Nikki's antics. "It'll be the perfect cover. We can travel anywhere in her circus, no questions asked. Hiding in plain sight."

That's not what's worrisome, and she knows it. But how can you argue with her logic? Men are supposed to be the rational ones, not the emotional ones, so I grunt something about it being cool.

That's about all the alone time we get in the Nikki road show. There's always some new town, some new hotel, some new performance with its own quirks and kinks to work out. While I'm busy fetching coffee for everybody, the star and her stage crew practice.

Photo still, courtesy Last Burn Films © 2006

Her show consists of a mind-numbing series of costume changes. The wardrobe bill must be insane, that's all I can say. Every song is a chance for her to be reborn, a new chapter in her evolution. You wouldn't recognize her on stage if you didn't know it was her concert. They tell me it's a success; her *Chameleon* album is breaking all of Mexico's sales records.

The women, they're busy debating stuff like the correlation between sex and death in entertainment. That is, the center stage women—the backup dancers spend their time stretching or eating tofu pudding or sharing fitness tips. The long African American one, she's Vi. Leena says it's short for Viagra. The bleached blonde is Demi, short for Demerol. The Korean is Flo, short for Flonase. There's even one named Perky, after Percoset. Everyone is naming their kids after products these days—it's as if your kid isn't worth the DNA they're printed on unless they've got a corporate seal of approval.

Enrique, he comes and goes; his business calls for a lot of traveling. He's got a crib further south filled with refrigerated rooms to store his product, and even though the bugs can go awhile without food somebody's got to swing in and feed them worms occasionally.

On the tour bus I'm reading murder books when Leena comes by and tells me I'm "gigolo cool." Way too much time is spent trying to figure that one out, giving me the mother of all migraines. We're on the train, only we're not going from jail to prison, not technically speaking, even though we're prisoners of Nikki's lifestyle. And while we're running around playing pop star, who's taking care of my babies at home? Who's going to dust and wax them, talk to them in soothing tones? And what about my living babes—is the whole death row thing going to come to an end now that their "independent contractor" has run off?

Days and towns continue to blur on our whirlwind tour. As part of the program to "hip me up" Juanita has me listening to something called POJO. She informs me that it stands for "Post Organic Jungle Outburst, an' ya just cain't fuck wit dat, ese!" Speaking of Juanita, she is only tolerated in the group because she "blends" so well, and is a good "handler" for me. There's some bad blood because one time she pointed out that Nikki is 34, only two years younger than Juanita's mother.

The one constant in my life is the man down trigger. Somehow I've managed to hold onto this thing through my travels. Must be good luck, since I never had to use it on the job, never got killed during all the stupid things that have happened. When Perky isn't looking I snatch a small chain from one of her stage costumes to make a necklace for this thing. It should stay close to my heart as a reminder of where I come from, what I've been through.

Prep time for the next show. Everybody's lives are on hold while Nikki rummages through today's clothing selection. "Okay, what's this—prom night molestation?" She takes a dress and rips it down the middle, throws it on the floor, stomps on it. You can assume that means she's paying for it. "Hmm...nope, not this one either. That's still too mofo-ish. This one's minorly lame, and this one: who do I look like, Billie Holiday on crack?" All of this just to go out and shop before the concert.

After dismissing the wardrobe dude she bosses some more people around, including us—that is, me—and gets on with her preparations. It's almost like she's afraid to show her face outside. Who knew that celebrities were so close to being shut-ins? She makes like this big philosopher, always spouting off about karma and all paths leading back to one and the Kabala, but she's just as scared and confused as the rest of us. Part of her big routine is yoga—anything from the East is *enlightened*. Seeing Nikki go through her warm-up stretches is a little too, uh, well it can't be called sexy exactly, and I have to look away before getting disturbed by the thought. Too late for that, though.

Leena's watching me, all suspicious-like, so I ask if Nikki's ever considered a workout video or book. She mulls it over and nods, genuinely impressed. "You know what? That's a good idea. She ought to turn her money maker into a money maker, if you know what I mean."

When Nikki's done primping and getting her body ready for action, she comes over with my instructions. "All right, boy toy. You're coming with me this time—everyone else just be cool and eat some fruit. We can't have too many of you being seen in public at once."

"Right," I say. "Like four of us waiting around for a big tour bus to pick us up. And why do I have to go with you?"

"Because you're *so* entirely grateful for everything, you're good at opening doors, and you look like a scrub. Now let's go—Nikki stays in motion like the ocean, honey."

What I want to say is that still waters run deep, but Leena's scowl convinces me not to.

On the way to the elevators she adds, "Oh, in addition to opening doors you have to cut through crowds, or it's your ass. Lead on, McScrub."

Maybe it's just my sense of humor, but I don't get it. Either way, this prison guard turned gigolo turned fugitive is actually pretty good at the scrub routine, even though it sucks to be near her. After stepping through the front doors the media goes into full gear, all microphones and cameras and questions at full throttle. The limo is only ten or fifteen feet away, but there's got to be two hundred folks here, if you count the fans too. Nikki smiles and waves, I start chopping through the horde, but for whatever reason a hail of questions stop her. Actually, they all sound like the same question.

"Oh, who—him?" She turns to me, indecision bubbling in her features. "This is my fiancé, K-Ill. He's a rap star up in the States." A second later Nikki's brown eyes and sculpted eyebrows are zooming in, her fingers pressing at the back of my neck. It's a huge, deep wet one, a Big Red Moment. The flashbulb assault leaves me dizzy, as does this bizarre turn of events. *Oohs* and *ahs* abound, and the hail of questions is deafening. She fires off a few monosyllabic answers before prodding me into cutting through the crowd. I open the door for her with a flourish, some teen girls cry out while waving to me, and I jump in beside her.

Our limo gets moving, and after putting up the divider Nikki slaps me. "Don't you even get any thoughts, you son of a bitch."

"*You're* the one who kissed *me!*"

"And you better get used to it," she replies, checking her lipstick. "You heard the response. They're already calling us the couple of the year, Venus meets Adonis—*duh!*—and we've got to play it to the hilt. You want to keep hiding out on my tour? You gotta put out for the public. And no tongue, got it?"

So that's how it is. Here, she's the tank boss. Here, I've got to be somebody's sister. Sonovabitch! It's all I can do to keep myself in check while she prattles on about the publicity ops this twist opens up. Her entrances will have twice the impact now. Already she's trying to figure out how many big film debuts we can make it to—what's Salma's number again?—and how many big restaurants are in the area, what will be the most successful kiss/embrace/ hand-holding ratio, and on and on.

I groan, "But why K-Ill?"

"Just be thankful," she sneers. "I actually started to say your name, then came up with that off the top of my head. I'm used to improvising—interviewers have been called me an oral jazz musician."

"Oh, I'll bet."

That earns me another slap, the sound of her palm against my cheek like a gunshot. This is how Nikki and I "bang the skins."

In prison, when you *roll out* or *roll up* it means you're moving to another cell, another facility. Lately our personalities are on the roll. Juanita, of all people, has been remade in God Nikki's image, hair infused with all manner of styling gels, lashes emphasized, high fashion suits hand-tailored for her. This makes Juanita an *interpreter*. She is our tongue, giving our hungry mouths access to all things Mexican. Leena is decked out with fashionable steel-toed boots and a plain yet ridiculously expensive suit, with dark shades and slicked back hair. This makes Leena a *body guard*. Our shield against the ill effects of our status, protecting us against who we are. Nikki is at the center of it all, looking fabulous while pulling our strings. This makes her *rich*. Yup—no matter how much influence they flaunt the whites still ain't right.

We're rolling with the seven-figure clica. That means all kinds of fancy meals that don't even look like food, endless parties and going from this place to that, that place to this. Despite the sensitive nature of my stay here Nikki has insisted on me sitting in for mind-numbing interviews conducted in Spanish. Me, I just sit there nodding and grinning my fool head off. I'm a cheerleader, an extra.

So now every time I go out in public people are following me. Taking pictures from a distance with freaky telephoto lenses. My hair is dyed different colors every day—Nikki's beautician task force tries new hair styles to alter the way my face appears to be shaped, using different facial hair configurations. Sunglasses are mandatory, of course, and they've given me colored contact lenses. It's disturbing how they fawn over me for hours in their throne of appearance alteration. What's worse is when Nikki herself has to go somewhere, because I have to be on her arm, the two of us posing in all sorts of fake-me-out lovey-doveyness. The photographers keep asking us to kiss and we oblige them. Busting out fake affection and rhymes comes as second nature now. Got to go with the flow. I'm no longer just leading a double life but a triple life, a quadruple life.

...My name is K-Ill and I'm just K-Illin', step to me son and ya suffer loss of feelin', I'll throw ya off the roof and burn the whole damn buildin', you're laid out on ice while I'm just chillin', cause I'm comin' with the malice from Nogalas to Dallas, punk I'll show ya how much ballast it takes to weigh a body down, yo don't fuck around cause you'll wake up underground, while I'm wakin' up with Sanka, cause when it comes to spillin' blood I'm like a Hexxon oil tanker!

Okay, so Juanita's been helping me with the rhymes. Juanita, whose hair is growing out, she's starting to look ladylike. Leena the bodyguard, she's already put the hurt on a couple guys—one a reporter and the other a stalker—and she's made a point of slamming a number of female admirers who got touchy-feely with me. She really needs to chill out. Thankfully nobody's recognized us yet, but if one of these people gets the law on us we've had it. Nikki the diva, she couldn't care less about any of it. K-Ill, the hottest guy south of the border, he just wants everything to level out, to go back to normal.

There's been a lot of talk about adding some kind of "intergalactic" or "alien" angle to K-Ill's "music" but so far I've been able to veto all that. Juanita insists it's the major untapped source in hip hop. "DJ Q-bert and his crew, they know what time it is," she tells me. Apparently there's a school of thought among certain DJ's centering on the theory that hip hop music unleashes your "God self"—sorta building on the whole tribal drum thing from ancient ceremonies, and launching it into the next millennia. The theory is also based around trying to match their "turntablism" to what technologically advanced civilizations from outer space would consider "music." Personally, I can't imagine a break dancing Ziggy Stardust, but what do I know. Too bad for me Nikki and her set are all hot about the idea. In fact, she's even having some "alien" stage outfits designed for her next tour. Different porn...or is it?

On top of all that, there's talk of a music video in Español—a K-Ill video. There's talk of K-Ill and Nikki doing a duet, maybe even an album together. Where does it end?

K-Ill on Ice.

Jesus K-Ill Superstar.

K-Ill For A Day, the hip new reality show. Sure, why not? I haven't been K-Ill for too much more than a day myself.

And the pictures. They've started trickling in again, a few here and there. Threatening, ominous? No. The first is a middle-aged chick trying to look twenty years younger, hair badly bleached, revealing she doesn't have a bra on. The second is a darker woman and her toy. The third is from a shy young dude topless in a walk-in freezer of all places. A smiling woman in an office displaying her limberness. A couple showing their appreciation. Another young guy, beating off to the beats, painting his sound system white. Isn't this what agents are for? Screening this kind of crap?

Right now I'm playing a prison-wannabe rapper hanging on the set of a hot new international production. It's a horror flick, but that's no surprise. Thing is, somebody found out about my mad massage skills. Nikki's loose lips sink my ship again. The producers of this "international production"—B-movie makers from Bolivia, Florida, and Italy—decided to up their star factor by having me do a cameo as some rich woman's private masseuse. She's the star, the rich woman, well the actress playing a rich woman, but she's rich in real life too so there ain't a whole lot of acting involved. Lady's come on to me like seven times now and we don't even speak the same language. Not bad, considering I've only been on the set all of forty-five minutes. Maybe it has to do with the fact that my costume is a loincloth, or that my muscles are all oiled up. Or maybe it was that demonstration massage the producers made me do on her. As if this movie really depends on authenticity.

The Masseusing.

How do I get talked into these things?

Maybe it was the catchy tag line: *He'll relax your muscles...forever.*

Yes, the trailer was quite a piece of work. They showed it to me, all confident smiles and moneymaking assurances. You know how some horror promos show blood dripping down the screen while creepy music plays? This one had massage oil dripping down the screen. Come on.

It figures that Nikki insists on milling around the set—charming everyone, she's sure—making contacts and impressions and yada yada yada. Also figures that her figure is close to the female lead's figure; they're almost inseparable, at least for these last ten minutes now. Some bogus former CIA dude who saw action in Nicaragua is advising me on how to fight against The Masseuser while those two busty ladies pal around. Nikki informed me the lead "posed" for some "magazines" in Europe. "It's different over there," she told me.

"What about all the subjugation of the collective female identity or whatever you and Leena were talking about?"

"Gimme a break," she said. "Those photos were hot as hell."

Me, I'm just wondering how it is all these people don't know a *masseuse* is female and a *masseur* is male.

"Look," I say to the CIA guy, "do I get to learn how to break necks and stuff? All those cool ninja-type moves?"

"I'm a commando not a ninja, son."

"Well, commando moves then."

"Hell no. You just need to look like you can fight is all. You go around breakin' peoples' necks and my ass is in a legal sling."

From the corner of my eye, I'm watching a red-haired pop diva playing with a certain Italian sex symbol's black hair. "Dude, if we're talking money here, I can have her cut you a crazy check."

He looks at Nikki, then at me. He grabs a passing Mexican camera-man. "Okay, first thing you do is put your right hand on the jaw, like so..."

The Bribing. He'll relax your morals...forever.

Does the local massage union give legal advice about carpal tunnel syndrome? The CIA dude is sure that's the problem with my fore-arms and wrists. After three full days of the Italian cover girl flubbing her lines, insisting on shooting scenes over, and strong-arming the director into shooting additional "massage sequences," well, my forearms are about done. Don't get me wrong—okay, get me wrong. I *am* saying that being all over a sex symbol 24/7 can be a shitty proposition. If I never have to smell those funky aromatherapy oils again it'll be too soon. Another brilliant idea on her part. Hey, her body totally conforms to what the media says the "perfect woman" should look like, but damn her personality!

I tried bringing the subject up when talking with Nikki yester-day, but all she had to say was, "With bazoombas like that who gives a damn!"

"Excuse me," I said to a Bolivian crew member. "Could you fetch this woman a bib? She's drooling."

"Oh, you made a funny!" Nikki giggled up a storm. Her and me, I don't think we're ever in the same conversation.

Miss Italy giggled too, eying me up like a one-eyed dog in a meat market. She said something about "big bone" and "long time"—who knows, with that accent.

"See? She doesn't mind. She thinks it's cute."

"Well I don't.

Miss Italy muttered something about "oh yeah, baby" between giggles, something about "candle wax" between shaking her hips and her shoulders.

"That's right, candle wax." Nikki put an arm around her, giving me the thumbs-up. "The ho gets *like that* like that."

Tomorrow we're supposed to do the frontal scene. All my CIA kill training, for what? So Miss Bazoomba Italiano can force the producers to allow full nudity? It's usually the other way around—producers forcing nudity on the actors. I'm getting paid by the day to grope and knead foreign flesh while practicing how to make compound fractures between takes. After today, who knows. The pay is sweet, but with hours of applying the "main squeeze" to her back and legs and, mostly, her butt cheeks, all I want to tell Bazoomba is lay off all the refried beans she must be eating. My God.

Yep, maybe tomorrow we can tell the producers K-Ill is committed to another project and has to wrap things up. That'll work. When I get back in I'll bounce the idea off Leena. It'll still be a while, since I opted to walk home tonight—just couldn't take another limo ride with Nikki, and the thirty minutes of posing for cameras that comes with a fifteen minute drive. Of course, I know Leena'll just go on again about how this Italian lady is a prisoner of society's expectations and how her mind is in desperate need of liberation. What would she say if she found out about Nikki's desperate need to liberate Bazoomba's clothes from her body?

Wait. What was that?

Am I being followed? I'm being followed.

A casual look around at the city's nightlife: God damn if they're not following me!

Who is it this time, or does that even matter? Hell with it, they don't know they've given themselves away. There's a little break in the wall around the corner, if memory serves. Sure enough, here it is, with plenty of shadows to conceal one pissed off CIA-trained mofo. Don't they realize who they're dealing with now? This is *K-Ill*. Or is it?

I snatch the first one and slam his ass, penitentiary-style. The second one is almost too shocked to make a move, or maybe he's stoned. They're both in suits, the second one has a laptop computer, but they're not geeks. More like X3 dudes trying to pass as businessmen. Okay, they aren't cops, cultists, or radical feminists, and it's doubtful they're with Diaz. That means they aren't packing heat, so I can probably take them out if it comes to that.

"What the fuck do you want!"

"Yo, yo, yo!" the second one says. "Chill one time, yo!"

His buddy nods as much as he can. "Peace, pot, and microdot, my brother of another color. Naw mean?"

"No. No I don't know what the fuck you mean. Start talking sense while you still can, punk."

The second one says, "Look, Mr. Ill—or, uh, can I call you K?"

"*Kay* is a girl's name."

"Okay, Mr. Ill, our bad. You saw us right away though, got's ta give you props. That's some mad eagle eye action my man." He sort of chuckles like we're old school buddies having a drink.

"What my associate is tryin' ta say is, we just want ta talk and shit. Got a business proposition, you could call it. Cool?"

My hold relaxes. "You have thirty seconds, so make it good."

"Let's just say it involves your lovely fiancé. Drop the bomb, homes." The second one nods and opens his laptop. There's some kind of porno site on the screen and I almost laugh, thinking they got sidetracked on the Internet while they followed me. "We realize mister, uh, Ill, that you know your woman inside and out, so to speak. But let's just say you ain't the only one."

In this shadowy little alley the screen is crystal clear—as clear as their game. They explain the "streaming videos" were lifted from old videos made by Nikki's failed past musical endeavors. Several of the clips show her dancing around in what's next to nothing, with tiny glued-on pompoms just barely covering her "pompoms"; the other clips feature a harder-edged look, this time with bombshells partially covering her "bombshells." Photo stills come from an old nudie calendar she did. These guys figure this would ruin us if it went live on the Internet.

"Think about the news coverage, the canceled appearances, the effect that would have on her tours and contracts, and then how that would mess with your own career, Mr. Ill. You know if we launched this site it would rake in millions of pesos the first week alone."

The thought is disturbing. Sure, you've got to be realistic about the fact that teen boys all across this country are killing Nikki every hour on the hour, night and day—hell, not just the boys, but the men and women too. As a people they buy the magazines and videos, grab their petroleum jelly and vibrators and ooh-la-la-sundries, fantasize about shooting her, then get on with their lives. She's a diversion, a steam valve. A mattress for the collective siesta. Different porn with the same face they know and love.

But this, what these fools are spouting off about, it doesn't even matter if it's real or generated by some pimply computer nerd. This will ruin everything, make Nikki a hypocrite, a fallen icon. Chingada in the flesh.

"So what, you boys want me to pose for a site or something?"

"Naw! Hell naw. We're talkin' 'bout what this shiznit be worth on the street. *Naw mean?*" They look at me intently.

The Bribing. It'll bounce back on his ass...forever.

Back at the Hive I manage to catch Queen Bee in one of her solitary moments. "Nikki, we have to talk."

"If it's about the sex scene you're supposed to do with slut-bucket—"

"Is it really necessary to refer to her as 'slut-bucket?'"

She sneers. "Yes. Absolutely."

"First of all, I'm not doing a sex scene—"

"Oh yes you are. I was talking to the DP and he said it had been added to the schedule. It'll play as a 'fantasy-sequence' your character has right before getting killed."

"Oh, sex and death again. No, look, who even cares about that, it's—"

"Well you better start caring! Rumors will start. You know how the paparazzi are about things." She stops to smile. "Look at us. We're arguing just like a real couple."

Right now Pillory Clinton and the branks would be very useful. "I'm trying to give you a heads-up on some bad shit."

"Bad shit? If you mean that was bogus weed I bought, I'll—"

"I'm talking about the kind of bad shit you don't want the public knowing about. Or Leena, I'm guessing." Finally she shuts up and I can explain the whole thing to her.

The effect this has wasn't expected—it's sort of like a cork pops, unleashing everything she's been wanting to tell people about herself. The hidden face of Nikki revealed. Oncoming confession in three, two, one: "I wasn't always this glamorous bastion of pop culture."

"You're only popular in Mexico, but whatever."

The himbo is ignored. "The way I put myself through school was being a Knockers waitress."

"Never been to a Knockers restaurant myself."

"It's a national chain. Some of the others and I, we were featured in the *Girls of Knockers* calendar one year, with my solo pic showing me topless, except for the massive door knockers they put on my 'knockers.'"

"How original. You sure know how to put the 'titty' in 'identity.'"

Did the himbo say something? "Turned out the photographer was in with some up-and-coming record label, did cover and PR shots for them. Guy fancied himself as having a nose for talent and put us girls together as The Pom Squad, an all-girl group. My name in the band was 'Kinki.' Our songs were about high school romances and partying, and the videos featured plenty of cheerleader-type dance moves and 'pom pom' action. When that album flopped they repackaged us to have an image more in line with the emerging hard-edged element in pop music. Thus, The P.O.M.B. Squad was born: Posse of Mad Bitches. And hey, no more of those stupid comments, got it?

"Anyway, this time we ran around in skimpy bulletproof vests and thong fatigues with explosions all around, singing and rapping about eliminating the competition, bumpin' and grindin', bangin' the skins, gettin' highway nasty. That album was titled *Blowin'*, of all stupid fucking things! Long story short, after dancing around wearing little more than bombshells on our chests the label pulled The P.O.M.B. Squad's life support. Four of the others went on to perform as a barely-dressed Gospel act called G.I.R.L. Squad: God's Intermediaries of Redemptive Light. One other girl and I, we followed our own paths. That involved me bouncing around as a backing vocalist on various studio projects for a few years before finally landing a solo album."

"And what about the other woman? She sour on the whole music thing?"

"Not exactly. You know the Notorious T.I.T.?"

"Sure, who doesn't?"

"There you go."

It takes a second to sink in that Nikki used to be in a group with the USA's hottest female rapper. "Wow. So what happened to the rest?"

"I don't know. One got married and had kids, another's modeling for lingerie companies. What's important is none of it is something we really want to bring up again."

"All right then. We pay them what they want."

"Are you out of your fucking mind? They'll just keep sucking our blood until they suck us dry. No, this is some bunch of loser geeks bluffing us. You know how much it costs to run a commercial website?"

"You didn't see these guys. They aren't just geeks." But I'm a himbo, a body with no brain. Why bother opening my mouth? "Okay, what about Leena at least?"

"Kenrick, I met her on the set of P.O.M.B.'s 'Freakism' video. She was doing demolitions consulting for films to make extra cash on the side. The record company actually blew up two square blocks of condemned tenements making that video, with LA's blessing of course. Still, the minorities said we were committing psychological genocide, whatever that means." Her eyes glaze over, seeing nothing but the past, and she chuckles to herself. "I watched this Army butch scouting out where the charges should be placed, telling the director how far away the cameras needed to be, and one day I walked up to her and was like, 'Hey baby light my fire.'"

"All righty then. That's more than enough info, thanks."

She grips my shoulders, eyes wide. "They don't have the other video, do they?"

"What other video?"

She looks away, suddenly concerned with checking her nails. "Oh...nothing. It's nothing."

The Shame snort slips out again. "Just when I thought you were all out of surprises."

"Look, that's about enough out of you, Mr. Gigolo."

"What's that supposed to mean?"

"I think you know, Mr. Brim*lay*. I mean, Brimley."

"Hey, I've got *my* past under wraps, sister. You just better make sure this Knockers business doesn't blow up your precious image."

She smirks and shoves today's newspaper in my face. On page three is my photo, blown up, grainy and kind of scary looking. "You have it all under control, huh? Think again, himbo."

The article is about a renegade prison guard who kept a home full of "torture implements the likes of which rival Vlad the Impaler." Right, so much for journalistic integrity. Apparently, "Kenrick the Terrible" is on the run with serial arsonist Leena Manessah, or "Mad Dog Manasseh" as the press calls her. State prison officials refuse to comment on the situation.

"Don't worry, little himbo," she says, patting my head. "It's already being taken care of."

Nikki has her minions scouring the country's newsstands, buying up copies of any papers running my story. Sad tale is this backfires on us, causing news agencies to think the buying public is wild for more dirt on Kenrick the Terrible. One night I'm out with Juanita, incognito, burning a fat stack of newspapers somewhere in a network of alleys, each one more funky smelling than the one before it. It would be easy to get lost in here without her. Or, the fashion accessory version of her.

Nikki has found the public response is even more positive when she keeps Juanita by her side. Reminds me of those rich women who carry fluffy little dogs everywhere they go. In the attempt to make

Promotional image, courtesy Last Burn Films © 2006

Juanita "fluffy" her eyebrows have been trimmed, sculpted. Lasers removed 85% of the scar tissue across her throat; our make-up wizards handle the remaining 15% before she goes out in public. Her suits were thrown out in favor of form-fitting leather dresses that build up her cleavage. Cherry-Popper Red lipstick has now been cashed in for Loose-Flapper Burgundy lipstick. Then the leather dresses disappear, replaced by styles played out in the 1920's. The straight hair has been curled. This phase of her evolution is the "personality" phase. First they "feminized" her, next they say they're going to "sexualize" her.

Hefting another load of us out of the crate and onto the fire I ask, "So... what's with the new look?"

"Whadda ya care, Mr. K-Ill, sir."

"What's that supposed to mean?"

"I dunno. I'm just all flattered and shit a big star like K-Ill's taking his time to ask me about things."

"I'm not complaining or anything. In fact, the nose ring is cool." No response. "All right. I'm sorry about the way things've gone. It's just, you know, trying to keep up this cover, it's gotten way outta hand."

She flips through the entertainment section. "Check it out...can't them fools put two and two together?"

There's a feature article on the "fabuloso" Nikki, with an insert about her mysterious interpreter, showing Juanita posed in 1920's gear on a velvet couch. Page cinco of the main section features big pictures of us supplied by the prison, and a dozen pages later there's this freakin' color photo of her.

I whistle, comparing the two pics. "Oh yeah baby, so maybe this whole makeover is a good thing after all."

Suddenly we're up against a brick wall. Fingers are gripping my hair, burrowing into my muscles. For just a second it's too much like that messed up run-in with Kirkmoor. Luckily, this is just Juanita unable to control herself. And, for whatever reason, my hands have also lost control. They're sliding all over her thighs like eels on acid, getting trapped by her garter straps. The way we're kissing could get someone's teeth knocked out. It's enough to send her weird little plumed hat into the muck on the alley floor. If anybody asks, we can truthfully report that she's been successfully "sexualized." She forcefully grinds my hands into her hind side, and I squeeze like there's no tomorrow. Of course, this causes the tendons in my forearms to feel like they're ripping through my skin and my throat makes a noise that suits the feeling.

"What," she yells, shoving away from me. "What the fuck's wrong *this* time?"

"Look, it's all me, it's not your fault. They've got me rubbing down this actress on the set like 24/7 and my arms—"

"'Rubbing down?' Like how?"

"You know, giving her a full body massage, and she keeps screwing up her lines so I'll have to—"

"And is shit naked and shit?"

"Well, yeah, but—"

"And what'chu be wearin'?"

"Um, like a little towel. Around my waist. Actually, they let her oil me up so my muscles and all look bigger on screen. But—"

She just looks at me.

"You know, rubbing some Italian sex model's ass all day long isn't what I want to be doing. It's my job."

"Ya know what? Just fuckin' forget it, I don't give a shit anymore."

Continuing with the explanations only causes her to curse up a storm and run from the alley. Damn, how the hell am I going to find my way back? Hot air whips around between the cruddy walls, trying to escape, carrying ashes and soot with it. In the fire Juanita and I are burning. Leena's eyes glare out at me, then turn black and disintegrate.

Thugs keep lurking, lesbian beatnik hippy chick Bohemians keep popping up and preaching, New Agers keep hovering a bit too close for my liking. Nobody needs to know how those weirdos hounded my family when I was young, how they nearly kidnapped me, or Shame, or Greg so many times. And our goofball mother, the less said about her the better. All our clica needs to know is we have to keep rolling out, keep it on the move.

Tonight the tour bus is taking us to Isla Mujeres. "Place was some kind of resort island or something until a telecommunications company bought it all," Nikki says, still impressed by the sound of her own voice. "They turned the whole thing into the TelSec Entertainment Complex, hosting all the major sports events and concerts and such, broadcast exclusively by TelSec, or its subsidiaries."

Me? I don't give a damn. It's Leena who gets into it with her. All the way into town they debate the "proliferation of weapons of mass distraction vis á vis the exponentially increasing corporate mergers." Leena's comment about the public's adoration of Nikki's own natural pair of "weapons of mass distraction" pretty much kills that conversation. All the while, Juanita and I steal glances at each other, our libidos bruising in the exchange. Hey, she stole a glance first.

Trying to ignore her pouty lips I tell them, "I overheard some tourists talking yesterday about some excavation project that's going on near here. A ridiculous amount of ships went down in the Caribbean and the Gulf of Mexico, like 1,600 ships, and the government is working with some firm out of Florida to find them on the ocean floor. Sounds to me like something worth checking out."

Leena replies, "That all just amounts to the unbridled greed of corrupt officials and corporations, trying to profit off the lost treasures of the slave trade and New World holocaust. As far as I'm concerned those explorers—like anyone else profiteering from slave labor—deserve to be lost to the sands of time."

Vi walks past to use the bathroom at the rear of the bus, and Nikki slaps her on the ass. Leena's too caught up in her tirade to notice. Nikki adds, "Let the past stay buried." Probably she's thinking more about her own situation when she says that.

The conversation shifts to business, like usual. On the up side Madbo—"Da Angriest Nigga in da World"—wants to make a cameo appearance next time I'm in the studio.

"If that's the up side I'm not sure I want to hear the down side, ladies."

The down side is that Hexxon plans to sue over my "oil spill" lyrics. Apparently they only provide oil from domestic reserves and own no oil tankers. The general consensus is: more free publicity. It seems good, at least until we get to the hotel. Enrique is already there, waiting for us. Somehow he always manages to stay three steps ahead.

"Ladies and gents," he says, a tarantula perched on his shoulder, "Brace yourselves. The latest media spectacle is about to hit us like a tsunami."

"Well?" Nikki hates being in the dark. "Spill the beans, short stuff!"

He ignores her. "Kenrick, a couple weeks ago some smartass reporter overheard a member of our group calling you Suicidio and did a write-up about it in their entertainment column. What's happened is it set off a wave of suicides—in some cases single, or as pacts, or in crazy stunts and crimes of escalating wackiness in the attempt to be remembered as *Rey Suicidio*, the Suicide King."

Leena and Nikki get deep on it, talking about instant penitence and unforgivable sin rolled up into one action. Me, I don't care about all that. To me it would be cool not to be the one "causing" all these people to die. They assure me it's not *me* but my *image*.

"But, aren't I responsible for my image?"

The answer ain't so simple, it turns out. Meanwhile, people are attacking police with water pistols, orchestrating demolition derbies on the highways, using electrical wires to swing around like Tarzan. The K-Illers of the world are uniting in death. As for my public image, record burnings are causing sales to skyrocket. Whatever.

If people kill themselves in my name, do the souls stick around? Do they cling to me like plastic wrap, spying on my every move?

In the days that follow K-Ill is reported to be set off in meditation. No interviews, no public appearances. This only causes the suicides to increase; a rumor goes around that K-Ill pulled off "el suicidio grande" and my fans want to join me, or top my self-extermination. Leena, the reason I'm down here to begin with, keeps as distant as she's been ever since Nikki hit the scene. Juanita has gone out of her way to avoid me. Nikki, she forces herself to spend time with me in order to keep up appearances. That, and pick on me. Miss Italy, she's left something like fifty messages since we checked in here. "Sad no ass-master," she says. "Want to play," she says. "Ooh," she says. "Kill you with knife you no call," she says.

And the photos. Mexican women in varying states of undress, some smiling but most of them trying not to look nervous, with plenty of buff men mixed in too. Couples going at it like there's no tomorrow. Couples preparing for suicide pacts. Couples beginning their suicide pacts. Loners who aren't naked, but posing all the same, sending me their promises to kill themselves. Photos of the dead sent by angry relatives. Death threats.

Every time I turn on the TV it's the K-Ill show, reality TV and drama and comedy and music video all rolled into one. Every time

I look out the window there's reporters and earth-tone-clad college chicks and K-Illers and New Agers and pale men in dark suits with sunglasses and aggressive mofoism in every single face. Every time I pick up the phone there's incoherent muttering about "hot" or "slut-bucket miss daddy" or "oh yeah, baby" or "candle wax" and what sounds suspiciously like suspicious sounds.

Not like there's time to talk with anybody. The women have been drilling me on Spanish grammar and vocabulary and all that. Trying to keep me from being such a "himbo." The frustrating part is all of Nikki's jokes about oral exams. If I ever find out who told her about my old job I'll...I'll...well, it won't be good. And I'm not their only target. The think tank keeps lobbing shells: the current big idea is to have a bleached-blonde Juanita dancing around as one of the backing performers on stage, wearing next to nothing. Whatever, man. Who could keep up with caring about every crappy idea to come down the pike? Like this committee thing. They want to judge my rapping, my dance moves, the whole performance. Juanita and Leena and Nikki sit and observe while I posture and spit game. Who will win on this edition of *Outlaw Idol?*

"The rhymes is good, ya got the groove. But I just can't feel it, naw mean?"

"Technically very good—but work on the personality, it's a little unpolished. Overall I really liked it though."

"The long list is enunciation, projection, breath control, charisma, and sex-sex-sex. The short list: you need a lot of work."

If K-Ill had a pay site loaded with his own naughty pics and vids, would he have to go through all this nonsense? At least I don't have a dozen corporate execs breathing down my neck, rewriting every word. Still, Nikki has Juanita get up and show me the ropes.

"I know how to dance!"

"No, no you don't. Not like this. Not the *right* way. What you do only qualifies as dancing at karaoke bars and strip clubs." Nikki, the smug wankster. Did she dig up my male dancer background too?

Juanita gets up and starts to shake her thing like the drums of death are beating and she's the only one in earshot.

"Uh...you want me to do *that?*" Yes, they do. My best imitation isn't good enough, no. Nikki insists Juanita give hands-on instruction. What's up with this? We do as asked, players in the world that is Nikki's stage. This whole time Juanita and I avoid eye contact. Do this and this, she tells me, her back to my front, reaching around, her hands on my hips. It's not clear if this is a dance as much as it's some kind of weird simulated sex—well, that's what most dancing is, isn't it? She never got to take advantage of my "full services" on the eve of her execution, and maybe this is the closest we'll ever get. A look at Leena doesn't reveal much, except that she's trying not to reveal much. I'm on the run with my girlfriend and her girlfriend, doing fake sex with the person who wants to be my girlfriend at their command. Part of me hopes the FBI will come busting through the door. Another part of me forces my attention back to the task at hand.

Fashion update: her hair is platinum blonde now, partially covered by a knit bandana you could probably strangle a person with—worn not prison style but feminine style; her bottom lip is pierced to compliment the nose piercing, and her lips are a glossy bruised purple. It's kind of horrible looking.

The dance moves still aren't good enough. Nikki claps her hands and tells us to let the music take over, even though there is none playing for us. But you can't argue with the boss. We gyrate more and more ferociously. Is any of this worth it? One look at the boss lady and I can tell. She knows just what's going on. She knows we're having some kind of awkwardness and wants to find out if it's of a biblical nature. What a punk.

Juanita, Nikki's tongue, starts to slink and slide over me, her hips a little too energetic, her look a little too removed. Our diva brings the session to a halt, abruptly thanking us and saying we have to get ready for something or other. Juanita's sent off to arrange something with someone, still never making eye contact with me, and Leena skips out without saying anything at all.

On the table is a stack of today's papers. Tests revealed blood in my home, confirmed to be that of a missing coworker. The investigation has turned up my little dispute with Ritchie, leading objective reporters to ask: *How many others have fallen prey to Kenrick the Terrible?*

"All right, Kinki, or Nikki, or whatever you're called. You think you're real cute calling all the shots, don't you. Well you and me are gonna have us a little talk."

She jerks to her feet with breasts stabbing at me through her skintight top like daggers from her heart. "And whatever is the problem, dearest?" When she pokes me in the chest she hits the necklace under my shirt. "And hey, what the heck is that thing? I've never seen any-one wear their pager like jewelry."

"It's a man down trigger, not that it's any of your business."

"Man down? Some kind of remote control for oral sex from your old job?"

One, two, and breathe. "Don't try to change the subject. What I wanted to say is this isn't working, not for any of us. We're free, we're rich, but we have no say in how we live. You ever hear about a prison with golden bras?"

She laughs. "Riiiight. A prison with golden bras."

"That's not what I said, and you know it."

"That would be so much more convincing if you could stop staring at my chest when you talk to me."

"Golden *bars!* We're in a prison with—"

"I get it, I get it." She smirks. "The only one who *won't* be getting any is you."

The rack she has, it's not lethal, but just the same it's a safe bet many men have spent time moaning and groaning on it. Me, I'm ready to scream. The latest statistics indicate that in the time it's taken us to bicker another kid has killed themselves in my name.

We're having an intervention. Just me and Leena and Nikki, plus some of Nikki's scrubs—but they never counted as real people before, so why start now? Juanita, she's pretty much been banished after our sexy little performance. If our diva has her way we'll probably never be seen in the same place ever again. Can't have rumors, you know. Anyway, some of Juanita's family is in town so she's running interference to keep them away from any ungrateful desert vagrants who might be lurking around.

"I mean, *Jesus* Ken."

The heat is doing me in, anybody can take one look and see that. In fact my sallow skin and weight loss are starting up the Mexican rumor mill. Is K-Ill strung out on brown tar, aka Mexican heroin? Cortical region and maladaption, please allow me to introduce you to Cortez and Malinche...

"You've got to get cleaned up. Drop the heroin or I'm leaving you!" This, from Nikki.

We're backstage at the TelSec Center, the big night. I'm lounging on a huge cushy something or other, shades on, staring at the ceiling. "Now, would this be a fake breakup or a real one?"

"I'm serious!" Nikki stomps her foot and the peons flee to safer areas of the building. "I won't let you screw up my image. This is my public appearance we're talking about!"

"Appearances aren't always what they seem. You ought to know that better than anybody."

Leena chimes in with, "You could at least spend some time getting a tan, Kenny. Just look at you."

"What, you too now? I'll roast alive out there. Tell you what. How about imaginary rehab for my imaginary addiction, to save my imaginary relationship. We can top it all off with an imaginary wedding."

Leena's sarcastic laughter is no surprise, but what the hell is Nikki thinking? She looks to be happier than the horse's shit. All of a sudden she's thrown herself next to me on this cushy thing, arm wrapped around my shoulders. The enormous jiggle at her chest reminds me of the breaststroke, if you know what I mean.

"Think about the copious press coverage our relationship has received. If my stock soared by being engaged to a himbo, just consider what a marriage would do. Move over Trista and Ryan! It's time for the K and N connection." The *what?* "Or maybe Nik-Ill is better."

"Um, a nickel might be all that idea's worth."

"Hey, I'm serious!"

Leena noticeably tenses. "Nikki, I'm warning you..."

"Oh what? It's just a little fake fling is all. We're talking about my career here."

"And where does it stop?" Leena stalks over to us, leans down with her hands crushing the cushion to either side of Nikki's head. "Is the 'honeymoon video' going to 'somehow' make its way to the Internet? You going to have his children? How far are you willing to sink for some shitty publicity!"

"Well, wouldn't have to have kids right away I guess..." It's not enough for me to play sister, no, now the tank boss wants to shoot me for real. Nikki gulps, bats her eyes. "Leena, honey—"

Leena grabs Nikki's throat. Something is smoldering in her eyes that she hasn't shown me before, making me gulp too. "Listen, bitch. This crap can only go so far. Bad enough you turned this whole thing into a public circus when I'm trying to conduct a mission. Now fucking drop the routine. Your beloved rapper is gonna get gunned down back up north or something, move to Japan, who cares—and you will go on with your precious career down here, solo. Got it?"

Nikki stutters the beginnings of several different responses before settling on, "We could, um, get you a public hubby or something. Would you like that, baby?"

A look of disgust on her face, Leena brushes Nikki aside like yesterday's rubbish. "You don't have any idea what I *like*." She embraces me in a passionate kiss and, despite everything, there's no way to keep from pouring everything I have into it. Only after we separate do I realize we were moaning like teenagers messing around in the back seat of a car. Leena straightens up, smoothes out her suit, turns to the gaping pop star. "You have a decision to make, and when I get back you better have made the right one." She storms out and the temperature drops to a tolerable level.

Nikki looks at me, horrified, her lower lip beginning to tremble. Oncoming maladaption in three, two, one: "You...you and her...when you said you two had a special relationship, I never thought...*motherfucker!*" She throws herself at me, all snarls and curses and ripping claws. Hasn't she heard any of my lyrics? What's she doing messing with the K-Ill?!

We roll to the floor, a tangle of limbs and dislike, my shades crushed under us as we rock back and forth. Not like I'm looking, but she's spilled over the top of her dress. If it weren't for my sore joints and muscle pain this would be no contest, but even so it only takes a second to pin her wrists down. That's not the end of it though. Her knees ram into my sides, globs of her spit are launched onto my face.

Then, the MO hits her: *malicious orgasm*. That's not something either of us wanted, but at least she finally calms down.

"All right then," I say. "You going to be good if I let you up?"

"Fuck you."

"Right." As we sit up she delivers my umpteenth slap. After failing to find a handkerchief my face has to be wiped on some cushions to remove her spit.

Standing over me, adjusting the straps of her gown, Nikki says, "Don't go anywhere, asshole. After the show tonight, you and me have *a lot* to talk about."

She makes a dramatic exit before I can even fire off a sarcastic remark about three of her nails being broken. Hey, that's a first: fake concern for my fake fiancé's fake nails. We've been here *way* too long.

"Aye carumba! Check this out, man." The fish's head is cut down the middle like in some biology textbook. It's not the smell that worries me, or that this is the hotel kitchen. It's the fact that there's some freak-ass thing where the fish's tongue should be. Enrique talks excitedly with the chef. "Here's the deal, Suicidio. He says more and more of 'em are being shipped in like this lately."

"Dude man, what the fuck is that?"

"Parasite. Gets in the fish's mouth and eats out the whole freakin' tongue, right? Then it anchors itself into the muscles and *replaces* the tongue. The fish can actually use it to grab food, to swallow, all that."

There's a big pile of fish that needs to be gutted and cleaned, and the chef doesn't look bothered in the least.

"Dude, this rap star is vegetarian only from now on, got it jack?"

Enrique's getting a little too into it though. "Lookit, man, check out those little eyes. Damn thing's cute as a button." When he bumped into me in the lobby and tried to talk me into dinner, this isn't what I thought he had in mind. The plan was to slip out through the kitchen's exit and find Leena. "Word, I told you crustaceans were versatile."

"That thing's a crustacean? You mean, like a scorpion?"

"Or a lobster or a crab or whatever. Yeah."

"Okay, that's it for any hope of dinner." I leave him behind to study parasites all on his lonesome.

So the fake rapper goes out on the streets in a country that's been conned into thinking it's his home, worried about his bogus relationship, doing his best not to look like he's trying to score drugs for his nonexistent habit, hair dyed red with green contacts in his eyes, and a whole bottle of MonkeyTan on his skin. The newsstand has rows of headlines about Mexican stars, European royalty, international wars, and the latest dirt from up north. *Man Disfigured By Lye* is one. More importantly, there's an update about Kenrick the Terrible. Now he's the "Sexecutioner." Yep, that's right. They found a bunch of "voyeur cams" set up in my apartment—the ones I put there to watch S.I.S.T.E.R.'s private snuff fest. But that lead them to investigate my old locker and the cells I "worked" in—even the execution chamber and the planning rooms—and I'll be damned if they didn't find a hell of a lot more web cams waiting for them.

Somebody else was getting themselves their own private snuff show, that and more.

Investigations quickly turned up an adult website called The Sexecutioner. Over three thousand members worldwide logged in on a regular basis to download pictures and videos of yours truly "sadistically abusing death row captives" and even to see clips of the women dying. The site has been shut down and authorities are searching for the culprits. Prison officials still have no comment.

What kind of sick, fucked up bullshit lies are these?! They think they can smoke me out with this bunch of nonsense? No, they can just plain smoke me. One, two, and breathe...K-Ill will be the picture of calmness. He will not draw any attention to himself. He will go find Leena, then get the hell out.

Enrique catches up to me. "Hey man, that's some bad stuff. We better get you out of the public eye for a while. My pad isn't too far— want to crash there?"

"Sounds good to me."

His place turns out to be in walking distance. The whole way there I rant about how none of these reports are true, aside from me owning a collection of antiques, and he listens patiently. People on the street turn and watch, wondering if I'm really me, checking out Enrique's crazy black cowboy boots with the silver chains, his crazy silver belt buckle. The apartment is your typical bachelor den: a busted up table, two chairs, a computer, and a mattress on the floor. That's all in the front room. His other rooms, they're divided up by what type of insect they hold.

"No guest rooms?"

"Not unless you like yourself some mild refrigeration."

I consider the argument with Leena and Nikki. "Might do me some good. This climate is totally killing me."

He looks me up and down. "That's not the only thing doing you in. Sooner we get you out of the circus the better. Now come on, if you're going to stay here you've got to help with dinner."

My appetite still hasn't recovered from those freaky tongue parasite things, but the dinner isn't for me. It's for the hundreds of guests in Enrique's terrariums. *Pandinus imperitor* and *Microtityus waeringi* and *Hemiscorpious lepturus*, as if any of that means a damn thing to me. *Hadogenes troglodytes* and *Heterometrus*, they're like eight inches long and I don't want anything to do with them.

"Don't be a sissy, Kenrick. Scorpions used to be three feet long, bigger maybe. These modern-day scorps aren't anything."

"I'll keep that in mind when they're stinging me to death."

"Shut up and hand me the worms."

"What makes insects better than worms, anyway?"

"Arachnids aren't insects. They only have two major body sections. And anyway, they've got longevity. Some tarantulas live twenty, thirty years. The females anyway. Males only live about a year."

"Sucks to be a guy spider I guess."

"You're catching on."

"You know, in prison a *stinger* is a metal plate hooked up to live wires."

He sort of looks at me, then laughs. "The student becomes the teacher."

"What am I here, the bug man's Tonto or something?"

"Yo," he laughs. "Don't say that around here. *Tonto* is like 'idiot' *en Español*." His pager goes off and his mood darkens. "Sorry bro, I got to split."

"It's cool. Need some time to think things over anyway."

"You do that. And, do you mind...?" He gestures to the bugs.

"It's no problem. You go ahead. Nothing serious, I hope?"

Instead of answering he grabs his stuff, tells me the human food is in the refrigerator, and practically runs out the door. Whatever that's about.

There's only so much a man can take of playing with worms, and my host probably wouldn't mind if his computer got a little workout, so I hit the Internet. And, it only takes a little while before the Sexecutioner comes to mind, then comes to the screen. There's all kinds of sites out there now, perpetrating on my good name. Stuff that's obviously a bunch of cheese ball porno companies trying to cash in on this guy's misery. Then there's something else that pops up. A Russian web site featuring a picture that makes me choke on my drink. I click through to the main site, to their "free tour" section just to see if...

That's Kirkmoor, all right, her angry eyes staring, her face all contused. That strong jaw of hers, it's as rigid as ever. She's nude on a bed in a dim room. When the hell did she do this? Guess I'm not the only one with a questionable background.

A man enters the frame. He's pretty much average in size, but with all that leather bondage stuff on you can't see any skin. He sets his drink down on a little night stand and stays motionless for a bit. She refuses to acknowledge him, choosing instead to keep her eyes fixed on whatever it is she's looking at. What's going on here? With those bruises, and the way she's acting, this isn't...I mean...

All of a sudden the guy whips out his pecker and flings himself on top of her. Before you know it he's jackhammering away, pounding like there's no tomorrow, pounding like the pulse beating against my eardrums, the heart hammering my breastbone. Then he wraps his crinkly black fingers around her throat, fucking her so wildly that the frame of the bed lifts off the floor. Why doesn't she fight back?! Is she doped up?! Either way, it's clear why she had a chip on her shoulder. Now his fist rises, descends, meets her cheek, feels like it's punching through my stomach.

Kirkmoor's head moves to the side—other than that, she has no reaction. Those eyes continue to stare. The bed continues to rock. The leather maniac continues to punch her, choke her. Still no reaction.

And the little night stand, it's shaking too. The guy's drink sloshes around. It's tea. Tea in a mason jar.

And now it's clear what this is, who really put Kirkmoor in this position. Bart, he can keep choking her from here to kingdom come but she won't ever feel a thing.

He grabs her ankles and forces them up over his shoulders until the toes are brushing the walls—the sound from her hips is like somebody's fingers being caught in a meat grinder. Or, in this case, a corpse grinder. He howls and begins to fuck like a baboon on PCP, fangs bared through his zipper-mouth, howling like the ghost of a vivisected lab animal. If you're paying attention you notice her toes breaking on the headboard, the wall, one by one becoming postmodern architecture in the flesh. Her tits continue to jiggle.

No wonder he was so enthusiastic about the Internet during our chat in the graveyard.

The video cuts off; if you want to see more you have to pay. The words BROUGHT TO YOU BY THE SEXECUTIONER pop up on the screen in dripping-blood letters. A close-up of my smiling face drops down and bounces across the words, hitting every syllable. Then my face rolls down and lands between Chauntelle's dark breasts. Her angry, tear-filled eyes are familiar—that's when she was telling me about her dead son. My head rolls along, spinning toward Blossom as she posed for that nudie snapshot she wanted me to take. The backwoods blonde does her best to strike a "glamour pose" and her smile is heartbreaking. My head rolls into her crotch and she falls away like a bowling pin. The word SCORE pops up, and a robotic voice proclaims *"All your bitch are now mine."*

The next thing I know Enrique's computer is gone, just fucking gone. So is his window. Yep, it's down there on the sidewalk. Nobody's around, thankfully. The last thing we need is a bunch of people hit by falling glass, on top of everything else.

The cellphone starts to whine, demanding my attention. It's Nikki. "We have to talk," she says.

"Look, if it's about the latest video—"

"What video?"

"Never mind."

"Look, we don't have time for this. I'm supposed to be on stage in a little over an hour. You know where there's that palm tree that looks like a giant dick? Right behind it is a Todo Bell. Meet me across the street from the Todo Bell."

"They have those here?"

"Todo's everywhere, *darling*."

When she says that word it's like the drums of death are beating for my skin only. "Look, why can't we talk about this over the—"

"Just be there in ten minutes, got it?"

Normally, this is the part where I make a smart-ass remark and she slaps me. Instead the line goes dead, and it's a little too much like those talks with Shame. What the hell is all this about? Kirkmoor's tits are still jiggling in my mind, like Juanita's hips, like the napalm gel Leena had me create for our escape, like the worms being torn apart by Enrique's scorpions. Instead of dealing with all that it's time to manage another of Nikki's blowups.

Man on the Street Opinions

BRANDELL, 35, WASHINGTON, DC: Kenrick the Terrible? Sure, I heard about that. Messed up scene, man. No wonder the President is out of whack—if that's how things are run in his home state then I don't know. Tell you the truth it doesn't just make them look bad, it makes the whole country look bad. Especially if it's true what they're saying on the news, about how other countries run their prisons compared to our prisons. And don't even make me start on how we have over two million folks locked up.

LULU, 19, ANCHORAGE: If you ask me it's about time all these liberals got a wake up call. They wanna act shocked? Sad? Outraged? Hell-o people. This is what happens when you relax all the standards and let anything go. Total lack of discipline at every level of society. Everyone knows you can't just have words on paper, you need to back rules up with action. Equal opportunity employment my foot. There's no way a suspected serial killer should have ever been allowed anywhere near a correctional facility, unless he was being locked up there. Never proved anything? It was years ago? Like those arguements even matter. The fact is the state fell for his fake I.D. and never bothered with a real background check. As for the death row felons he "abused," well, big deal. I say you get what you ask for. Don't go around killing people if you can't handle the consequences.

SIMIAN, 28, CORPUS CHRISTI: As if it's not tough enough for playas to break 'em off some. Now we got mad wenches fired up 'bout this here fool? Come on now, that ain't correct. Brothas don't wanna be hittin' it like that. Feel me? Leave that noise in the house o' freaks. This fool obviously got no respect for the female species. Gots ta treat a queen like a queen, naw mean? Might be a nice scam if you wanna get like that like that, but peeps need ta recognize. 580, we's best catch out 'fore we's catch a case, and don't come wit the package neither cuzz!

DANIELLA, 44, FT. WORTH: Personally, I don't know how he got away with it for so long. That's kinda impressive in its own right. But with his looks, you know, why should he have to resort to that kinda thing? Ain't right. There's plenty of God-fearing, law-abiding women out here in society that would kill for a night with that kind of...I mean...have you seen those videos? The things he can do? Shoot. He doesn't have to be on the run. I'm sure there's plenty of women, middle-aged women, maybe even here in the Ft. Worth area, who have a spare room and would appreciate the...company. Know what I mean? Some of these middle-aged women might even have a nice savings account, maybe a waterbed and alligator clamps and Freon 12 and—

Even down here Todo Bell's menu is en Inglés. From a distance you can make out the huge ad for their brand new Huevos Cracker Sweet Omlette. A cardboard cutout of Humperdunk glares out at potential customers, with a word-bubble containing "Get chipot-layed...tongiht! Yeah!" If memory serves, he legally changed his name from "Stephen Humperdink" after becoming successful in the NBA. Now he spends a lot of time starring in movies.

Not that any of that matters now, not with everything gone haywire. I adjust my glasses and try to be cool, try to ignore all the hives breaking out on my arms. It's been fifteen minutes and still no superstar tantrums, no paparazzi.

Somebody whistles from down the street and I turn just in time to see a smiling face. A smiling, unwelcome face. There's about a city block between us so I keep turning, looking all around as if I didn't see her, then start walking in the opposite direction. This inspires a second whistle, in turn spurring me on to a quicker pace. Still no sign of Nikki, unless...

"Big daddy!" a voice calls. "Hallo! Hallo! Is me!"

The Italian accent goes in one ear and out the other. Not quite at the level of a jog I power walk down the sidewalk. Heads turn, and continue to turn when my pursuer calls out.

Isn't that the famous gangster rapper? they're all wondering.

Isn't the woman catching up to him that super model with the perfect body?

"Is me! she calls. "Nikki, she give us together! Stop! Is okay!"

Nikki what? Holy crap, is this her solution to Leena's ultimatum—to foist me off on some bimbo? "No autographs," I call over my shoulder.

"Is okay! Me love you! Long time!" The clicking of her heels draws closer. "Stop, stop! Nikki, she is giving us together!"

"No autographs! No autographs!"

"Stop and make me rubdown! I command!"

We're trotting, then sprinting, through crowds of confused people. Every time we come to an intersection I turn down the path of least resistance. The fewer people the better. And damn, who would ever figure her condition was good enough to keep up with me? Or maybe it's not her; burnout isn't any joke. How long have I been out in the open now, out in public?

Too long, it looks like. I only say that because of the gun muzzle that comes out of nowhere, pressed against my neck, the four burly types surrounding me, the car with tinted windows speeding up to the curb. It's those X3 wannabes and their friends, only they don't have a laptop with them this time.

The man in the back seat, he's all smiles. The ring on his finger bears a fist gripping a lightning bolt, and the bullets in his gun all have my name on them.

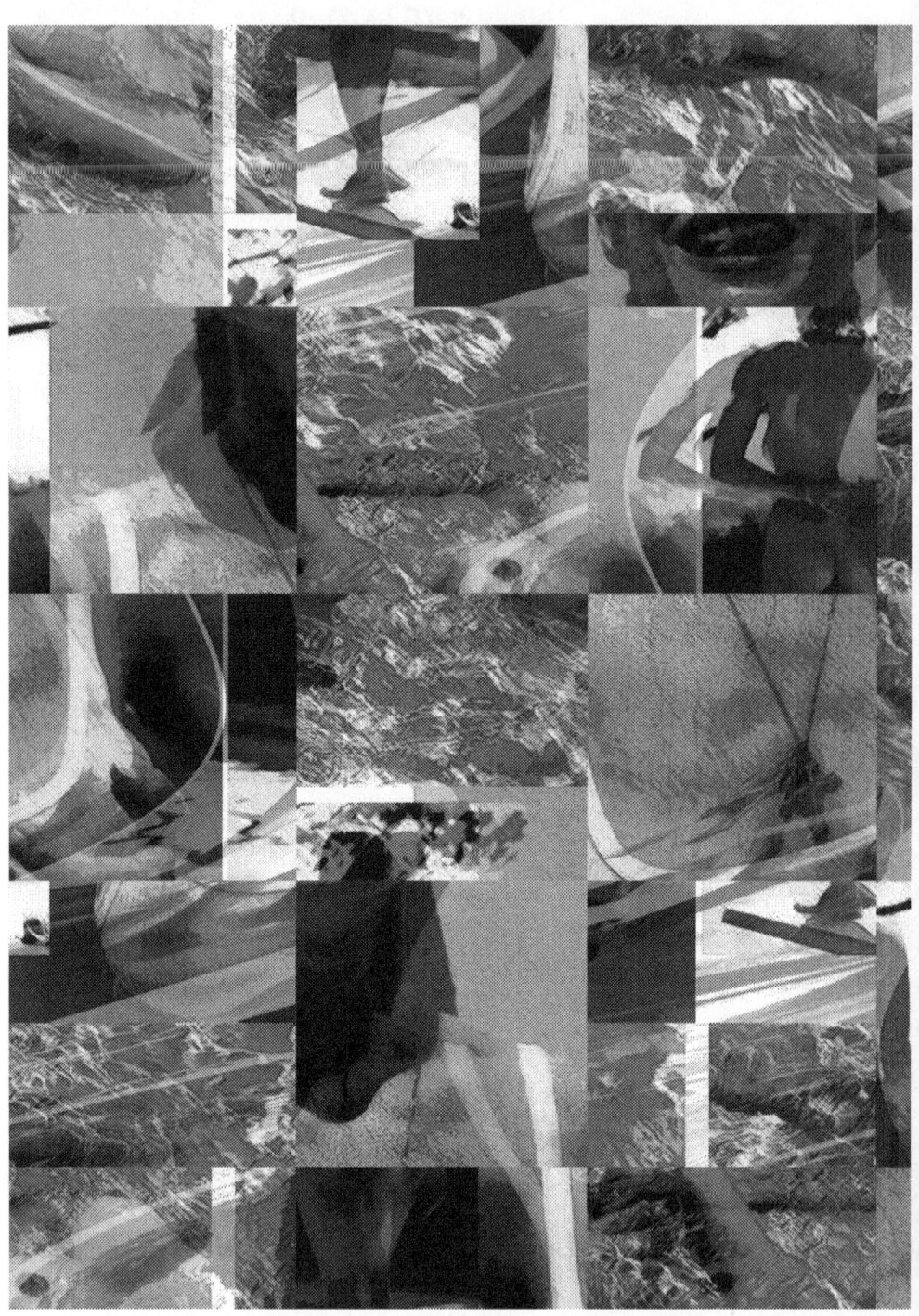

Promotional image, courtesy Last Burn Films © 2006

PART FOUR:

FLIPPING THE SCRIPT

"If Prometheus was worthy of the wrath of heaven for kindling the first fire upon Earth, how ought all the Gods to honor the men who make it their professional business to put it out?"
—John Godfrey Saxe, circa 1850

"When the well is dry, we know the worth of water."
—Benjamin Franklin, *Poor Richard's Almanac*

Promotional image, courtesy Last Burn Films © 2006

H UGE SMOKESTACKS PUMP OUT a sea of smoke that hangs in the sky from horizon to horizon, a curtain blocking out the stars. This factory we're in, it's abandoned but the neighboring ones haven't stopped running, not for something as minor as a riot. Outside there's shouting everywhere. What looks like an elite security force in full riot gear forms several solid lines, blocking the progress of protesters. The private police force is shouting something about scrapas. From here it seems they're calling the protesters *scrapas*, whatever that means. The protesters, they're just nutting up. Already some of them are throwing trash or even stones, but they're not brave enough to get anywhere near the security force yet.

Nice of my kidnappers to have so many monitors set up in here. Gives us a chance to watch the hostage standoff play out. There I am on TV, a freeze-frame of K-Ill striking gangster poses in a commercial for FizzyPiss. Seems like some weezo tipped off the media that K-Ill had been kidnapped by a rival gang or some such. Funnily enough, the protest was already in full swing when we got here. Some sort of labor dispute or other political thing. After the news, though, now the number of protesters has doubled, tripled. They might just be an army of K-Illers, each trying to prove who's the K-Illin'est. The K-Ill reality show has officially debuted, at the top of the charts no less.

When the cameras zoom in you can see several kids who may or may not be about to sacrifice themselves for me. When the camera pans to the right you can see the insignia on the security uniforms more clearly. It's a fist grabbing a lightning bolt. When the camera pulls out you can see a new commotion in progress. Never one to miss a publicity op, a limo pulls up and delivers Nikki into a spotlight even bigger than center stage at a concert. Hey, isn't she supposed to be *doing* a concert? Immediately she starts bossing people around, demanding to speak to the perpetrators. The crowd cheers, the security force is confused, record sales go up 5%.

There's all this to watch, and Leena. She's lurking in the shadows behind a forklift and some crates. I don't look right at her, no, just sort of keep track of her in the corner of my eye. None of these other fools has picked up on her being here, not yet.

They're too busy making sure everything in the factory is secure. Who'd of thunk if you kidnap a celebrity people might be watching? Diaz orders his men to run here or go there, but mostly he's worried about all the gold bars. That, and a bunch of junk piled in the corner. When we first pulled up it looked like some kind of abandoned factory from outside, but it's clean as a whistle inside. Diaz/Date Rapers logos are all over everything. Damn fool must've bought this place to run his criminal operations out of. It's right on the water, so he can probably smuggle like nobody's business. Just look at all the boats and diving gear. He isn't taking any chances, whatever he's using this old factory for. Damn thing's equipped with the exact same lockdown tech we had at the prison: motion detectors and sniffers and what looks like dispensers for nerve gas, automated doors that can trap people in each room on a second's notice. Anybody tries to storm the place they're in for a "kiss"—that's how we in the trade refer to KSS, or KillVector Security Systems.

Men with machine guns mill around, glaring at me. So far they've only dealt out a few punches here and there, just to make a point. "Uh, look," I start. "There's got to be a way we can work this out. Work-o out-o?"

Diaz slaps me. "I speak *Ingles* just fine, asshole!"

"You do?"

"Of course. How could I own a basketball franchise and not be fluent in the language?"

The room in his house full of Daytona Date-Raper merchandise. The scuba equipment all around here and rotting wood and barnacles. The stack of gold bars in the corner. The Florida corporation contracting with the Mexican government to recover all the lost ships from the slave trade! Son of a...

But me, I'm a prop, an afterthought. Nobody has time for a washed up never-was when there's thousands of people ready to throw down outside your door. Worse, the police are starting to trickle in, keeping a safer distance than even the reporters. Last time I saw a riot situation this bad was when the Boston Booty Bandits beat the San Diego Wetbacks on a technicality. One dude is obsessed with something called the Charada China. Another guy is waving around feathers and blowing cigar smoke like mad. What a freak show this all turned out to be. The others, they're checking their guns, their knives and walkie-talkies and explosives.

On TV Nikki is working the crowd, coordinating cheers and shouts, spitting plenty of game and giving the guards hell. The screaming, fist-waving masses look like some third world militia about to invade the industrialized nations. A few of Diaz's thugs finally go out to speak with her. Damn it—would it kill them to run English subtitles? At first it looks like a successful celebrity negotiation, but before Nikki can finish announcing her demands one of them slaps her. Another grabs her arm and yanks her inside, while others grab the camera crew. That's when all apeshit breaks loose. Mad scrapas and K-Illers surge toward the line of guards. The security force replies by cutting loose with tear gas. Batons crack skulls. Rocks bounce harmlessly off Plexiglas shields. Gloved fists and steel-toed boots have their way with protester teeth. The security people at the edges of the lines slowly get overwhelmed and taken down, like black-armored alien invaders being torn apart by rabid native animals.

Cars are burning, the windows of surrounding buildings are getting smashed, bottles and rocks fly through the air in every direction. The chaos spreads to reporters who are stupid enough to be on the streets. Scrawny kids and adults rampage into the wall of news vans, some getting smashed in the head by heavy cameras. One newswoman gets stole right in the face while five dudes split her audio man's wig. Another reporter is crushed when his van gets flipped over on top of him. The news helicopters swarm like vultures on PCP, diving and circling madly, all jockeying for position. One collides with a police helicopter and the fiery heaps crash down onto the rioters. A tail blade spins maybe a hundred yards through the air and slices through five armored guards. All the way at the far edge of the mayhem the police have emptied their guns into the crowd. Out of ammo, out of luck, they are overrun and stomped into wine.

And those X3 dudes that sold me to Diaz? They were some of the first ones to get slammed in the middle of it all. The security force wouldn't let them through after they got paid and left the factory. That's one less dumb-ass web site we have to worry about.

Diaz applauds, says something to his buddies. Seeing my expression, he says, "We celebrate because now we can slip out with you, the goods, and not even leave any fingerprints. You know what I mean? Fingerprints?"

While they're breaking out the champagne I'm like, "Huh?"

"Oh come now, Mr. Brimley. *Fingerprints of the Gods.* You of all people should know what I mean." When I insist that I have no idea he laughs harder. "I was hoping this wouldn't be a pleasant talk, after the way you dishonored mi familia. Keep on playing dumb, it'll give me the chance to work you over."

"Listen, why'd you save me to begin with if—"

"You ought to know the law of the street by now." The law is: *what goes around comes around.* "The life of my niece for your life. But then it came to my attention some very interesting people are looking for you."

"Right, right, everybody knows the cops—"

"I'm not talking about them." His meaningful look turns my blood cold. He knows this and smiles. "You are not the only one they look for. Now how about this woman of yours, this Leena. Please, don't give me a straight answer; I want to enjoy getting it out of you."

They toast each other, even stopping to give me a glass. "Jesus," I say after sipping. "Is this champagne or champiss?" Before they know what's hit them my glass is thrown into the closest guard's face. Feet, do your stuff!

Couldn't help cheering for myself there, but what was I thinking? It only takes them a second to slam me. It takes all of one more second for them to pull out a nasty-looking set of alligator clips.

And I watch as, from the shadows, Leena pulls the trigger...shooting me in the chest.

Some of us guards had a rabbit's foot or lucky boxers we wore to work every day, whatever it was you never changed your routine. I've always had my man-down trigger. So far it's worked, so why should now be any different. Alarms shriek, lights flash, and nobody else seems to know why. My lucky charm was hanging down under my shirt and took the bullet for me. Otherwise it would have been a perfect heart shot. The result is it triggered a massive security meltdown, commencing in eighteen, seventeen, sixteen…

Leena is pinned down in what really isn't the best position because of a few thugs she didn't see coming up a staircase when she opened fire. Diaz, he took one in the shoulder and isn't looking too good. Me? If I could get over the shock of what just happened maybe I'd cause a distraction to help Leena out, but if she's going to turn all skeevy on me she can sweat it for a while. First she ditches me outside the prison, now she shoots me. How long does it take for a guy to get the hint? Anyway, laying here like this I can't take my eyes off the sky-light. Something that looks suspiciously like a UFO is hovering over the building, watching over everything. Must be a helicopter, a trick of the lights…

Leena stops firing and Diaz orders his men to take a break. Maybe they finished her off? A few of them cautiously inch forward. At least the pain has finally stopped—it's so much easier to breathe when it doesn't feel like you've got a bullet stuck between your heart and your lungs.

We're entering the final stages of the KSS sequence. Doors slam shut on arms and legs, the system switches over to red lights, gas starts to pump out like stage smoke. In all the chaos it's easy as hell to sneak around to Leena, who almost jumps out of her skin when she sees me. There's a tense second when it's not clear if she wants to shoot me again or jump my bones. In the end we end up hightailing it to the door that looks most secure. My trigger allows us to pass through, but not without Diaz spotting us.

"*Chingada madre way!*" he shouts, looking like he might have a heart attack.

His men jump up from behind their cover only to catch some bullets with their faces. Just before the door slams shut Nikki slides through with the cameraman and sound guy. The reporter who was with them doesn't make it, and through the little window in the door we watch him get gassed with the rest.

We're in the control room. There's a slew of bullet holes and some blood, but no bodies. The news people, they speak hyper-Español and check their equipment. Everything seems to be running. There's this weird tension between Leena and Nikki, who mad dog it while I slump to the floor.

"Got a problem?" Nikki sneers.

Leena's jaw flexes, she makes a noise with her gun, then she steps up to her girlfriend's face. "What do you think you're doing?"

"Hey, it's a free country—"

"I gave you a direct command and you disobeyed it."

Angry men are on the other side of the door, cursing in their language, choking on gas. We ignore them.

"I'm not one of your army flunkies, commander butch."

Leena grabs a handful of hair, whispers something in Nikki's ear. The cameraman gets excited and swings the camera toward her. She drops Nikki and bats the camera away, presses the barrel of her gun into the dude's throat. After whispering something to him she moves on, starts barricading the control room.

The camera guy, there's a big indentation in his throat from the gun's barrel. Nikki, she recovers her wits and starts talking to the newspeople, pointing to me and indicating camera angles and framing. Me, I'm feeling my chest trying to figure out which bones are broken.

The monitors that didn't get shot up show all the craziness is still in full swing. Police helicopters are dropping nets on people, guards and rioters fight tooth and nail. The few remaining journalists go wild. It doesn't take too much imagination to see the headlines now: *Sexecutioner Goes Down*.

And the feed from in here, it's the award-winning moment. Nikki, the biggest music sensation, kneeling at the side of my "corpse," wailing, while flames leap in the background like her sup-porting dancers. The beat is maintained by shotgun blasts, there's a chorus of sirens, and the struggling masses harmonize with Nikki's cries. The truly hilarious thing is that on TelSec her concert is going on strong as ever—the music is pumping, dancers are gyrating, and Juanita is singing/jiggling, holding the microphone to her mouth in a manner you can only think of as "suggestive." From one skimpy outfit to the next her tattoos are fully visible and nobody seems to notice, or care, that it's not exactly Nikki performing.

The K-Ill in me is thinking: no rapper ever caused a riot this bad. Taliban, eat your hearts out! The Kenrick Brimley in me is thinking: my girlfriend performed the ultimate betrayal.

All of a sudden everything is quiet in the streets. There's huge monitors set up way at the edge of things and everybody's watching them, the rioters and security force and police alike. They're watching the K-Ill show, watching Diaz's men dropping in the gas-haze through our observation window, watching the remaining men gather in rooms adjacent to ours.

The authorities have cordoned off the area directly around the fac-tory. Emergency workers are pouring in, trying to help the injured. About two blocks away you can see the barricade holding back a gath-ering crowd, hear their rage. The networks, they've got all their top people on the ground, interviewing police spokesmen and rioters and their fellow journalists who survived round one. A Todo-Tron has been set up over to the side, its screen the size of a building, carrying the live feed from inside. There she is, the pop diva cradling her man as he watches his Todo-Tronned self on a monitor. His hand slides off cam-era, groping for the microphone. He's alive! Is he going to speak? Everything goes so quiet you could hear a hair-trigger drop.

You find yourself in front of a mob hovering at the edge of chaos.

They wait for you, the tourist, the transient, and knowing you need to buy time you gasp, "*Me cago en las tetas de la Virgen María para que el Niño Jesús chupe mierda.*" The hobos' words, the ones Enrique warned you about.

You just told them you took a dump on the Virgin Mary's tits so that baby Jesus would have to suck shit.

So much for calm and quiet, peace and recovery. The riot starts up again twice as strong, with mad jawas surging forward to storm the factory and knock the offending words from K-Ill's mouth. They rampage over and through the emergency workers, the fallen and injured. Diaz and his men, they won't get away as easy as all that. On the monitors you watch a construction tarp slide away from a section of the factory. The only thing being constructed was a gun turret, and the hail of bullets cuts the angry horde to ribbons. All I did was lure them in for the kill. A mass suicidio grande, with extra green card chili on the side.

The guns have started going off again and Nikki, she's lost it. The gibbering newsmen are useless too. When somebody starts to ram down the door the other three split, choosing to cram into a closet and leave me laying on the floor. I sit up and the pain shooting through my chest speaks the language of broken ribs. By the time it passes and my sense returns the door is caving in.

Leena carefully aims, fires three shots through the door, smiles when two different voices cry out. "You're coming with me," she says, yanking me to my feet, dragging me away while Diaz's men fire through the door. Nikki and company don't dare follow, so it's just the two of us again. The two of us, and Leena's gun pointed at my gut.

We're in another huge storage space on the other side of the factory, loaded with all kinds of pirate booty. Gold nuggets, carved jade, silver trinkets, shattered pottery, corroded slave shackles, giant stone statues, and what looks like busted plane control panels—only they're crusted with as much deep sea crap as everything else. Leena's had me helping her barricade the door with this stuff for minutes now. It would be easy enough to pocket some slave-trade treasure if it wasn't so likely she'd blow me away.

Before I can think about any of it she has me pressed against a wall with the barrel of her machine gun under my chin. She's back to having that maniac thing going on like every other time she's been away from me too long. "You need to ask yourself which side you're on, because I want an answer right now."

"*You* asking *me* questions?"

"You don't always get a chance to be on the winning team."

"I'll keep that in mind." How is it possible for everything to change so quickly? One minute I'm a hot rap star, then I'm capped in the chest by the woman I thought was my sig other, then I'm back with my sig other again like nothing ever happened.

"What, Kenny?"

"Don't Kenny me. Just come on out with it. No more smoke screens. Who's it going to hurt now, anyway? The damage is done."

She removes the gun, has me help her roll a stone wheel in front of the door. "Look, it's like this. I did a job for my superiors and went into the layaway program. When it was clear that gig was up I busted out. End of story."

Arms crossed, I nod, staring at the gold, trying not to count the bars. "*Lay*away program. I get it." After a moment she catches the innuendo and chastises me for not taking this thing seriously enough. "Convince me then. Who are your bosses? What kind of job are we talking about? That was the lamest explanation ever."

There's a hesitation. I can tell what she's thinking. *Do I need him around enough to rationalize giving away secrets, and if so how easy will it be to kill him later to prevent him spreading the truth?* It turns out honesty is the best policy, for now. According to her she's been an operative on a slew of missions in her time, the last being the destruction of "materials" that had "fallen into the wrong hands." The string of arsons was her cover. And Governor Pollock, he didn't die of coronary problems, he was assassinated for being a puppet of "the enemy." Before that she had death row as her personal safe house, but after his death there was actually a chance she'd be executed. That's why she broke out when she did.

"Jesus! You mean I worried about you all that time for nothing?!"

"It's not like we didn't have a good time, Brimley."

Brimley! Of all things! "Roger that, captain."

"Look—"

"Or is it 'roger you?'"

"All right, you know how it works. I showed you mine so you show me yours. What do you really know, and what's the Diaz connection. One of his smugglers? Maybe you're in on recovering all these artifacts?" She shakes a carved jade trinket at me. It's a face, one that reminds me of my father. "Come on, we don't have forever. And none of that story about some ridiculous insults a hobo gave you. Nobody's stupid enough to fall for that."

Good to know she thinks so highly of me after all our years together. "You were out there, you heard him. He's Juanita's uncle and what comes around goes around. Karma."

She sneers. "Did you know he uses prisoners from the Mexican jails as 'volunteers' for his neurotoxin experiments?"

"This is fucking useless. *What* experiments? And you're welcome, by the way."

"For what?"

"Me being stupid and busting you out!"

"Right. Listen, Ken-baby, don't let your emotions get in the way of being smart."

"Oh, I didn't realize I was capable of being 'smart.'"

She bites her tongue, then her mood changes drastically. "Hold on a second. Something's up."

I tense up. The siren stopped. I click the man-down trigger; my one trick pony has gone lame.

"Middle of the room. Now!" She drags me by the collar but after about fifteen feet the wall blows in, spraying the area with fragments and dust. We break for the other side of the room, for the huge stone bodies and the crates stacked around them. We almost manage to cover all forty or fifty feet before they open fire.

After we dive behind the sea-junk I scream over the gunfire, "Why the hell did you try to shoot me?!"

"I didn't *try*, I did it," she says, taking out one or two of them as they rush in.

"No shit, but why?!"

"Why? Because you became a liability. There aren't any prisoners in this war."

"Oh yeah?"

"Yeah!"

"Then what do you call *us?*"

"Temporarily indisposed."

Very clever. We get another label and whammo, we're good to go. It's not like Diaz has us captive in his warehouse or anything. Another burst of gunfire comes our way, followed by another burst and another until it's two solid minutes of keeping our heads down. We're both covered by splinters and shards, with dust clogging our superficial cuts. Looks like a bullet even grazed her side.

"Still think we can't bleed too hard?" I ask, expecting her to tell me to shut up. Instead she looks my way and gives me a throaty laugh. "What the hell's so funny?"

"I'm not alone on this, Kenny. Don't you worry your pretty little—" Something catches her eye. "Phosphorous grenade! Run!"

We both scramble in separate directions and the door to hell opens behind us. There's a flash of heat like I've never felt before, like trying to carry the weight of a thousand deserts on my back, and then suddenly the ground is gone and some wooden crates are coming at me. After that I'm through the crates, smacking against the floor, with wood and electronic gadgets crashing down on top of me.

Before I can get my bearings some guy kicks me in the ribs, tries again but I pull on his foot when it comes my way. He lands with the back of his head on a hunk of metal—not good. Before I'm even all the way standing another runs at me with a knife. Right hand grabs wrist, left hand pushes down elbow, hips twist to the right, and just like the CIA dude said this one goes face-first into the concrete. The motion of your arm and hand that propels you along the water, that's sculling. The motion of my arm and hand propelling a brick, that's skulling. Okay, I guess they're fed up with hand-to-hand. The floor shakes like another explosion's gone off. Bullets start spraying the area wildly. Are they even trying to hit me?

The lights go out. I swear, that's the cheapest trick in the book. What's next—are they going to scare us by having a cat jump out? Trying not to think about the blood in my mouth I focus instead on the sound of more gunfire, of explosions and it hits me: no, they aren't trying to hit us after all. They're fighting somebody else. And hanging up above it all, through the skylight...

It's clear Diaz's men are fighting off police or rioters or rabid fans. While they're distracted by that ruckus I jump up, unable to take it anymore. I'm running around this place screaming, "*El aliento!*" and pointing back to the lights. Hey, I've learned *some* Español since I've been here.

A hand grabs me and drags me into the shadows. It's Enrique. "Shut it, man."

"But—"

"*Aliento* is *breath*. People aren't going to know what the hell you're trying to say anyhow."

"But...what the hell are you doing here anyway?! You're gonna get yourself killed!"

"Sorry to burst your bubble, but I'm CIA. Now simmer down." He drags me back into the shadows. "Come on, we've got to get you out of here. There's a back door to this place."

We start down a dimly lit corridor. "Wait. Did you just say what I think you said? CIA?"

Up ahead there's another form shifting in the shadows. For a second I freeze up, then recognize the silhouette. You've got to be kidding me.

"What it is, shark boy. Ya look, like, all messed up."

"Juanita, for the love of...what do you think you're doing?"

"I ain't gonna leave my boy hangin', naw mean?"

"But...you're back at the concert!"

"Naw I ain't, that's my cousin Rosario all done up to look like me an' shit." She grabs my collar and my chest throbs. "An' about you and her—"

"Hey!" Enrique waves his gun around, gestures to a stairway. You can see shadows dancing back around the corner, fire-shadows. Smoke is in the air. "Hey! Earth to dumb-asses!"

"Okay, okay!" Juanita turns, takes a step.

My hand clenches her elbow, my eyes lock on Enrique's. "I'm not going any fucking where. Not until I get some answers."

"Answers?" Juanita starts. "What we need is to—"

"Well, I need some answers."

He checks his gun, checks to see if anybody is wise to us yet. This is the first time I've ever seen him sweat. "It's not that simple. Have you ever heard the saying, 'The truth is a lie that has yet to be revealed?'"

"I'm losing my patience here, man." Then a memory rises to the surface. "When you were talking about that hyaline layer or whatever, with the fluorescent stuff in it. You were testing to see if I was in the know."

"That's right. I knew who you were at Diaz's ranch. Special case—every agency has wanted a piece of you for a long time. So when you got mixed up in all that mess with Manasseh red flags went up. Those dudes at El Monumento a la Madre, the men in black?"

"The suits."

"Right. Like I said, special case, and they want you the worst. By the time I took a couple of them out you'd already run into the rest. When I caught back up with you something was obviously up with Manasseh and her pop-star girlfriend so I had to hang back to let them play their hand. Sorry, but I couldn't tell you the real deal 'til now. Okay, you happy now? *Vamanos*!"

"But what was the whole bug-smuggling thing, what's the deal with Diaz, what—"

"Kenrick man, I already told Juanita all about it so ask her. She can explain it while you get the hell out of here. Now get going. These stairs are the escape exit. Under the factory there's a network of canals."

The sound of gunfire draws closer. I hesitate, finally take a few steps. "Okay man, okay. Take care of yourself."

"One more thing. Stay away from Leena, whatever you do. Got it?"

"Yeah, Sharky." Juanita punches my shoulder.

"You don't have to tell me twice." With that we head into the darkness.

Please state your name for the record.

I get paid to have my voice on records.

We've asked you five times now, Miss.

And five times later you're still a pasty freak in a cheap suit. You look like you belong center stage at a funeral.

[pause]

Bernadette Waldmann, correct?

[pause]

Your defiant-oppositional behavior problems would be best suspended until you find yourself in more tolerant company, Miss Waldmann. They are ill-timed at best.

Your face is ill-constructed, your suit is ill-fitting, and your breath—your *breath*—is just plain ill.

So Bernie—mind if I call you Bernie?—how many secrets did your fiancé confide in you?

Do you see these nails? You see them, right? Six-hundred dollars of upkeep every week. You call me Ber...that *name* again and I'll stick them in your eyes. Got it?

Duly noted. Now: your fiancé.

We didn't talk much.

Oh. Your relationship was of a more physical nature then.

No. No it wasn't. We just didn't spend much time together. You know, like most couples.

Are those your real breasts, Bernadette?

Well, they sure aren't yours, now are they?

And would Kenrick the Terrible be able to confirm whether or not you have implants?

[pregnant pause]

You and he had little to nothing in the way of a relationship, correct?

You don't have to call him that.

What?

Terrible. He wasn't all that. He was just a regular guy.

That, Miss Waldmann, is proof positive you know nothing and are, for our purposes, less than useless.

When my eyes open I've got a dark-skinned angel over me. My hair is warm and wet between my neck and her thigh. Laying here with wood pressing in against my back, my head in her lap, the first worry to make itself known: is she looking up my nose?

"Thought ya was some kinda swimmin' somebody. Almost had me worried."

I smile up at Juanita's faded scars. "Tit for tat I guess."

"Huh?" She checks out her chest.

"No, I mean...never mind." Everything slides and weaves and for a second it's like we're in the middle of an earthquake. Then I hear the water, see the torches and stone ceiling drifting by, and realize we're in a canoe or something.

"Where's Enrique?"

"Dunno. Dragged your drowned butt down a ways an' found this boat. Just been floatin' an' ain't seen no one since."

"Wait. I blacked out and you saved me?" She smiles, nods, is embarrassed by her pride. All this time I thought I'd taught her something that would save her life, not mine. What comes around goes around.

And I remember. The stairwell that was supposed to be an escape route was an old one, made out of stone. In our mad dash for safety we forgot to take into account the light, or lack of it, and fell right into the open hole that the stairway became. Fifteen, twenty feet and we hit water. After panicking a little I got my bearings and made it to the surface. There was enough light to see with from the lamps set up further along. The whole "escape route" turned out to actually be some kind of underground canal system. There was a walkway along one side, with lights rigged up over it, but they had all gone out.

Meanwhile, I realized Juanita was nowhere to be seen. The fact that she couldn't really swim came back to me. Then I realized my feet weren't touching the bottom and started to flip again. Spinning around with my arms searching the water I didn't care that my chest was killing me, that the water was freezing.

A huge splash behind me almost stopped my heart right then and there. Instead of some guy wanting to kill me, or stones crumbling away from above, it was Juanita. She took in a couple huge lungfuls, bobbing in the water, then laughed.

"Lookit, I'm floating like you showed me, all by myself!"

Just as I sighed in relief a shot rang out. Juanita went down, and in the shadows I saw Leena, glaring, her gun trained on the water.

"No!" I dived, trying to search for her under the surface despite the fact it was dark. Afraid to go up for air I stayed down long, too long, and instead of Juanita all I found was darkness.

Now, looking up at her, the gunshot wound is plainly visible in her shoulder. "Okay, thanks and everything, but let's check you out."

"We caught up in this foolishness, and all ya wanna do is check me out? Ya's a hardcore playa after all."

"Always a joker, huh?" This get-up of hers is ridiculous. She must've run right off the stage to come here once she heard what was going down. She's in fishnet stockings and, well, that's about all. Her boots are leather, leaving only her lingerie, so I end up tearing up my shirt. She tries to keep a smile up for me while I bandage her, but I can hear her teeth grinding together. After she's patched up we flip flop and she wraps my ribs with what's left.

"Enrique said he explained things to you. What's going on?"

"When I got here shit was all bad and whatnot, so he snatched me and kept them fools from cappin' me."

"What fools?"

"His crew and my uncle's crew. And the other stuff, it don't make much sense."

"Such as?"

"The whole smuggling thing. He said those scorpions are for my uncle's people to make neur...neurotoxin-based weapons."

"Crap, using the venom from their stingers?" She shrugs, then winces. "Leena said something about that but it didn't make sense before now. He say what it's all about?"

"Top secret, he said."

I nod, watch the walls go by. "You seen any other stairs, any exits since we've been in this thing?"

"Nuh-uh."

The longer we talk the more I realize what a complex old canal system we're following. The further we go, the better the lighting and condition of things. There's even more excavation equipment down here. I tell her about the stuff up in the warehouse, the sunken city suspected to be of the pre-classic period, around 2,800 feet below the surface, similar to Teotihuacan urban planning. It's smack dab in the middle of a chain of underwater volcanos where Cuba's western tip once connected to the Yucatan peninsula. Before a series of massive eruptions and earthquakes that entire strip of land was once above water. Where I'm getting all this from I have no idea, probably that article I read.

Something changes in Juanita's eyes while I talk. No, it's not boredom setting in. It's something a little too familiar.

Before I can turn around what looks like a giant arrow goes by, and I know our smooth sailing has come to an end. The faces of the people surrounding us, and the way they're dressed, it all dredges up the past I left behind.

I woke up groggy, with the world spinning and my clothes halfway on. It took a while to register where I was. Mood lighting and lava lamps and trip-out pictures and the smell of incense and dirty clothes all over the floor and furniture: a dorm room. A young woman was in the corner, on the floor, her knees drawn up to her chest. She was crying. Me, I was on the bed.

We had been drinking together, of that I was fairly sure. Her name was Su; that slowly established itself as a fact. Right, Su short for Suphedrine. What kind of situation had I gotten myself into? What had happened?

It was just my second semester of college. Well, community college, but it still counts officially. You hear all sorts of stories about bad things going down, things getting out of control, but you never expect to find yourself in the middle of a statistic.

"Su? Uh...Su?"

She didn't respond.

"Su, what's going on here?"

She only sobbed harder.

So I tried harder. I sat up, tucked in my shirt, buttoned and zipped my pants. Rubbed my face, again and again, smelled the sex in the room. A sticker on her dresser read *Don't Be A Victim*.

"Su—"

"Can't you shut the fuck up, you stupid piece of ass?!" After that outburst she went back to her regularly scheduled crying.

"Su...whatever happened here...I'm sorry, and let's not mention it to—"

"Fuck, I'll tell whoever I want that I broke off a piece of that beef-cake! If they're not all fucking dead already!"

"Huh?"

"My *friend*, you idiot, my *best friend* was just found fucking *murdered* on C Quad, and all you're worried about is that stupid rope!"

"Whoa, whoa, whoa—hold it. Your friend was killed and that's why you're upset."

She stopped crying all of a sudden and looked at me, wide-eyed, with something like awe. "*No shit!*"

"Look—"

"No, you look. I want you the fuck out of here. Now."

I started looking for my shoes, then stopped. "Rope?"

She stood, grabbing me by my collar. "The fuck! Out! Now!"

"Okay, just—"

"You dumb—"

"Okay, okay, *okay!*"

I half stepped out into the hall, half fell out as she shoved me. When I turned to ask about my shoes the door slammed in my face. It was late, how late I wasn't sure, but pretty much everyone had gone to sleep already.

And I was thinking. We all knew that *rope* was the street name for *rohypnol*. Standing there trying to figure it all out I was overcome by a dizzy spell. Being on the swim team I was the picture of health. The last time I'd been ill was before my brothers and I had run away. Mom liked to keep us sick. Thinking about my mother, and the drinks Su bought for me, I threw up on the wall.

My legs started pumping, carrying me away, with no destination in mind. Just running. Outside, in the moist predawn air, I had to stop and catch my breath on a bench. The world was spinning and my stomach felt like hell and my muscles were sore already. It was just a shitty little sprint! Then it occurred to me that maybe they were getting sore even before I ran. Confused, getting more scared by the second, I sat and shook for minutes.

The haze lifted from my thoughts and another dark notion hit me. Her friend had just been murdered, but she didn't say anything about them finding her killer. The psycho could still be lurking on campus. It would make sense to get back to my apartment as soon as possible.

The next day I was all fucked up. In class I couldn't concentrate—well, the classes I remembered to attend—and at practice everybody could tell I was off. Trying to bring it up to one of my teammates in the locker room was useless. Soon as I opened my mouth it was like the ability to speak ran out the back door. He gave me a weird look and left me to get dressed alone. The coach, he came back and lectured me about "partying too hard." With my speech impaired I could only nod.

What would I say to those people anyway? That maybe some chick I met in a bar drugged me and did things to me when I was out of it? If you're a guy that kind of thing doesn't happen to you, not as far as the public is concerned. If you're a guy, having sex is something you're supposed to boast about, whether it was conscious or unconscious or whatever. The only other option was to admit being victimized, which would be to admit weakness, and men simply don't tolerate weakness in other men. The idea of the other guys piling on the agony wasn't attractive.

Instead, I spent that night and the next morning trying to get ahold of Su. Text messages, e-mail, phone calls, knocking on her door, none of it got me anywhere. I even stopped in at the bar but there were these chicks in the back staring at me so I split. Su wasn't around anyway.

The next afternoon campus police stopped by my apartment. Den answered the door so they spoke with him first. He was my house mate, and his full name was Denzoprin. My stomach and muscles were still giving me shit, and since I had started seeing things I decided to stay in for the day. When Den knocked on the door he didn't wait for me to reply. He barged in saying that the police wanted to speak with me.

"About what?"

"Dunno. They asked me a buncha questions 'bout stuff I did the other night."

"What other night?"

"Two nights ago. And they asked where you were, so I told them you were out the whole time."

"Fuck, thanks man."

"Well, they asked. What was I supposed to say?"

Out in the living room were two surly-looking types, a man and woman, both middle-aged.

"Hello officers. Is this about the complaint I lodged?"

"Complaint?"

"Yeah, people following me and all."

They looked at each other, clueless, so I showed them a photocopy of the note left in my swim locker the week prior. The original had been taken by the police and put with their report, wherever that was.

"No sir, I'm sure the department is handling that matter already. We're looking into the murder of a one Alikah Laine. As we understand it you were at The Maiden's Head two nights prior?"

"Well..."

"We've spoken with several witnesses who place you there."

"Okay. Yeah."

"Can you tell us roughly what times you were there?"

Another dizzy spell started coming on then, and images of the New Agers started flooding my mind. They'd been following me my whole life and had recently caught up to me on campus. There was nowhere to run. With no memory of when I got to the bar or left I made up some times. My only alibi was Su, who not only was way too much like the New Age freaks, but wouldn't let the police know what she did. The detectives asked a few more questions, but overall seemed to be satisfied.

On day three Su continued to be evasive, and everything cleared up except for the general muscle ache. Coach was watching me like a hawk, and when I went into a seizure he'd had enough. He had the medics check my urine, and after they cleared me he called me into his office.

"Close the door, son." I did as he asked. "Now, I'm going to talk and you're going to listen. After I'm done talking you're not going to say a word. You're just going to leave. Got it?"

"Ye—"

"What'd I just say?! Zip it!" He sat brooding for a bit, watching to see if I would have the guts to speak up. I didn't. "Your swim log indicates muscle pain, intestinal troubles, the whole nine. At first it seemed like burnout. But then you go and start convulsing like that. Know what the urine test showed? Flunitrazepam. Rohypnol. Roofies. And don't look at me that way son, 'cause you haven't even seen me hit the 'roofy' yet. I don't know what kind of depraved scum you are, and frankly I don't care to know. Every member of the faculty and staff has been advised of what to look for in the fight against assaults on coeds. According to the literature the end-stage sexual predator actually starts using that shit on themselves, mixing it with cocaine and what all to get these crazy narcotic effects. But why am I telling you this, you already know about all that.

"As of this minute you are off the team and blacklisted from participating in *any* other activities within the athletic department. You're just lucky I don't have evidence about the things you've done, or else there'd be cops all up in your ass right this very minute, you sick motherfucker. Now get out of my sight. Looking on scum like you is personally offensive to decent folk."

He threw the book at me—my swim log, that is—and it bounced off my chest. I stood there looking at it on the floor of his office, pages spread and spine damaged, before stooping to retrieve it. My eyes found his, then went to the floor again. What point would there be in trying to explain? I left and cleaned out my locker.

It soon came to light that another coed had disappeared the week prior, and a few days after being kicked off the swim team, when another coed was found murdered, that's when things started getting a little too hot. The pictures were all very familiar. They were the same unfriendly faces that had been following, staring, threatening for the last two weeks. When I first saw them I pretended it was a coincidence. *There's New Age people all over the place*, I told myself. *Not all of them are psycho cultists*, I told myself. *This has nothing to do with the ones that screwed things up for me in high school*, I told myself. *Those sacrifices are in the past*, I told myself.

But in real life the past and present and future overlap, no matter what we tell ourselves. One builds on the other, builds toward the other, creating a circle. It's always the same cycle of shit.

The police came round more frequently, began calling at all hours, even started following me. A fourth new age hippy chick went missing. She was called Illy by her friends. It was short for Il, or Paxil. When the police searched her dorm room they found photos of me along with personal info, like my address and phone number and the names of my brothers. I skipped town before they could drag me down to the station.

You can get away with a lot on the road, but finding legit money is almost a hopeless prospect. Crime just draws unwanted attention to you, and no businesses hire without doing a background check. Well, almost none. There was an ad in the classifieds for a club in search of male dancers—no experience necessary. I was young, on the run, and needed cash. What was I supposed to do, go to the bank and ask for a loan?

The place was basically a strip joint trying to pass itself off as a restaurant and lounge, probably because it bordered on some fairly nice suburban neighborhoods. It was called The Tender Loin of all things, and in addition to dancers and beer specials they had an "all you can eat" lunch buffet. I can't tell you how many health code violations they had. The few windows were small and had bars on them, as if people break into establishments run by organized crime.

Eventually word spread about an arrest being made in my case. For once in my life fear settled in, fear for my brothers. The fact that we were triplets would mess things up for them. At the same time we all hated each others guts, so maybe them taking a fall for me wasn't such a bad thing. Pretty soon, though, it became obvious they hadn't nabbed Seamus or Greg. No, they'd thrown my mother in jail.

One, two, and breathe...

One day you wake up and it seems like the world is against you. You know what they're all thinking, that you deserve this. Okay: who really deserves to be strung up over a bubbling lava pit? That's what you want to know.

Three, four, and breathe...

Today's one of those days loaded with tons of useful insights. Such as, the worst part of hanging a hundred or more feet above molten lava is that chains chafe your wrists like nobody's business.

And you know what they're all thinking. They're saying to themselves, *this guy's in for one hell of a bath. Hey buddy, don't drop the soap!* Prison humor, like that isn't old. I'm starting to think all of life is just a punch line aimed at your chin. An arsonist, a singer, and a prison guard walk into a volcano...

Juanita, she's over to the side out of harm's way, half angry out of her mind, half scared to death. Enrique, they slapped him around some and left him on the floor, handcuffed. Leena, she's nowhere to be seen—maybe she'll make another dramatic appearance, or just shoot me from the shadows again. Nikki, who knows what happened to her. Maybe she made it out and is bringing help. Yeah, right.

The circling enemy warriors, they want to know: *Have the delusions started yet? If not there's still plenty of time for that. It only takes so long before your brain boils inside your skull, like those raver kids on ecstasy. Like those lab monkeys on the news, trapped in cages under hot water pipes that busted. Like all those people you left behind in the factory...*

When you learn breath control exercises and visualization, you never imagine you'll be putting it to use under these circumstances. You're told it makes you a better competitor, not that it keeps your freaked out interrogators from giving you a heart attack. Interrogators who want to know what happened in the factory. That and more.

How did you come to be there? How many died because of you? What lead you to become aligned with our enemies? You had sex with them...what do you think about having sex with us?

Their minds are easier to read than a freakin' porno mag. No matter what I tell them they're going to finish me off here tonight. And they know I know it. That mind reading, it's a two way street. One without clear lines, without signs or crossing guards, filled with head-on collisions.

One, two, and breathe...ugh.

Down there below me, that's what they call the terrestrial magma ocean. I know this because *they* told me so. What they didn't have to tell me is that it's made up of liquid rock, metal, and gasses. The key word here is *gasses*, at least when it comes to breathing. Damn, they don't call it the bowels of the Earth for nothing.

In prison, when an inmate throws a container of their collected urine and fecal matter at you, you've been *gassed*. This usually happens when a new fish is put in the tank, walking to their cell for the first time with an armful of state issue clothes, toiletries, and grudges. If you accept being gassed then you're a punk and a bitch, and whatever hap-

Photo still, courtesy Last Burn Films © 2006

pens after that nobody will care because you asked for it by not striking back. My employers, they were too humane to use gas chambers.

The women circle with their spears and their knives and their guns. A few of them are recognizable—they've been shown running away from cops on TV, or their photos sneered at customers from the post office wanted posters, and some are even the same ones who tried to kill me before. One beats a drum, another pulls on the chain, making me wobble in midair. This whole place is a special effects show out of some Hollywood producer's wet dream. The reddish glare from down below gives everything an eerie glint, with ancient temple ruins more authentic than any CGI, and a whole slew of angry natives calling for blood. One of them notices me taking in the surroundings and says, "These ruins were built with igneous rock, rock made out of solidified magma. It's a temple of the mother goddess Tonantzin but it can double as a crypt for you and your friends just as well."

"Igneous rock, huh? Wow." My friends, they're shaking their heads, worried that something worse could possibly happen. "So that makes all this like an igneous crock, right?"

"Maybe an igneous *crock pot* if we don't hear you talking."

Know what a person looks like when they know they're going to die? Like a person who knows they're about to die. No, it's not a joke.

One, two...every gasp brings in less air.

Even people who have made their peace—religious fanatics satisfied with their atonement, or sociopaths who don't care what they've done one way or the other—every person is the same when they know it's only a matter of seconds. The mentally challenged can tell too, they pick it up off of everybody else around them. Inhaling the vibes right out of the air. Reading minds. Their veins begin to bulge as the heart rate increases, eyes bug out, facial muscles contort with the exertion of staying conscious, the entire body tenses, muscles flex where you didn't even know people had muscles. Like Olympic level athletes on the final lap. And all they're trying to do is figure out how to hope against hope, praying to whatever gods will hear them. But the only one that matters in the temple of death is God Captor, finger on the switch. Reading my mind, and asking so many damned questions.

How did we get here anyway? And, if there is some kind of escape, how can I face the rest of the world—with everybody thinking crazy things about me? This will all be tabloid fodder from here to eternity, even if I don't make it out of this thing alive.

It's right there bubbling under the surface of their eyes, even with the distance and the waves of intense heat it's still visible: *Maybe we're offering you a merciful alternative*, they're thinking. Dr. Kevorkian with access to the terrestrial magma ocean. They play asp, I play Cleopatra's bosom. Okay, so I'm a boob now. Everything's asp-backwards these days. The victim roasts to death and they're really angels, angels of mercy.

Isn't that what you told yourself? That you were easing the misery of others?

One, two...

Is this any different?

Nobody likes a smarty-pants, especially a smarty-pants toying with your life. Maybe that's all I am. We live by our labels, don't we? That's what Leena and Nikki were always talking about. The definitions society places on us, that we place on objects or lifestyles or types of entertainment. *Boy toy*; that's how everybody sees Kenrick Brimley. These folks have simply decided to pull a crank to wind the toy up, make him speak, make him dance. Kenrick Brimley has become a monkey on a chain, playing the organ grinder at his own execution.

Here I am, facing the Big Burnout, thinking that burnout is mostly from psychological factors, so there are no real tests for it. That it used to be considered a copout for wussies. That low levels of serum ferritin—better known as iron—are often associated with poor performance and maladaption.

Did you enjoy it? What did you hope to gain? Are you a traitor to humanity or not? How long do you think it will take us to find your family?

"Why doncha just do whatever it is ya gonna do?! Huh?" This outburst earns Juanita a couple swift kicks.

Start from the beginning, one of them says.

Can reliving it all be as bad as the magma hot tub they've arranged for me? There's nothing else to lose. Watch as the boy toy gives them what they want, like always. *Work will set you free.* Or, better yet, *working it will set you free.*

Wait a minute. The one that told me to start from the beginning, with the intense eyes. She's one of the few whites here. And, she didn't move her mouth when she spoke just now.

"What the—!" That can't be. The freaky lady is in my head!

Don't be alarmed. This is just the full extent of what you and your brothers always tried, and failed, to do.

"You mean...? Hold on—what would you know about it anyway!"

You already know the answer, Rocket Man.

"Only one person ever called me that, Rocket Man. I always hated it."

What could be so bad about her? She was your own—

So, that's what all of this is about. This is going to be a lot more painful than I thought.

There's one thing I don't talk about with anyone, one person I don't even allow myself to think about. Mother. In her blood-red swim-suit, her lime green swimsuit, her white swimsuit. One pieces, all of them, except when she would embarrass us by swimming around our backyard nude, or the odd times when she would skinny dip with a swimming cap on. What was up with that?

Mom, the Olympian, the model, the New Ager, the one who was out of the popular loop after she went off about her alien abduction. Mom, always in her room cussing as she waxed herself, muttering under her breath about conspiracies while burning our toast. Mom, who made it so we couldn't invite friends over because of all the "charms" we had to wear around the house. Of course, our friends wanted to come over and watch her topless in the hot tub. Pretty soon we stopped having friends. Pretty soon we stopped having a mother. We told people that she was dead, we were orphans, we were grown in a test tube or something along those lines, whatever it took *not* to have a whacked out Area-51 mama. And you know what? After every-thing was said and done, her weirdest hang-up was that she never blinked her eyes. Not once. At least, not that me and my brothers could ever remember.

Her black one piece, her cammo one piece. Maybe wearing only swim attire is a sign of insanity. Come to think of it, Ma wasn't so different from Nikki in the looks department. Not a redhead, I guess you'd call her a "raven-haired beauty" if you wanted to get all fruity, but other than that they could've almost been twin sis—no, it's a little too disturbing to think about, even after everything that's happened. One thing Ma had, that Nikki could never possess, was the butcher knife incident. After chasing us around the house threatening to cut our father out of us, well, it doesn't take much more than that to con-vince teenagers to run away. The fucked up thing about it all was how she didn't try to get us back. Instead she followed us around snapping shots with a ridiculously long telephoto lens, as if we couldn't spot her or the people following her, taking photos of their own.

We scraped by okay though. We all worked night jobs, all forged papers and pretended to be our father if somebody called about one of the other brothers. Back then we didn't hate each other yet, not completely. No, the problem was the older we were the harder it was to tell who was who. It's called "proximity effect" and only happens to powerful telepaths and empaths. Us, we never went for any of that. Our official story was simply that the other two were in our way. Whatever we called it, the end result was the same: our experiences and thoughts all mixed until the water was so muddy we started hitting sandbars, rocks, each other. Together we were the perfect schizophrenic, one with multiple bodies but only a single personality, a mundane trinity.

My family was a four-person cult. Our initiation ritual involved aliens messing with you. Our doctrine was back to basics, a re-envisioning of old fertility religions. Our rituals involved the opposite of filial piety—we attempted to ward off our "father." Mother always said the lights came and took her in the middle of the night. Sometimes she called them angels, sometimes she called them aliens, but me and my brothers were supposed to call them "Dad." We always figured she was nuts—I mean, she *was* nuts, don't get me wrong—but maybe she was nuts *and* she was right. Even with all the other weirdness we never allowed ourselves to believe the "sexual experiment" story.

When she was younger Mom was pale, dark, green-eyed and intense, if not strung-out looking. If she ever smiled it was the mischievous kind, the type of smile most people save for private moments like successfully shoplifting or looking sexy in the mirror. Her smiles always preceded trouble. The naughty look is what made her perfect for the covers of sports magazines despite the fact she never won any medals, made her perfect for local gal makes good news segments, made her transition from athlete to model a natural evolution. That was all before we were born, though, or when we were too young to remember. Very few, if any, photographers called her after the nervous breakdown. She always blamed it on our eighteen month gestation instead, as if such a thing really could happen. The smiling, buoyant mother that stared at us from musty old covers wouldn't have recognized the paranoid glances being cast at us from the shadows, from doorways, from around corners when she thought we couldn't see her.

The woman at the arraignment, she was a far cry from the mother creeping through my memories. Her features had softened to the point that she looked somewhat approachable, not like my pre-escape mother. She wore glasses and dressed schoolmarmish and was polite to those speaking in the court, completely unlike the danger-vixen who could enrage a room full of people within seconds. When she spoke, when she told her story, it was restrained, almost embarrassed, the exact opposite of the UFO-rants I ran away from.

The authorities held her in contempt, so we had something in common. The difference was they thought she actually killed those people, and I knew she couldn't have. She was a vegetarian for God's sake. She might've tried to kill her sons a few times, but other than that she wouldn't hurt a fly. Them, all they knew was the cockamamy story she spouted in the courtroom and in interrogation, it was hogwash. Bunkum. Far as they were concerned she was stonewalling, trying to either get an insanity plea or buy time. They threw her in the slammer until she could respect the court.

It turned out not to be a big deal that I was this wanted dude waltzing into their proceedings. With somebody in custody under suspicion of the murders the police didn't give a tinker's dam about little old me. When they let me back to speak with her she was just sitting on the bed staring at the wall, her favorite pastime. She was dressed in simple black with a white blouse. Always white, never, ever gray. When she heard me enter her eyes shifted, and instead of sarcasm she greeted me with a gaping jaw. I tried not to think about the creases on her forehead, the laugh lines around her mouth, the fact that she could get the death penalty.

"It's me. It's Kenrick."

For once the concern in her eyes wasn't directed inward. "My son. My beautiful, beautiful son." I did a quick double-take, but nobody was standing behind me. "Look at you. So handsome, so magnificent."

"Uh...Mom, you ought to take it easy. Obviously you're—"

"I know what I am, and I know what you are, which is not your father's son. That's more than I can say for the other two. I can't believe you came back for me."

Then again, being the oldest, these duties always fell to me. When you're a kid it's one thing to lord popping out first over your siblings, but another thing entirely to live up to the responsibility. I always had to play "father"—make dinner when she wasn't around, make sure the others did their homework, massaged Mom's shoulders and rubbed her feet when she got home from the few odd jobs she could hold. Hey, you don't get crazy masseur skills like mine over night. All my life I took care of other people, had it instilled in me to always put myself second. In the end what does that get you? A one-way ticket to Hate City, population one.

I took a look around. "Pretty cushy setup you've got here."

"It's the conjugal cell. It's cleaner and they even give me a TV and VCR. No reception, of course, you can only play video tapes."

"I don't get it. Con...conju..."

She leaned forward and whispered conspiratorially, "It's where inmates can have sex with their spouses."

"Oh!" I jumped back, straightened my clothes, looked around seeing things a bit differently this time. "So it's like...oh."

"Come here. Come sit next to Mommy, Rocket Man." I rolled my eyes and sighed, but did as she asked. "You know why I'm here, don't you? Because I told the truth. Those people have been after my boys for years, but now that you're older they don't want to kidnap you anymore. No. Full-grown alien offspring are too hard to brainwash. They want to kill you now. I was only protecting my family."

"Mom. Come on. Why do this? You didn't kill those people, and neither did I."

"Can't a mother protect her son if she wants to?" Strange that after all those years of only caring about herself and her bizarre stories she could change into this maternal savior type. "All this talk is only making me more tense. Come on, rub Mommy's shoulders like you used to."

I took up a position behind her, began to knead her muscles. "Why couldn't you marry some guy we hated, who could hate us back. There were plenty of 'em lined up to give you shoulder rubs back in the day."

She laughed, shook her head. "Don't you know? I wanted to keep all that hate to myself. Which just makes me a normal parent."

A guard peered in to check on us, donut in hand, and froze mid-chew when he saw me rubbing down my mother in the conjugal cell. "So it's like…oh." He forced his bite down, then added, "Five minutes."

After that things felt a little strange so we stuck to just talking. She refused to listen to reason though. She stood by her story, they stood by their logic, and the stalemate left her rotting in that cell for days, then weeks, then months. I stayed nearby, visiting when I could, despite the fact that people in town still treated me like a potential killer. The more they pressed the more she insisted it was a conspiracy of cultists bent on taking her alien progeny, and the more her health deteriorated.

Then, one day, she was dead. Just like that. The headlines read *Suspect Dies Under Mysterious Circumstances* and *Escape From Justice* and *Colorado Coonskins Scandal Erupts*. They never let me see the body, just gave me the cremains when they were done with her. Who knows what really happened to her in there.

My brothers, they were phantoms during all this. Nonexistent. The old proximity effect thing that made us move away from each other might have kept them at bay, but I doubt it. Shame and Greg were always slackers, which explains why they came out second and third. And during all of it, during all the crazy shit that went down through our childhood, our teen years, not once did our real father show up—alien or otherwise. Lord knows we could have used a male role model, some kind of stabilizing force. Thinking about the impossible, sometimes you can't help asking: if an alien turns out to be an unfit parent, should they be forced to have their test tubes tied?

Because my mother died they never officially closed the case, but never investigated further either. And because they never closed the case it haunted my every step. Eventually I had to give up on my old life and become somebody else altogether.

That's it. The end. Roll credits. The most important events of my life, all spilled out. In what—seconds? Minutes? This speed of thought stuff still scares the crap out of me.

You'll get used to it, she assures me. She seems to be the leader, if they even have leaders.

"Well, for you it may be natural, but for me—"

Only for the Enemy is this an inborn ability.

"Hmm."

I have implants. My eyes wander to her chest and she yells, "Cybernetics!"

The heat of the lava pit below me is starting to be not so bad. "Hey, maybe a person could get used to this—it's sort of more like a sauna than a dungeon."

It's not a dungeon, it's a ritual execution chamber.

"And the difference is?"

Don't be obtuse.

Oh, so now they want to start bickering with my thoughts. What really doesn't make sense is why should these freaks still be chasing me after all this time?

Rocket Man, I know for a fact you're familiar with the natural law that water seeks equilibrium. Do you think other facets of Creation are any different?

"Don't call me that. And I've got no clue what you're trying to say." The rest, they've got no idea what's going on. The chanting dies down and they look at each other like the heat has finally gotten to me.

You should know that I was your mother's friend. I was there when they took her, and helped nurse her back to health. Then, *You may not want to hear it but she really was abducted.*

Shit. So there it is: I'm not even human. I'm a test tube human wannabe.

You're human, but not just *human. You're so much more than that. Go ahead, you can do this too.*

Well, why not. I try it. Seems like she receives all my thoughts: physical sensations and emotions and excitement and hostility all rolled into one. For her it's like reading the funny pages, but for me it's like I'm looking at the Dead Sea Scrolls. We go back and forth like this, locked in a mental exchange for who knows how long, until a movement distracts me.

Enrique is on his knees now, elbow against the wall propping him up. Seems like he's sizing up the situation. The women, they're ignoring him now, starting to chant more ferociously. With the pain clearing up it's easier to focus on our surroundings. All around this place there's what you'd call friezes—don't ask how I know that—depicting all kinds of funky ancient people or gods, crazy buildings and animals and plants. Around the very top of the room are statues of birds, and of all the animals engraved on the walls two scorpions keep drawing my attention.

He thinks we're going to die down here, knows it. What he's got no clue about is the fact that I've got the blood of little gray men floating around in my system, making me some kind of supernatural dude. If that's true, why can't I just levitate out of here? Or do some kind of mind-bolt thing on these chicks like in the movies?

The women start beating on their drums even harder, faster.

You can say what you want, I don't believe you about my mother. *Just admit it. Let go.*

"No...uh...that is..." Okay, so if I start listening to myself I kill the flow. If I just let it happen it'll pour out, like a faucet. My brain is turning into a thought sponge, soaking up things left and right. Now, can me and these whacky ladies give each other brain sponge baths?

The only phenomena that is unexplainable is your abundance of life-force. We can see your aura, and we all agree. Something is wrong here.

So what's the big problem with being healthy?

The problem is that only Masters could attain what you have, and you are not a Master. If your story is to be believed—and, obviously, you are not sophisticated enough to deceive us—then you have involuntarily acquired spiritual energy from the deceased.

Uh...is that common?

No.

My babies come to mind. The rack, the branks, the iron maiden, all of it. The women on the eve of their death, their bodies tangled

Promotional image, courtesy Last Burn Films © 2006

with mine. Those same women the following evening, staring at me as they drew their last breaths. The nameless hordes staring up at me from the instant photos in the mail. The legions of people who killed themselves in my name.

Juanita, she's near the wheel that keeps my chain in place, and inches closer to it every minute. Those scorpions on the wall keep screaming for attention. The one on the right is a little bigger. The one to the left has more detail though. The stone bearing the tail is round, with what seem to be rays of light emanating from it, jutting out from the wall. Checking out the size of the tail and pincers it hits me: that's the male. And those aren't rays of light so much as grips for turning the round stone the tail is on.

Trying to stall for time I say, "Well, you didn't need to do anything so drastic. You could've just asked me about it up front."

This is a war, you must understand.

"Love and war, the trusty standbys in our storied lineage of excuses." Whoa—this doesn't sound like me at all! I'm grabbing more stuff out of the air by the second.

There's got to be a solution. Maybe my mind can split, can function as two separate but equal parts. Concentrating, I think: Hey lady, if the penal system sticks people with syringes to kill them, does dropping people into a hole make this a vaginal system?

Oh! How dare you!

No, still not there. Concentrating even harder I think of the way Daphne screamed when we were together, even while focusing on Enrique. Those distinct shrieks of hers left my ears ringing for days after her execution, and they cause mother's "friend" to shake her head once, twice. *The scorpion's tail,* I'm telling him, *focus on the power radiating from its tail.* Just when the New Age mind groper seems to recover I start to replay some of the more questionable requests

Daphne acted out with me, and her look sours. *Those aren't rays of light, they're handles. They're not looking, go ahead and turn it!*

Daphne, she had been in the psych ward more than once. She was what you'd call a biter. The leader shakes her head again, disconnects. Enrique, he's staring intently at the wall, at the tail, and looks like he's scheming.

I've been revolted before. We all know what you did, and it comes as no shock—

Gizelle, she'd really been something to look at in her youth, but when a person does twenty-five years on the inside it's like fifty out in the world. Her skin was weird and blotchy, her smile didn't hide her sick desperation, her former hardbody was loose like an ill-fitting suit, which was worse than just being saggy like a normal middle-aged person. Thinking about my lips on her varicose veins does the trick. While the interrogator is distracted I urge Juanita forward, distract the woman guarding the chain with thoughts of my abdomen.

And Enrique, he's in position. Nobody sees as he twists, not until one hears his handcuffs scraping stone. But it's too late now. He has separated the tail from the body and, more importantly, released a massive flood gate.

Surfing the Terrestrial Magma Ocean

Grab your boogieboard. Throw that shit in the fire. Grab your surfboard. Get you a running start and jump on that terrestrial magma ocean. Learn you what big kahuna be all about.

Whoa dude. Magma ocean? Yup.

The proto-Earth was formed by continuous collusion—I mean, collision—of celestial riffraff and castoffs, a veritable prison colony of the solar system's undesirable elements, until it grew to become the most important planet. Important to us, at least. This proto-Earth was impacted by something the size of Mars or the Moon, was originally a much larger planet, the remains of which are scattered throughout the asteroid belt, along with the ejaculate spewed by many other celestial bodies during "banging." Never fear, even the largest of impacts wouldn't melt our planet completely. Gnarly.

So, this giant impact melted a large amount of surface, a whole hemisphere. Heavy, dude. Turned half the planet into a deformed blob of surging magma. A magma ocean. Isostatic adjustment redistributed the mass to form a more symmetric spherical configuration...natural law say: *the circle must be maintained at all times, mon.*

Be surfing that shit? Be true. Magma ocean contains large amounts of water. Be talking the union of water and fire. Low-viscosity convecting magma ocean behaves more like an atmosphere than a solid mantle. That be: even though it's *under*ground now it's not *ground*, fool. Them convective velocities are roughly the same as in our atmosphere. Imagine gale-force lava whipping around at 60 mph, 100 mph. Talk about a rip tide. Be a wet atmosphere where evaporation and condensation are present in the form of melting and crystallization of lava. Scrum-didly.

So you're hanging ten on a Mt. Everest-sized tsunami. Because fluid dynamics and physics of suspension in magma oceans are radically different, floatation doesn't function in the same manner, and you begin to sink. That's okay, go with the flow. But how easy be it to roll with this flow? We're talking liquidus vs. solidus. Crystallization = solid stuff forming. Flow starts to suck dog nuts at 40% crystallization...in other words, when things start getting hard life don't go smoothly, but so what? Work that surfboard like your daddy showed

John Edward Lawson

you. Rocket on around those rocks, those hard places.

Watch out for the iron bars separating the magma ocean from the mantle. Liquid iron, or Fe, is a foreign, or alien, substance introduced by that nasty intergalactic "banging." Injected like sperm into egg during artificial insemination. Be getting nasty on the periodic table.

Radioactive potassium be likely the main source of heat in Earth's core. At low temperatures iron and potassium refuse to interact, but when you turn up the heat on them, increase the pressure they're under iron actually draws potassium out of the silicate-dominated mantle. Makes the beast with two isotopes, and they come out on the other side as an entirely new compound never experienced on the Earth's surface. This new potassium in the core acts to generate the heat and the magnetic field. That's right, magnetism. Animal magnetism.

About a tenth of a percent of the Earth's core be potassium, the same ratio as in a banana. When you chomp bananas for a potassium and B vitamin boner you're getting your radioactive grind on. Radio, active. You catching this transmission? The info rocketing through the air? Be checking out Abe and Matsui, and that Solomatov be dropping knowledge like *Deep Impact*.

The pressure for metal/silicate equilibrium be the pressure that corresponds to the bottom of the magma ocean...in other words, the weight of this fire ocean be linked to keeping things equal, to maintaining balance.

The magma ocean be the only part of the planet to go through substantial transformation. 1,292 F to 2,372 F, and it's not a dry heat. Already done told you, the union of fire and water. It's a wet heat. Crystallization of the shallow magma ocean takes more than one hundred million years. Who cares, you won't be surfing that long anyway.

223

☯

A faceless corpse bumps into me and I shove it away. The water that poured into the pit, first it all evaporated and this shock wave of crazy steam blasted everyone by the pit. Luckily they had swung me all the way to the side by then. True, they did it so quickly my ribs slammed into the wall, but I'd rather be crying curses at the top of my lungs than have all my skin melted off. At first the funky-ass water pouring in was ice cold, but now it's like a hot tub in here. We don't find a way out and eventually it'll heat up to the point that we cook to death. Even after minutes of full-blast flooding the water keeps on coming, keeps everyone at its mercy. When you get your footing it's swept out from beneath you. When you find a notch to hold on the wall the water rises above it, pushing you toward the ceiling.

"This shit's insane!" Juanita shouts. I agree. Enrique, he's busy firing shots at the few women who managed to hang on to their weapons. When he runs out of ammo he throws his gun, smacking one upside the head.

"She's the first you actually hit, CIA man."

"Hey, eat it buddy! I'm an intelligence officer, not a marksman!"

"Well why don't we make it back up to the factory, where your buddies—"

"Dead," he says over the roar of the water.

"Huh?"

"The fire. Everyone in the factory is a goner."

Well, maybe Nikki didn't make it out after all. It's not like we'd know how to get back to the factory, even if we could make it into the corridors that led to this temple. They're all submerged now. The ceiling, it's inching down toward us with each passing second. Hey, at least the chains are off my wrists. Juanita might as well be some kind of secret agent, the way she handled the women around the winch.

The flow of water forces the corpse my way, making me deflect it again. "Good thing I spotted that scorpion tail, huh?"

Enrique wipes the smelly water from his eyes. "What?"

"The scorpion tail, I—"

"You? What do you mean, you?"

"What do you mean, me?"

"I mean I was laying there and saw that relief of scorps on the wall, figured out the male had something fishy going on. If it wasn't for me you'd still be getting slow roasted up there."

The women, in their panic, have mostly forgotten about us, but one makes a lame attempt to spear us. The weapon goes five feet to our right and Juanita shouts some choice words in Spanish.

Me, I'm still trying to figure out what he means. I'm the one who—

"Yo man, it's not like ya did all the work. Ya see me splittin' wigs up in this bitch? Dint nobody hafta tell me to raise up."

"Okay, okay, much respect." They high five.

They say how worried they were getting when I started babbling up there over the lava. They tell me it's okay, that I'll get back to normal soon. Sure. I see how it is. I'm either totally delusional or powerful beyond my wildest imagination, so powerful people don't even realize it. "Yeah, go ahead and celebrate. That doesn't help us get out of here. In case you hadn't noticed this place is going to fill pretty soon."

"No way, the water's gotta stop sometime."

"I don't think so. You smell it? We're talking some kind of underground lake or something. Try not to swallow any, who knows what's living in it." The body comes at me again and I kick at it. Just as my foot connects the body sinks out of sight. Almost as if...

Enrique points. "Check out these Quetzal statues around the ceiling."

"The birds?"

"That's right. Kenrick, give me a boost. I'm going to get on one."

"What for?"

"Check it, the water's about to snuff the torches. Got to assume a superior position while we can see what we're doing."

I help him out, and pretty soon he's on the statue. We work to get Juanita situated up there, then me just as the light dies out.

The women, the ones who didn't get swept away or roasted, they've been screaming their damn fool heads off the whole time. It doesn't make sense. Can't they swim?

Here in the lack of light we make out another sound. The water is coming in below surface level now, but still we hear the faint sound of rushing water, growing stronger.

Juanita leans in. "What's that?"

"There's a break in the masonry, somewhere close. Sounds like..."

"Up above us," I finish.

"Damn you Kenrick Brimley!" one of the women hollers. We ignore her.

"Yo, what's this?" Juanita has snagged a bag full of stuff floating on the water.

"Muchos gracias," Enrique says. "This might just save our asses."

"What've you got there," I ask, wondering why my mental powers are failing me.

"Just a sec." He rummages around, then chuckles. "All right, these waterproof bags really work! Still got my blacklight from the smuggling trade. Not the best, but we'll be able to see enough to get out of here."

Huddled together in the darkness we strain our eyes to see if it'll work. There's a click and even though we're expecting it the dull blacklight surprises us. The water is murky, but you can still see halfway across the chamber. Studying the water, trying to zoom in on the screams, it's clear why the women are so upset. There's something fluorescent in here with us. Not cute little buggers you keep in a terrarium. These fucking things are like three or four feet long, with freaky paddle-legs, swimming around like heat-seeking torpedoes. Water scorpions. Giant ones, all around, and now we know what that lever was for. It is an execution chamber, after all, and the women have been screaming because they knew what was coming. One of the monster bugs passes right under us and its stinger is six, maybe eight inches.

None of us has the balls to comment, except Juanita, who says "I hope they ain't attracted to shit, 'cause there's a bunch of it in my drawers now."

Did I really need to know that?

"Right, that's it," Enrique says. He shines the light up above us. "Yep, must be some kind of escape chute. You, we're boosting you up to that hole." He grabs Juanita.

"Wait, I won't be able to see!"

"That doesn't matter."

"But what if it's more'a them up in there?!"

The scorpions, they start tearing into the women. That right there is what you'd call a discussion killer. Juanita, she hardly needs our help. She's already scrabbled halfway up on her own, nails breaking and tearing off on the stone. With us giving her a hand she disappears through the hole. We listen, don't hear her screaming, give each other the thumbs up.

"Okay," I tell him. "Let's get up there."

"No, you first. If we don't catch up to each other out there, just remember what I told you before."

"Stay away from the suits and Leena."

"Right." He moves to boost me up. We're still too far down for one person to make it on their own. Without the help of the rising water that is, and there's no way you want to be in that water.

"What about you man?"

"Don't worry about me, I've still got a mission to complete."

"Oh yeah?"

"Yeah, getting you out of here. Plus, I'm a scorpion expert. If I can't make it up there I'll know how to handle these things."

I hesitate, then let him boost me up to the hole. It's smooth inside and steep, nearly impossible to hold myself here. Still, I manage to turn back, extend my hand. "Come on dude, I can't stay like this."

He sighs, reaches for me. "Hallelujah. I was just about to—" And the quetzal breaks. Plummets into the water. Enrique, he drops like a stone, and as his black light sinks out of sight it illuminates all the monsters swimming around him. Then it flickers, goes out.

For a second, just a second, I think about jumping back in, but I lose my grip and it becomes a moot point. I'm speeding down a dark tunnel, some kind of escape chute or overflow pipe slick with algae, and the sound of rushing water grows closer and closer. I barely have time to take a breath before hitting a wall of water.

Surging through swirling waters like some kind of maniac rocket, it's all I can do to just follow Juanita's red boots. Hopefully she's heading toward the surface and not the bottom. *If* there's even a surface here. Wait—we just hit warm water, and all of a sudden the crazy tide is more like a tiny tug. There's light here, and Juanita doesn't need me to tell her where to go.

We burst through the surface and spend who knows how long just trying to catch our breath and stay above the water. By the time our panic fades it becomes clear that everything is a haze. There's no sun, no sky, no way to tell where we are. Just this funky fog blanketing everything.

I swim over to her. "Hey, you okay?"

She spits out some water. "Does being shot and sunk and popping up in the middle of Atlantis count as okay?"

"No, no, like this," I say, grabbing her under the arms. "Just stop for a second. Keep going like that and you'll burn up all your energy in fifteen minutes. Now do like this with your legs," I say. She studies mine, then adjusts her technique. "Now do this with your arms," I say, using one arm to demonstrate and the other to help support her.

"Okay, okay, think I got it now."

"Yeah, that's better. And remember what I showed you about regulating your breath?"

She nods and starts treading water like a pro. She looks around. "What about...?"

"I don't know. He might've made it out, but I don't think so."

We nod to ourselves, avoid eye contact, try to keep our spirits from sinking completely. The real battle is never against nature, not in a situation like this. It's a battle against yourself. Even after everything that's gone down I'd say I'm in pretty good shape, mentally and physically. Always been more at home in the water anyway. Juanita, her silly little costume is in tatters but her makeshift bandage is holding up. This is the first time I've gotten a clear look at her—the bleached hair now has fake black strands woven in, loaded with black and white beads and braids, all caught up in the rows of piercings lining her earlobes. In addition to the jewelry they stuck in her nose and lip there's more tearing through her soaked brassiere. Where they shaved/plucked her eyebrows and drew on fake ones, that's all washed away now leaving her with nothing. Kind of makes her look like an alien.

"Hey, you're looking good. You been practicing in the pool when I wasn't around?"

She tries to smile. "Don't be simple. I just, ya know, don't wanna drown an' shit like that."

"Well, don't worry. People have been known to tread water for whole days."

She makes a dismissive noise. "We out here that long I'm a'hafta kill somebody." We share a nervous laugh. "Where she shot me...the blood, I mean..." She looks into the water, searching the area below us.

"Like I said, don't worry. Sharks don't like to eat people, because they don't know what we are. And even when they do mess up and bite us, it's no big deal—been there, done that, remember? It's more likely a barracuda will attack, but even that's a stretch of the imagination. The water's warm, the freaks are all dead, there's just you and me. Everything's cool if we keep ourselves in check."

Leena, who knows where she is. She's dead to me now, and me I'm plain dead to the world. The way things were going with my reputation this is a good thing. Only after we die can we have a chance to build decent lives for ourselves.

"So when's a boat gonna roll up? I don't wanna die..."

"I told you—"

"I don't wanna die a virgin." She looks away, pretends to scan the water some more, twists up her lips and hums one of Nikki's tunes.

"You're still...?"

"Mm-hmm."

"Well, I guess they didn't do such a good job sexualizing you after all." We laugh some, a bit easier this time.

"So...ya think that situation'll ever change?" She moves a little closer.

"All I can say is that boat better damn well have a waterbed." I move in and kiss her, and she embraces me. It's only a second before we start to sink. We break away, wipe the water from our faces, laugh some more.

"Where we at, Sharky? This fog shit ain't kosher."

"Kosher?"

She splashes me, and I return the favor, and before we know it a full fledged water fight is on. Of course, we start to sink again and have to stop.

"Yo, don't be messin' 'round like that! Gots ta conserve energy, ya feel me?"

I tickle her. "I feel you all right."

"Stop playin'! I done tol' ya: ya's so simple!"

A look around doesn't reveal much. If anything, the fog is even worse than before. "Dumb-ass fog. We can't be that far off the coast. I mean, the tunnels were underground, but we couldn't have traveled *that* far."

"Shhh." She pats my shoulder and tenses up, which makes her start to sink yet again. "Listen. Birds."

We listen for ten, twenty seconds. Salt water sloshes, we hear each others breathing, and then a seagull calls out somewhere in the distance. The distant distance.

"Fuck yeah, that's a good sign. Even though sound travels far on open water we're still close to land. Somewhat."

"Groovy. Ya down for a little swim?"

"We've got to figure out what direction it's coming from though. Who knows how long that'll take."

"Awright. So we'll chill for a while. Come on, Sharky, don't look like that. Go with the flow."

Too true. You can't fight nature. We could tread water hoping, praying, for even a single ray of sunlight to find our way with. Instead we close our eyes and listen, waiting for the bird to cry out again and tell us where we need to go.

Promotional image, courtesy Last Burn Films © 2006

BONUS MATERIALS

-Isolated Soundtrack
-Deleted Scenes
-Alternate Ending
-Previews

ISOLATED SOUNDTRACK

Last Burn in Hell: Da Soundtrack* [recommended listening]
Talibanized Records
$25.95, 2-disk set with multimedia features

Disk 1
1. TECHNO ANIMAL — Blood Money
2. DJ SPOOKY — Post-Human Sophistry
3. DJ SHADOW — Midnight in a Perfect World
4. TECHNO ANIMAL — Monosphate
5. TECHNO ANIMAL — Freefall
6. PANACEA — Jacob's Ladder
7. DJ SPOOKY — Riddim Warfare
8. TECHNO ANIMAL — Beheaded
9. TECHNO ANIMAL — Demonoid
10. CRACKER — Low
11. TECHNO ANIMAL — Anti Matter
12. BILLY IDOL — Eyes Without a Face
13. TECHNO ANIMAL — Piraña
14. TECHNO ANIMAL — City of Glass

Disk 2
1. TECHNO ANIMAL — Hydrozoid
2. PANACEA — Stormbringer
3. HELIOS CREED — Tele-Vision
4. TECHNO ANIMAL — Self Strangulation
5. DJ SPOOKY — Dialectical Transformation II
6. PANACEA — Tron
7. DJ SPOOKY — Galactic
8. TECHNO ANIMAL — Intercourse
9. DJ SPOOKY — Scientific
10. LOVE AND ROCKETS — No New Tale to Tell
11. DA TALIBAN — It's Da Taliban
12. DOWN FOR DA COUNT FEATURING DRE-COOLA AND DJ RENFIELD — Women of the Night
13. NIKKI — Chameleon
14. NIKKI — Desconocido Estrafalario

ERROR
Your playback device is not compatible with this feature.

* Da Taliban, Down for the Count, and Nikki are fictional, while the other artists mentioned are real; we strongly urge you to track down their records for the most enjoyable *Last Burn in Hell* experience.

DELETED SCENES

Deleted Scene 1

ONE TIME WE RAN out of money. Mom had taken us on a cross-country amnesia spree, doing everything in her power to mold us into a new family. One with no history, no corrupting secrets lurking under the surface. When our bottom dollar was taken by a lotto machine we had no choice. It was time to visit "Dad."

My brothers and I, we were ten and had no idea what to expect. We were at that gawky stage where your arms and legs get longer, stretching the muscle out before it can catch up in growth, all knobby knees and elbows cutting through our clothes. As for Mom, she was at a crossroads in both a physical and mental sense. Her fits of odd behavior were growing longer and more frequent, and it seemed as though one day soon she'd speed toward insanity and find it was a one-way street. As for her looks, she wasn't middle-aged yet, but the signs of hard living were showing up. Wrinkles were hinted at, the skin holding her together had begun to loosen slightly, her enormous breasts hung an inch or two lower. But those piercing green eyes would stop anyone dead—when she was lucid—and a toss of her dark hair still got her free drinks at the bar.

We hitched a ride with a trucker who was called Wheezy even though he had an overpowering, booming voice. That ride took us into the godless part of Utah, where desolation was the norm. A hand shook me awake when we reached our destination. The town was called Mad King, and it looked like it had been resuscitated after a messy suicide attempt—the place had a right to be mad, far as we could tell. Even to a kid it was clear the town had no economic prospects. We realized then our father wasn't going to be some suave Hollywood bigwig with a mansion on the hill, despite all the years of speculation and fantasies. After making some calls from the grease-saturated truck stop Mom gathered us up and had us wait outside. The heat was unlike anything we'd ever experienced. It was the perfect excuse for Mom to wear her black bathing suit, boots, and a strange little leather vest.

Not too long after that a gleaming white Cadillac pulled up, and our hopes for a rich father got a second wind. Then he stepped out. The first thing I noticed about our father was that he wore a broad-brimmed fur hat, white, with a huge iridescent green plume stuck in the side. Oversized, oval-shaped shades covered his eyes, and his skin was unreasonably pale. Not only that, it looked somewhat powdery.

His ring-encrusted fingers struck a match, lit up a hand-rolled cigarette. "So this them or what?" When he spoke his mouth didn't move nearly enough.

Mom wasn't playing her scripted role in this happy reunion. Instead of joy something else trembled in her features. She hastily wiped at her nose, then nodded.

"Sheeit. You boys turned out to be some white bread mutha-fuckas!" He handed Greg the cigarette while shaking hands with Seamus. "Call me Pimpdaddy."

What psychologists would say about the situation one can only guess, but it probably wouldn't be pretty.

Pimpdaddy gave us a couple hundred bucks and told us to get ourselves squared away at the Queen's Head Hotel. "While you're at it get me a separate suite, huh bitch? I'm a'stir up some bidness." With that he hopped back in the Caddy and peeled out of there, leaving us to figure out how to find the Queen's Head.

We looked at our mother, but her red cheeks and watery eyes told us not to bother speaking. Greg tried the cigarette and doubled over from the coughing fit that followed. Mom snatched the thing and threw it to the gravel. Seamus and I considered picking it up, but

Mom raised a hand to slap us, her head cocked at an "I dare you to," angle. We left.

In our dehydrated state we almost passed the Queen's Head by. The place didn't even appear to have electricity. The exterior paint had been peeling for a good decade, at least, and the pavement around the building was badly warped by heat and desert weeds. The guy manning the counter inside, he was just plain warped. As he led us up the creaky stairs to our suite we learned he was actually the owner.

Halfway up he stopped and spun on us. "Fella came through last week...said the ol' lady was in a scandalous state of disrepair...well now, I tol' him this here's *historic!* Ignoramus didn't have no clue. On the National Register an' all that. Fools don't got no sense o'history no more, I tell you what." Then, only two steps later, "Called it *scandalous!*"

He stared, trying to squeeze a response out of us with his eyes. Mother was busy formulating exactly the wrong thing to say, so it fell on us to quickly toss the owner a bone. "Seems nice enough," Seamus shrugged.

"Nice enough? This here lady ain't never been scandalized!" He continued up the steps and Mom rolled her eyes behind his back.

Time seemed to slow down once we were settled in. Everything creeps along at a torturer's pace in heat like that. The window unit gasped mild air conditioning that reeked of mildew, but us boys crowded around it like vultures at a ripe carcass. Mom, she lazed on the lumpy bed until Pimpdaddy finally showed up.

We forgot the AC and stuck to him, our curiosity overpowering common sense. Like Mom, Greg always had an intuition for what was exactly the wrong verbal TNT to throw in the mix. "So, like, are you really our father?"

"Sure," Pimpdaddy answered. "Why don't we call it Pimp & Sons Space Ho Providership." He took a drag of something that wasn't a cigarette, exhaled. "Sounds kinda classy."

He clearly wasn't our "daddy" but we continued to call him

Pimpdaddy regardless.

He had work for our mother. It came in the form of entertaining men all day long. These "men" were quiet, polite, and like Pimpdaddy their skin wasn't altogether convincing. They never blinked, their lips didn't move when they spoke, and they wore their flesh suits badly. The "entertaining" took place in Mom's room; we were banished to the dud room of the suite, with Pimpdaddy overseeing the operation.

And so began the steady stream of not-quite-men who shambled into the Queen's Head. The proprietor was suspicious, of course, but since all the men wore suits and ties he must have figured they were upscale business types. The proprietor ended up being more suspicious of the three of us boys roaming the halls of his historic establishment. We always smiled and waved, spouted syrupy-sweet gibberish that only served to make us seem guilty of something. It warmed our hearts to stoke his paranoia.

And if we were up to no good, which of us would he blame? Our DNA had been filed in triplicate with God & Co. That meant we could get away with anything, except when it came to each other. One or another of us was always around to catch a misdeed. It's not like we could hide anything from each other anyway—in our circle we were open books, written in an alien dialect filled with creative profanity.

That first night in the suite, after the "entertaining" was done, Mother called to me. I entered her room; stench hung in the air. I gathered her things while she slid into some pants, and the other two played their stupid games. She glared hard at me. "How dare you come in here when I'm naked," she growled, covering her chest.

"Well, you...I mean..." I dropped her stuff on the bed and left. Out in the suite one of my brothers stood opposite me, red-eyed and seething, spoiling for a fight. It must have been Greg. I warned him not to stare at me, and he did the same, trying to cover my words with his own. It was something he did to annoy me, and that tactic never failed to work its way under my skin. "Stop it," I shouted, my anger escalating to match his. "Stop it, stop it, stop it!" My own voice overpowered his, this time anyway, and I kept yelling just to avoid hearing his venom.

Pimpdaddy's muted conversation with Mom stopped as they came to see what all the fuss was. My brothers watched me from a doorway, nervous. As my anger grew Pimpdaddy hawked up a lugie on the carpet, saying "What the freak-all you on 'bout, boy?"

For some reason that pushed me over the edge. I lashed out and the little boy in the mirror fell to pieces.

We all stood around looking dumbly at the shards on the carpet. The glass was painted black on one side. For some reason this disturbed me the most. "Why's it like that?" I asked, oblivious to my wound.

Pimpdaddy said, "How else it's supposed to work? What, you think it's made a'magic glass better'n a window, huh? You don't block it on one side the light just goes right on through!"

I considered the dark nights spent watching for cultists, for tabloid journalists, for father descending from the sky, and how strong my reflection was when I faced that darkness. Unless maybe it was Greg or Seamus standing out there looking back in at me.

Mother sighed, asking Pimpdaddy to take the others out for fried chicken. She lead me back to the sink in the master bathroom, the funky odor of her clients still permeating everything. Without a word she examined me, rinsing the blood away with a gentle stream of cool water. Thinking she might say something I waited, then when it became obvious she wouldn't speak I opened my mouth. That's when she gingerly plucked some stray shards of glass from my hand, and I kept to groaning instead of speaking.

Since all the towels were damp and drying she took me back into her bedroom to fetch some tissues from the box next to the bed. Sitting there on the rumpled covers we kept our thoughts to ourselves. She patted down the wound while the cool, damp flesh of my hand felt all wrong alongside the searing throb shooting up to my shoulder. Her tirade about my bad behavior never materialized. Instead she kissed my hand to make it better. Only she didn't stop with the one kiss; her lips stayed at my hand, kissing softly. Then I felt her tongue, and pain as she began sucking at the wound. I wasn't sure what her intentions were, so I tried not to cry out or protest.

Something shifted in her features and she yanked my hand away, sending a jolt of pain through me. "You sick fuck, what's wrong with you?!" She struck me full force, sending me to the floor.

Having learned to stay on the move at times like this I quickly gathered myself up off the carpet. "I'm leaving, and I'm taking Greg and Shame with me."

"No," she sobbed, suddenly vulnerable, quivering as she tried to keep from slipping into the abyss. "Please, just...please."

It wasn't clear what the proper course of action was. What were a son's responsibilities in this scenario? What was the path of least masochism? My body refused to move as she beckoned to me. Maybe this display was real, or maybe I should run like all hell. In the end my feet outvoted my misgivings, slowly edging back toward the sobbing wet person on the bed. When I was within striking distance her arms lashed out, dragged me to her, crushed my awkward angles into her frame.

"I can only make it if I have you. Without your support there's nothing to live for."

There's a thing psychologists refer to as *emotional incest*. The child becomes a surrogate for the emotional duties of a mate, a spouse, a father who never was.

"But...all those men...or whatever they are...how can you...?"

She stroked my hair. "It's something no person should endure. But you know what? When I'm in there, in the dark with them doing what they do, I can make it as long as I keep my mind on you."

Now that, maybe that's what you could call *intellectual incest*, but I don't think she meant it quite like that.

In the morning a disturbed calm had settled over everyone. Even the owner of the Queen's Head had stopped mumbling to himself. Pimpdaddy showed up, giving Mom her cut for the previous day's work. He sat down with a blunt and some beer, then checked his PDA. Greg and Seamus shuffled out the door to explore the hotel's scars, but I stayed behind.

Pimpdaddy gave me the chopped liver eye. "It's all right," Mom told him. "You go take care of business. Kenny will keep watch on things."

He stepped toward us. "Bitch, I call the shots around here." After emptying his beer and considering our disposition he grunted, adding, "Guess I'll go stir up Greyjohns. Hey kid, why don't you sit out here and make sure nobody gets outta line. Know what I mean?"

He left the two of us alone. I stared at Mom, hard, and she tried to put on a smile but failed.

Soon enough an almost-man came around, loaded with booze and cash and the password to get him into Pimpdaddy & Sons Stellar Hoing Service. Mother left the bedroom door cracked open, whispering to me to stay put and watch in case this one got rowdy. My heart sank...this was all too uncomfortable for me.

She was on top of him, facing me, her breasts free to do as they willed. A hesitation surfaced, the tip of some frozen wholesomeness lurking within her. As her body struck a rhythm the hesitation vanished, replaced by a mischievous look, the type shared between co-conspirators. A genuine smile cracked her face, the first she'd managed since Mad King surrounded us.

Looking at that grin, ignoring what she was doing, the little boy in me declared that my mother could still be really beautiful when she wanted to.

At the same time, there was an adult voice budding in the back of my head, one full of bass. It muttered something about her being too afraid to lose me, thinking that I might still carry out my threat and take her boys away, that she was buying me off with this show.

Psychologists, maybe they'd call this *moral incest*. Or, it's some kind of incest.

The voice continued: *look at her, that's not love—it's enjoyment. She's back in control of something in her life, keeping you here, even if it means throwing herself into the out-of-control part of her life headlong.*

No! Mommy loves me, the boy in me tried to cry, voice growing weaker by the second. *Mommy is thinking about my best interest.*

And that, even armchair psychologists would call that *bullshit*.

After a pep talk from our mother I started sending Greg and

Seamus on errands, penny-ante busywork to distract them from what was happening around us. Newspapers, laundry, getting the scissors sharpened, finding matching thread to mend our clothes, the list was endless. Since they had no experience in these tasks it took them a ridiculous amount of time, especially without me to keep them on track. Things were much quieter in the following weeks. Looking back on it now, perhaps that was the worst mistake I ever made. Shielding my brothers from harm at home led them by the nose to a lifetime of harm on the streets.

Seamus, he started returning with things he didn't have before he left. Sometimes it was candy, or a new toothbrush, and it seemed harmless enough so I didn't say anything. Then it was comic books, summer sausages, socks. Since I hadn't said anything to begin with it seemed improper to start—besides, it was pretty much basic needs type stuff, and he shared. Then it was a watch, and then a pair of Air Humperdunks.

One day they came back acting strange. I figured out why when, three days later, the stench in our room led me to dead mice. There were maybe four or five of them squirreled away behind the dresser. The most decayed one looked to be pretty much intact, but each of the fresher mice was more gruesome than the last.

Seamus was nervous when I brought it to my brothers' attention. I thought maybe the place was getting scandalous after all, filled with rampant vermin. But then Greg, his reaction wasn't exactly right. He giggled, looked like he knew a thing or two about the dark side of the mirror. "I'm picking up a weird vibe off you, Greg man...what's up with that?"

"It gets boring going to the store. Here," he said, pulling a mouse out of his back pocket. "You can watch me do this one."

My hand slammed into his from below, sending the animal flying. It was dead before it ever hit the floor—Greg had either crushed it by accident, or killed it before tucking it in his pocket.

Seamus jumped back. He knew it wouldn't end well. So did Greg. I was the only one in the dark on the subject, so I stared him down. Things started to flow through the air between us: all the resentment in his heart at being ignored by our mother, at being "bullied" by me, at our screwed up lifestyle. He slashed my shoulder with a sliver of glass wrapped in cloth at one end. It happened so quickly he must have practiced the move hundreds of times. It was anybody's guess where the glass had been hidden.

What he hadn't practiced was the aftermath of his secret move. Basically it entailed me beating the living Christ out of him, and then back into him again.

Seamus cringed in the corner when I looked up from our brother's unconscious form. "Hey man, I may not've helped you...but I didn't help him either, okay?" He flinched as though I'd swung at him.

I went into our mother's room to disclose the strange bent infecting in Greg. She wasn't there, but her bathroom light was on. I knocked at the door and listened for the sound of a sink, a shower, a toilet. After knocking a couple more times I opened the door. Mom was standing in front of the mirror over the sink, sullen, almost gone, staring at herself from some lightless place. She was losing the battle, no longer beautiful with her shoulders slumped, her hair tangled, her makeup gone, her head tilted like some self-hating librarian.

It dawned on me she was only wearing her athletic bra. My jaw jogged a couple times as though some words might follow, then I turned to leave. She clutched my shirt.

"Look at me, Rocket Man. Look at me honestly." She squared my shoulders so that I was fully facing her. "Am I getting old?"

That, psychologists would think of all the years of therapy ahead and call it *money*.

I tried to keep my eyes glued on her belly button to avoid staring at her dangerous parts. "No, Mom. You're not old." I don't think either of us believed I meant it.

She embraced me, pressing me to her then, not as an act of owner-ship like before. Something was different about her. "Do you love me?"

"Of course!" There had been no hesitation, and we both knew how serious I was.

"Sometimes I think you're the only guy who ever did." Her fingers caressed my hair, my neck, my back. Tears, hot from her eyes, splattered on my cheeks. "You've seen everything there is to see of me, and you still love me."

A pit tore open in my belly, in my chest. It was the realization of her as a person, not a parent. It was the comprehension of how fucked up and lonely her life was, even compared to mine. My mouth worked aimlessly, again unable to summon any words. There was a deep, overpowering shame in that instant: of my past hate for her, of relinquishing that hate in this moment of revelation, of not being able to comfort her during my short life. All I could do was hug her, rub her skin, try to communicate some understanding and affection through physical means.

Her voice cracked as she asked, "Do you think I'm beautiful?" Then she shook, gripping her head. "No, you don't have to answer that. Never mind," she said, wiping her face with the heel of her palm. "I'm sorry."

"But you are beautiful. You're prettier than anyone I've ever met."

She sank to the tile floor with me, her kisses rapid and rough all over my head, leaving saliva in my hair, rocking back and forth with me in her arms.

Psychologists, by now they're lighting a post-orgasm cigarette. A case like mine could build careers like Donald Trump builds towers.

Pimpdaddy stood in the doorway. "Bitch, what the *hell* is you doin'? This boy owe me? He been gettin' by without payin'?"

Before I knew it my fist sank into his face. I was suddenly standing, adrenaline pumping through my blood. It felt like my knuckles had sunk into foam rubber. He didn't react, just stood there with his hands on his hips. A hand shoved the back of my head, sending me stumbling out of the bathroom—it was my mother's hand. I looked back at them. She had covered herself with a towel, her face flushed bright crimson, eyes pools of napalm in the flickering florescent light.

I was exiled from her room after that—it wasn't clear if that was her doing or his. Either way, we all kept playing along with the script. My brothers stayed away, Pimpdaddy went out in the world finding

Greyjohn clientele, our mother kept watching me from the bed while the weirdoes and freaks did their part, and I let it all happen. At least none of the customers got out of hand on my watch; they were calm as mutilated cattle.

A week later the gig was up and we headed back north, loaded with enough money to keep us for the next year.

Deleted Scene 2

Mr. Barnes, why don't you start from the beginning?

Th' name's Triple-B, slick.

And how is it that you made Kenrick Brimley's acquaintance?

Didn't know he was no Brimley back then. Was at th' Playboy Mansion an' shit like that, chuggin' some back, spillin' some for all th' fallen homies an' shit, an some bitch stops blowin' th' pole on account o' some K-Ill rollin' up in th' hizzy.

The pole?

Fishin' pole, naw mean?

"Gnaw" mean?

[sighs]

Do you know what I mean.

No, no I don't.

[pause]

Awright, so I's up in th' Plizzy Mizzy wit' mad bitches ridin' my jock, an' this white bread mofo come strollin' in all cool an' shit, like it ain't nothin', an' the mood all changed. Sick ill peeps just all got pressed an' shit. All these mizzy-fizzies done TV an' movies and magazines an' what all. Just stone-cold trippin' thinkin' this dude might look at 'em.

And?

An' he gets all up in my grill, see? Straight from the door to my face, he's not even scopin' any of them fly bitches or that mad buffet with them fois gras and shit.

And?

An' he's all tense an' shit. Like I'm all wrong over that stupid bitch I done in th' parkin' lot o that place. So I'm just like, damn young, get you a grip on yoself, naw mean? But he's like, don't start none it won't be none!

[pause]

AND?

Whole time it's mad bitches tryin' to get they blow on, but he got his fly locked down tight like underage.

You don't say.

Sho' 'nuff! Bitches slitherin' around on they stomachs an' shit tryin' to get up his baggy-ass pants! I'm talkin' prime cuts of meat here, yo, USDA certified fillet of bitch.

Back to the point of the story, assuming there is one. You altercated with Brimley?

What you trying to say?! I don't get my grind on like that, fool!

Restrain him! Restrain him!

[muffled grunts and curses; the sound of furniture scraping tile, toppling, breaking; a long pause filled with pants and groans]

What I was trying to say is: you got into a fistfight with him.

K-Ill? Hell naw, I ain't stupid. I's just like, "Respeck." Then me an' my crew blow that scene, found us some bitches at th' 7-11.

That's your story? That's supposed to be worth it?

Word.

That, Triple-B, earns you a one-way ticket to Guantanamo Bay. Good-bye.

ALTERNATE ENDING
It's Miller/Ass Time: The Crowd Pleaser

WE LISTEN FOR TEN, twenty seconds. Salt water sloshes, we hear each others breathing, and then a seagull calls out somewhere in the distance. The distant distance.

"Fuck yeah, that's a good sign. Even though sound travels far on open water we're still close to land. Somewhat."

"Groovy. Ya down for a little swim?"

"We've got to figure out what direction it's coming from though. Who knows how long that'll take."

"Awright. So we'll chill for a while. Come on, Sharky, don't look like that. Go with the flow."

Too true. You can't fight nature. So, we tread water hoping, praying, for even a single ray of sunlight to find our way with.

There is none.

Water sprays everywhere while Juanita screams, and I'm screaming because I have no idea what's going on. Her arms flail and my grip slides off her skin. We separate. Something knocks against my abdomen and takes away my breath, doubling me over—salt water sneaks down my throat and panic sets in.

Juanita disappears completely, then before the water can settle she resurfaces, launching unnaturally high out of the water. Something is wrapped around her, something *alive*, and memories of the sand shark attack flash through my mind: the unbelievable force and speed and total lack of control, my blood visible in the water before the pain could even register.

Muscles constrict around Juanita's throat. An arm. A head visible behind Juanita, pale skin in stark contrast to Juanita's rich color. Strands of wet hair pasted across angry eyes. *Leena.*

"What...what're you—" It's impossible to move in on them on account of all their thrashing.

Juanita's struggles are cut short by a cry of anguish. Leena is digging in her wound.

"Hey lover boy. Why the long face? You can't really care about this little skank."

"Who ya callin' skank, ya—"

Another sharp cry. And this time, a knife breaks the water. Here in the fog, in this not-light, the blade looks dull, fake. Knowing Leena, though, even a piece of soft rubber could be deadly in her hands.

Her eyes lock on mine. "Fine. You can watch her die, and then it's your turn."

"You say it like you weren't planning on doing that anyway."

Instead of arguing she chuckles. Juanita, her eyes dart to me, terrified, and an idea floats to the surface. If the mind tricks worked on those Bohemian freaks maybe it could help in this situation too. Apologies slip out of my mouth while I concentrate on Leena. Flying on autopilot the begging starts, even as I try to crack through her layers of consciousness.

"Sorry Brimley. That voodoo mumbo-jumbo won't work on me. Implants." This time my eyes don't dart to her chest. That could just be due to the fact that I've already certified the organic nature of her boobs. "Now get ready for the dyin'."

The tip of the knife digs into Juanita's skin, but then out of nowhere a sound hits us full force: a motor revving like mad. It's a speedboat, hurtling through the mist, slamming down just feet from our ménage-à-terror, and the impact splits us apart. The boat's wake leaves us tumbling out of control. Nothing you learn at swim meets prepares you for this.

A quick look reveals the Diaz fist-gripping-lightning logo. Why not? While the three of us sputter and try to suck in more air than water the boat doubles back. Leena is the quickest to recover and closes in on Juanita again.

Diaz's boat is barreling down on me, and even if I dive I won't be able to avoid broken bones on the bottom of the hull, getting sucked into the spinning blades, no way I can stop that psycho from hurting the woman I really love—

A hand locks onto my arm and drags me along with the boat, then up over the side. A bronze handsome devil looms over me. Enrique.

"What're you looking at?! Get off your ass and do something!"

The boat swerves and I tumble from side to side before I can even find my footing. "What...how...?!"

But he doesn't need to answer. I can see it all as big and bright as a drive-in movie because there's no reason for him to keep barriers between us. The scorpions, he didn't pay attention to them swimming around him in that rancid water. In those last few seconds before his light died the frieze caught his attention. It was below the water level but still easy enough to make out. What called to him was the female scorpion, something about its tail. He ducked and dived in the darkness that followed, keeping his arms and legs still, pressed against him. He didn't want frantic limb movements to send a victim signal. The frieze, he rammed into it with his head and nearly blacked out. Even so, he managed to feel the tail, grip it, pull it out. A hole opened in front of him, sucked him out and rocketed him to the surface. Right outside Diaz's burning warehouse on the waterfront, a fleet of commercial and luxury vessels at his disposal.

He glances away from the controls and sees me staring off into space. "Son of a bitch, must've hit you with the boat after all...gotta do everything myself!" Before I can protest the boat swerves again, coming to a halt, and we fishtail into Leena. She is sent skidding along the surface, and I take advantage of this to drag Juanita on board. While anybody else would be down for the count Leena just shakes her head and turns to face us. In fact, it looks like she's preparing to throw that knife of hers. I shield Juanita, but Enrique doesn't notice the impending danger. Instead he's digging something out from under the control panel. Is that what it looks like?

Enrique is stooped, using both hands to support a bazooka. He shouts, "*Smoke this, you overgrown gorilla bitch!*"

A rocket shoots out and slams into Leena. The split second before impact there's the realization in her eyes, then: a wall of heat slams me into the other side of the boat, and for long seconds it seems we might capsize.

Scorched blood and flesh shower us. A length of intestine whips around Juanita's neck like a bolo—even in death Leena won't give up. In my effort to unwrap it I fall, taking Juanita with me. They're both screaming, all of us are...this only registers because the high-pitched whine in my ears is starting to fade. Leena's ropey guts are muscous-slick and hot in my hands. It doesn't even occur to me until moments later that vomiting might result. Soon enough the three of us have tugged and clawed Juanita free, and we lie gasping in a heap.

We all notice something in the same split second. There it is, in the rear of the boat, splattered with Leena's blood. It's a grimy tarp crusted with dried sand, lumpy due to whatever it conceals.

I yank the tarp back, expecting a horde of alien invaders, or at least a couple dozen S.I.S.T.E.R.s armed with castration tools. Instead there's a pile of gold coins, gold chalices studded with gems, gold and gold and gold...

The look on their faces could snag Best Comedy Oscars. I clear my throat. "You do realize, don't you, that Diaz is the owner of the company excavating all the slave trade treasure off the coast."

It takes a moment to sink in. "*Oh yeah, baby!*" Enrique high-fives me.

Juanita nervously rubs her neck muscles. "Don't matter if I's blood or not, he ain't gonna let that slide. We best get gone, naw mean?"

"Naw mean."

Enrique takes the controls and, after minutes of trying to remember how he got the boat under way to begin with, finally gets it in gear. We lurch awkwardly, trying to avoid supporting ourselves on anything that may be covered in Leena's taint. The ride smoothes out just as we break away from the mist. Surrounded by clear air we begin to relax. Juanita slows down the massage, lets her finger tips slide down across her collarbones, tracing a path down her sternum like some kind of sensual vivisectionist. "Yo," she says, the smile returning to her eyes. "Let's hurry up and find a place to ass."

I wrap an arm around her waist and nod to Enrique. "You heard the lady. It's ass time."

"Aye, aye." He tosses us both [*insert expensive brand name beer here*] and sets a course for the horizon. We all laugh, drink, watch the sunlight glinting off the gold, and laugh some more.

ABOUT THE AUTHOR

John Edward Lawson is an author and editor living just outside Washington, D.C. His poetry collections include *The Troublesome Amputee*, *The Plague Factory*, *The Horrible*, and *The Scars Are Complimentary*. Fiction includes the novel *Last Burn in Hell* and the collection *Pocket Full of Loose Razorblades*. While serving as editor-in-chief of Raw Dog Screaming Press and *The Dream People* literary journal, John has also edited several anthologies including *The Wicked Will Laugh*, *Tempting Disaster*, *Sick*, and *Of Flesh and Hunger*. You can spy on him at www.johnlawson.org.

www.ingramcontent.com/pod-product-compliance
Lightning Source LLC
Chambersburg PA
CBHW050503260626
47157CB00004B/1167